Justice Hunger

Justice Hunger

BY MEYER LIBEN

A Short Novel and Nine Stories

The Dial Press   New York   1967

To
the memory of
my Father and Mother

Acknowledgment
is made to the following magazines
in whose pages
these stories first appeared:
i. e., The Cambridge Review for
"Solomon's Wisdom" (Winter 1956);
Commentary for
"The Locking Gas-Cap" (December 1957),
"Homage to Benny Leonard" (June 1959),
"A Note on Chivalry" (December 1962),
and "Ball of Fire";
and
The Massachusetts Review for
"You're It" (Spring 1961).

CONTENTS

ix

Justice Hunger

Justice Hunger

1. *The Way We Met*

Sitting late one night on a bench overlooking the East River, I was suddenly aware of a girl who stood against the railing a little way off. I had not seen nor heard her come, but that is not surprising, for at these hours of the night, particularly at these hours of a summer night, I am given to reverie, or to wild dreams about my future. In either case I become so absorbed that, though I was surprised to see the girl, I was not surprised that I hadn't seen her approach. She was gazing at the river, which was quite dark, for the sky was cloudy, moonless; the river was lit up by a boat carrying sand or gravel, and this boat sailed calmly, with a kind of toy light, for all the world as though it had been pushed by a child from some unseen shore.

The girl suddenly stirred and moved towards me. As she did, I noticed the shadow of an approaching figure—it was a policeman, jauntily twirling his stick on the midnight round. There flashed across my mind the figure of the running girl at the beginning of Dostoevsky's "White Nights," and then she was beside me, saying: "There's a cop coming, and I haven't done a thing but it's late and he's bound to look at me questioningly, or to question me if I'm alone, so I'll just sit here with you until he goes by."

Though she was agitated, she spoke calmly, in the friendly manner of a girl with a young man in whose company she was very much at ease. As the policeman walked by, she pointed to the boat, and said: "It's like an illuminated toy."

"Yes," I said, "like a toy boat pushed by a child from an unseen shore."

The policeman passed, and then the shadow of the policeman passed. I looked at the girl more closely, for until the cop disappeared I too was play-acting, behaving as though I knew this stranger very well, and who would be looking closely at the face of a person he knew very well, even though that person was a stranger? I find it difficult to describe a person, a face, in a way that satisfies me; that is more the task of a painter (though most of the best painters are not attempting it today), and the author must be content with behavior, action, with camouflages of action, and the absence of action, out of which come an image of a character, a notion of what a person is like, what a person wants, what he fears, what he thinks he wants and fears. But I look closely at people, I remember them forever. If I were asked, say, for the purpose of police identification, to describe this girl, I'd say that she was about five feet four inches tall, weighing perhaps 130 pounds, with dark hair and dark brown eyes (but I forget the color of people's eyes, the only time I am sure is when I am looking into them), a full mouth, trembling and firm (according to the changing circumstances in which I had observed her), and a faded scar over the right eye, the remnant, probably, of an early fall. No doubt an adequate police identification, the kind of description that might help in the search for a missing person (particularly under a picture of that person!), but it does not add up to a living face. She was quite beautiful.

After the shadow of the policeman had passed, the sound

of his footsteps died. The girl moved away from me, a natural though disappointing movement.

"That was very kind of you," she said.

"Anybody would have . . . ," I started.

"You're quite wrong," she broke in, "*anybody* would *not* have done it. Any number of people would have been outraged, or scared, would have turned me over to the policeman as a come-on girl, or a prostitute, or as a nuisance."

"I don't think you're really as cynical as all that," I said. (But why not? I thought, what do I know about her?) "After all, you *did* come over and sit next to me, I *am* a stranger, so you obviously are more trusting than you make yourself out to be."

I was very much annoyed with myself for emphasizing the words "did" and "am" because such emphases betray an agitation which I prefer to hide, particularly before strangers.

"You have to take your chances," she said.

"Anyway," I said, "that cop wouldn't have bothered you. You were only looking at the river, and it isn't *that* late."

The emphasis again.

"I told you," she flared, "that there isn't a thing they can hold me for. I just don't like to be questioned."

"All right," I said, "in that case I won't ask you a thing, but it *is* difficult, I mean, it's difficult for strangers to talk to one another without some introductory questions."

Then we were both silent, gazing at the suddenly empty river.

"I'm going," she said. "Would you put me into a cab?"

Sure enough, an empty cab was speeding down the East River Drive. I ran to the curb and hailed it.

"I'd like to see you again," I said, as the cab slowed down, "I promise to ask you nothing."

She acted confused, uncertain, then she fished a pencil and notebook out of her purse, scribbled on a page, tore it out of the book, handed the page to me, and stepped into the cab, which moved off with the thoughtless speed of a machine. I looked at the paper. It gave a St. Mark's Place address but no name.

2. *An Unsuccessful Search*

On my way to the address that she gave me, I resolved, in my favor, her curious forgetting. I resolved it by thinking that her attitude had been so friendly that there was no question (in her mind) but that I knew her name, so what was the point of writing it down, especially with a cab waiting? It is what a friend does when he moves and jots down his new address; he certainly would not bother to write his name. Names are shared among friends. In this way I resolved her omission in my favor, but the resolution was by no means complete—the absence of her name on the slip of paper (though hastily written, and with a cab waiting) bore an obviously negative interpretation. It was rather comical too, the way it is when a crucial element is found missing from a puzzle you're sure you solved. But on second thought not quite so comical, for here were only two elements, and one was missing. And the matter would be even less comical if the address were a spurious one, if she had jotted down the first number, the first street that popped into her head. But if it *were* a phony address, she probably would have jotted down a phony name, too. So I was left with the resolution that she had omitted to write her name out of an attitude of friendship, if not an excess of that emotion.

For those who are not familiar with lower New York, St. Mark's Place, as you walk east, past Cooper Union, is an extension of 8th Street. Starting on 3rd Avenue (there by the Sagamore Cafeteria), St. Mark's Place goes to Avenue A, into Tompkins Square, after which it becomes 8th Street again, and so to the river.

The western part of St. Mark's Place has an Old World look about it: nothing has been torn down for a very long time, there are poolrooms on the street level (most poolrooms in the city are up a flight), and many of the shops are Ukrainian and Polish. Poolrooms on the street level make for an Old World look? Fair question. And it is one of those rare New York blocks (becoming rarer all the time) where the inhabitants spend their time; it is not merely a street on the way to another street.

I looked up at the house whose number she had given me. It was fair-sized (for the block), and I walked up the stoop into the hallway to examine the mailbox names. There were about a dozen names, one of which was Miss Walda Wankowitz, and that was the only name with a "Miss" before it. I had taken a leisurely walk from work, to give myself a chance to resolve her omission in my favor, and it was a quarter after six now, a good time to find people in. I rang the bell, and there was a prompt response; I walked up to the third floor. I knocked on the door (the number showing on the mailbox), and the sound of the violin I had heard on the way up stopped. A woman of about sixty opened the door and looked at me in surprise.

"Miss Wankowitz?" I asked.

"That is correct," she said. She spoke with the pleasantly precise accent of the Russian intelligentsia, who refuse to learn English without an accent and so hold on to a life smashed beyond repair, if not beyond recall.

"I'm sorry," I said. "I'm looking for a young woman about twenty-four or twenty-five."

Before she drew herself up (yes, in that split second) I realized how tactless it was to mention so youthful an age, so abruptly, to an older woman, and a stranger. It was like telling her that she was forty years closer to the grave than the girl I was seeking.

"I'm looking for a friend," I said, hoping to smooth

matters out by now making no reference to age, and proceeded to give her my police description, omitting the scar.

"You have the wrong apartment," she said, the way one says, *You have the wrong number.* "There's nobody here answering that description."

"Would you know if there was somebody in the house—?"

I hesitated long enough to make her inevitable interruption absolutely polite.

"I really don't. I'm sorry."

Then she closed the door, slowly (not regretfully), and I went back down to the mailbox, wondering why I had picked so foreign a name when the girl I was seeking was so obviously an American. I then found the name Warren, with no first name, and figuring that was quite an American name I tried the bell. The answer was more than prompt, it was immediate, and when I opened the outside door, there was Warren, standing at the door of his ground floor apartment. He was about my age, and I asked him about the girl.

"What's her name?" he said. His tone was antagonistic.

"Truthfully," I said, "I don't know her name." As soon as I said it, I realized that he thought I was a detective, or some kind of private investigator, and I certainly couldn't blame him.

"I wouldn't know anyone like that in this building," he said, and he was now less antagonistic and more cagey, but the use of "wouldn't" rather than "don't" made me suspicious. "You probably have the wrong house."

"Oh, no," I said, looking at the slip of paper again, "this is the address all right."

I recognized how absurd it was to carry a slip of paper with an address (even the correct address) and no name.

"Well, I don't know," said Warren. "Sounds to me like you got a bum steer."

He spoke with the kind of ungrammatical toughness that

a sensitive young man will sometimes affect with a policeman, or a taxi driver, or any threat from below.

"Where's the super?" I asked, and to my amazement my voice had the ring of a law-enforcement official.

"Down in the basement," said Warren, "the first door on your left as you come in."

So I went down to the cellar, knocked on the first door to the left, and a hefty woman filled up the doorway.

I told her what it was I wanted, and she was suspicious, though without any sign of fear.

"We haven't been here very long," she said. "I don't know nobody like that; my husband and I, we're only here a short time."

She stared at me, awaiting further questions, but I had enough. The possibility that this was a phony address loomed up stronger than ever, and I certainly wasn't going to every door in the building, looking for someone who probably didn't live here, who had jotted down the first number and the first street that came into her head. And I was tired of being taken for an investigator or private eye, so I thanked the super's wife and went upstairs, into the street.

3. *An Interlude*

I am the kind of person who is disappointed easily, but with whom hope dies slowly. As I strolled along 2nd Avenue, reviewing my unsuccessful search, I was very suspicious about the behavior of the tenants—particularly Warren—and of the super's wife. Nevertheless, I felt that I would have behaved in the same way toward a stranger who came seeking out a neighbor, a friend, in the absurd way that I was seeking her out. A stranger with a description, but without a name; what is a friend, a neighbor, to think? It is the way you look for someone seen fleeing from a crime, armed with a description of a suspect given by a passer-by.

The possibility of this being a phony address loomed down as I considered my behavior under comparable circumstances, and in a slightly more optimistic frame of mind I picked up a copy of the *New York Evening Sun* and went into the Café Royale.

This café, now unfortunately extinct, was at the time one of the glories of Second Avenue. It was the haunt of the East Side intelligentsia, of Yiddish journalists and theatrical figures, of merchants, kibitzers, and *luftmenschen*, an easy-going cosmopolitan restaurant which favored conversation, where one could sit at leisure, and where the food was tasty. Then Broadway produced a play about the café, called it *Café Crown*, and in trying to live up to this dramatic image of itself the Café Royale came to its end. Such is the power of art in our complex society. No doubt considerations of an economic nature were also involved.

I found a table in the corner, to obtain the best view of the lively and changing scene, and tried to conjure up her name. Eunice? Jane? June? I decided that she was half-Jewish, that her mother was Jewish. Sarah? Hannah? Miriam? Miriam sounded convincing. And her last name. Wells? Lawrence? But that last was by association with her first name. Jordan? Miriam Jordan. Why not Miriam Jordan?

Having solved this vexing problem, I turned to the sports section. Now it was no accident that I had bought the *Sun;* that was partly to annoy the liberal denizens of the restaurant. The paper was a bastion, if not a rallying point, of the dying, old-fashioned conservatism, and the sight of it would infuriate any self-respecting member of a W.P.A. Arts Project, of which this restaurant had more than its share. The fact is that I myself was annoyed when I saw someone reading the *Sun*, but never thought to think that he was reading the paper to annoy me. A more substantial reason for my reading the paper was my admiration for two of its sportswriters, Joe Vila and George Trevor, who to my mind were the Aristotle and

Plato of this sphere of journalism. Vila was the most knowl-
edgeable sportswriter of his time, his column was crowded
with facts, figures, comparisons, statistics—all of which he
used to build up a dense and convincing history. An analytic
coolness lifted these facts and figures from the statistical sphere
and made a world wherein stalked heroes of the past, even the
legendary past, and contenders of the present. The stories of
George Trevor, particularly his football stories, built up an
unusual aura of remembrance; his account of a game plunged
one into an ancient world, as of childhood, into a recall seem-
ingly beyond memory, a world of disappearing pasts on whose
surface shone the contingencies of this day and this struggle.

But it was in the heat of the summer—no goal posts were
being torn down in a manner to confuse the anthropologists of
a later day. I put the paper down. Miriam Jordan. Miriam
Fuller? No, Jordan was better, more Midwest than New
England.

"You're playing the market?"

I looked up somewhat in surprise at the waiter (though
one learned never to be altogether surprised by the waiters at
the Café Royale) who was bringing me a plate of soup. He
was looking at my paper, which I had folded so that the
financial page showed—it was not done on purpose, but
brought out the reaction that I had unconsciously sought.

I shrugged without comitting myself.

"Let me tell you," he said, "here is something you
shouldn't miss."

He jabbed the paper, down toward the bottom of the
page.

"Supreme Inc." (He said *ink*, not *incorporated*.) "Let's
see, what did it close today?"

He picked up the paper and swiftly scanned it.

"Ha!" he said, "seven and a half, already picked up a
half-point."

"What kind of a company is it?" I asked. "What do they make?"

"What difference?" asked the waiter. "There's a man has lunch here nearly every day, a member of the Board of Directors. I've known him for years."

"Do you know how the stock sells in relation to its earnings per share?"

"What kind of earnings?" asked the waiter. "You're looking in the mouth of a gift horse. Look."

He started writing on my napkin.

"You buy one hundred shares. Let's say, for an example, it costs you seven hundred dollars. I happen to know that this company is coming out with a certain development, further I can't talk. It has to go up six points, a three percent dividend it pays disregardless. So what can you lose?"

He put my napkin down triumphantly. I studied the figures.

"Do I have to tell you right away?" I asked.

"For your own good," he said, "think it over."

He rushed off to another table, and I started on my soup, which had cooled.

The meal was pleasant; the stir, the changing scene, absorbed my attention, and the waiter offered a few less urgent financial suggestions. When he asked if I wanted another cup of coffee (which he was either selling or offering) I told him a joke:

An investor comes to a market analyst.
—What should I do?
The analyst checks his charts, graphs, ponders, and says:
—The best thing for you is to buy A.T.&T.
—I already bought A.T.&T.
—*Then sell it!*

The waiter laughed, and on this pleasant note I made my way to the cashier's desk. In addition to the joke, I had left the waiter a tip in line with the prevailing standards. I paid my bill, glad that I had come to know Miriam Jordan in these pleasant surroundings. But I found the name rather cold. I regretted that she did not have one of those long Russian names, so warm and diminutive, on whose length one can play all sorts of chords, so that the very saying of the name becomes an experience, but Miriam Jordan it would have to be, and purchasing a fine ten-cent cigar, I went out into the heat and turmoil of the 2nd Avenue night.

4. *We Meet Again*

Though it was not on my way home, I headed west on St. Mark's Place, past the house that I had so unsuccessfully searched, and then saw the object of my search approaching that house. Not a phony address at all, I thought triumphantly, for I was never rid of this dark possibility.

Her eyes lit up with what I like to think was interest.

"How are you?" she asked.

"Fine," I said, "I'm not on this block by accident."

This remark was partly in reaction to her formal (though friendly) question.

I pulled out the paper with her address written on it and showed it to her.

"Just where I live," she said.

"It would have been easier," I said, "with more documentation."

"You mean the apartment number?"

"I mean your name."

She looked puzzled and said:

"But I was sure that you knew my name, didn't I mention it to you?"

Just as I thought, I thought gladly. In that friendly air, by the river, it had been as though we knew one another.

"No, you didn't," I said, "but I've been considering the

matter and concluded your name is Miriam Jordan, that you come from the Midwest, and that you have a Protestant father and a Jewish mother."

She asked me up to her apartment, and as we walked to the familiar house, she said:

"I do come from the Midwest. My father is Jewish, my mother is Lutheran. My name is Melanie Craig."

"It sounds," I said, "like the children's game—you know the one. *My name is Collisshangie, I come from Cardiff, and I sell coronachs.*"

"I remember the game very well," she said, "but I moved in different circles."

"Your father is Jewish, and your name is Craig?"

"My father's name is Bogen, which is short, I believe, for Ellenbogen. My ex-husband's name is Craig."

She didn't seem much interested in pursuing this line of thought.

"Melanie," I said, "I never thought of that one."

"It's German, of course, I'm named after my maternal grandmother."

As we were walking up to the fourth floor, I told her my name and mentioned that I was unmarried, never married. These are all details that must appear at one time or another. She explained that she had two rooms with kitchenette and bath, and she opened the hallway door into her apartment.

"It's very nice," I said, but I wasn't thinking of its appearance, but of the fact that I was in the room. What I really meant to say was: "It's very nice to be here, in your apartment."

She went in to wash, and it was very pleasant to be sitting in this room, waiting for the return of the girl who had brought this sudden interest into my life, a girl I might never have seen again had I told the waiter in the Café Royale a longer joke, or had I told him no joke at all.

It is very pleasant indeed to sit in the room of a girl who interests you, in a lived-in room absolutely strange to you, waiting for a girl who has brought a sudden interest into your life. Then I picked up a book and became entranced with it, the way you do with a book familiar or strange in circumstances pleasurable or hinting at future pleasure.

She came into the room, and we faced one another, really for the first time, on terms real and difficult; there was no policeman moving toward us and away, there was no lit-up vessel, no melodrama of an unexpected meeting, there were the two of us facing one another in a room, wondering whether this was a beginning or an end. We had no common friends, no organizational ties (though we did share—already —a small background of common experience), we had to reveal ourselves and then slowly see whether the interest was factitious or not. It is a moment that many newly met people seek to avoid, preferring movement, any kind of action, to avoid the human confrontation, the possibility of disappointment.

We spoke for a few hours. She told me something of her upbringing and of the death of her father (five years back) in an automobile crash. She spoke of her younger brother (a student at Ohio State) to whom she was extraordinarily attached (attractive girls are usually attached to younger brothers). She told me of her own schooling (University of Illinois and Hunter College), of her interest in the modern dance as well as in "reportage," a kind of reporting in depth with a social angle. She was supporting herself with a secretarial job at Con Edison, in the building at 14th Street and Irving Place. She spoke, in general terms, of her relations with her mother and of her own marriage; she had been married at twenty and just recently divorced, after four years.

There is a tendency in early meetings to an excess of self-revelation—we make up for the strangeness by offering an unusual range and depth of information, to close the distance. But we avoided that trap, we kept a fair balance between undue revelation and secrecy, understood one another in a way that developed interest without the unpleasant feeling that we knew more than we ought to, the feeling that sometimes makes the first meeting the last.

We both came to see that we were reaching a joyless stage in the conversation, that there can be too much conversation about the past, and this can become an escape, for the past is generally interesting (or can be made interesting in the circumstances of a first meeting), but the future is hard, and we must stop the present from dying. So we became restive, bored with each other's backgrounds (looking more for the meaningful look, gesture, than the detailed account, which can more easily smother the truth than reveal it), and the conversation, which had been rather spirited, began to idle, the way a waiting motor does. But what were we waiting for?

I stood up, walked to the window, moved closer to her, and suggested that we go out for coffee. I wanted to hold her in my arms, but I am very cautious, hate to make a move that can have a conclusive negative effect, for a girl may be well disposed to you and yet the last place in the world she may want to be is in your arms.

"Great," she said, and I couldn't tell whether she was relieved at the prospect of going out of the house or pleased at the thought of going out with me.

5. Sudden Jealousy

"I must say," I said as we sat down in Ratner's, the famed East Side dairy restaurant, "that you're either unknown in your apartment house, or you have the most fanatically loyal friends. Take, for example, Miss Wankowitz, the violin teacher."

"I haven't been living here very long," she said. "I think I know who you mean. I hear her playing on my way up, but I don't know her at all."

I was disappointed at this lack of connection, for I wanted to come closer to her on the basis of something shared, and was prepared to settle for Miss Wankowitz.

I then asked about the redoubtable wife of the superintendent, and Melanie grinned.

"That was nice of her," she said. "It's good to know that people are trying to protect you, though there's nothing to be protected from."

Ha! a bit of a connection. We spoke about the super and his wife; I learned that they had a son at Pratt Institute, a daughter at Seward Park High School. An interest in a woman will of course awaken interest in people who are in any way connected with that woman, and particularly if you have had any sort of connection yourself with the people so connected. Some connection I had with the super and his wife!

I saved the name of Warren for the end, out of a suspicion, a surmise, a fear, and her reaction justified these feelings.

"Oh, you met Sandy," she said.

But she said it in that pleasant, carefree manner which covers a closer bond.

"He's a poet," she said, "who works during the day in the Railway Express terminal."

She took a folded sheet of paper out of her bag.

"He occasionally slips a poem under my door," she said. "Here's one of them."

She handed it to me. I hesitated, and she went on:

"Oh, it's not personal, I wouldn't show you anything personal."

The poem was:

SEASIDE TOWN

Last night I dreamt of the seaside town
Where I spent my fairest days
I saw the faces of forgotten friends
The wind-ups of unfinished games.

I felt the wind and spray of the winter sea
In the streets of that buried town
I saw wondrous women, and stately men
In caps and ruffled gowns.

And in the summer, by the whispering waves
Of that blue and boundless sea,
We fought our sorrows and dreamed our joys
In the spray, the mystery.

Pale horizon, endless shore
Wave on wilful wave,
Figures of sleep, figures of shadow,
The lost, forgotten, and saved.

Last night I dreamt of that seaside town
Of homes, of street, of shore,
Where I spent my dreams, and spent my joy
And have them evermore.

We discussed this poem, which I thought had a nostalgic charm, but this discussion was bringing me further and further away from the object of my desire.

"I don't want to talk about his poetry," I said. "I don't even want to talk about *him*."

"You brought his name up," she said, "and is there any better way to tell you about a man than by showing you his poem?"

"I don't want to know about him," I said. "I wanted to talk about him a while back."

"That's no way to treat him," she said. "Would you want to be treated that way?"

I was angry with myself for this sudden and absurd fit of jealousy, and Melanie certainly was not pleased with me;

she said it was late and that she ought to be getting home. We walked home silently and paused in front of her apartment house. It was a moment when an ending was possible. Then Melanie smiled—it was an amused and understanding smile, and emboldened by this smile I shook hands with her (something I hate to do with a girl) and said: "Let's meet at the park bench tomorrow night."

"The day after tomorrow night," she said, and moved swiftly up the stoop stairs.

6. Criticisms

In the time between this unfortunate fit of jealousy and our scheduled meeting on the East River Drive, I thought a good deal about Melanie. I realized that I was disturbed by what I found to be a kind of carelessness or untidiness in her life—I couldn't think of a word that accurately characterized my feeling. I am rather orderly in my habits, but what did I know about her life, her habits? Her father dead in an automobile crash, her mother remarried—there was obviously nothing to criticize here. How many thousands of lives are taken in accidents every year? and her father a passenger in a car hit head on by a truck out of control. Then the mother remarried after five years. What is there to criticize here? But I am so used to a given family stability that these events somehow displeased me—my reasoning could not kill the sense that this was a wrong sequence of events for a family. And so with her own divorce—her husband apparently a ne'er-do-well, charming but couldn't hold a job, quickly bored, always on the move. Of course, it is not for us to judge the preferences of others, but I felt rather angry at Melanie for falling in love with so obviously shiftless a character, though where would I have been had she married well, and stayed married? The fact that she came from the Midwest also annoyed me—those vast spaces, prairies, so alien to my way of life. And all in keeping with a certain transiency about her. She said that she had not been living in her apartment very long; she gave the impression that she had not lived anywhere very long, though of course that could be attributed to the shiftlessness of her husband. And her relation to the law was troubling—her fear of the policeman and the curious protective attitude of the super's wife and of Warren, though *his* attitude could be attributed to jealousy, the sudden appearance of a rival on the scene. And showing me the poem—true, it wasn't a personal poem, except that every poem is a little personal, especially if it is given to you by the poet. Would Warren have approved my seeing it or approved her showing it to me? But it was an honest poem, and she showed it to me with a certain pride. What was wrong? And why was I looking so hard to criticize; how did I come to set up my kind of background as a basis from which to characterize and run down another style of life? Never had I criticized so soon and so severely a girl who had so swiftly interested me so much.

7. *An Impasse*

I arrived at the park bench early; when I am anxious, or guilty (remember my critical thoughts about Melanie), I have a tendency to arrive early at a meeting place, in fear, no doubt, that my keeper of the rendezvous, arriving early, or on time, will punish me by not waiting, and if I'm early I can be sure that she hasn't arrived yet, or at all. On other occasions I show up late to make an impression or to prove mastery; there is no end to the reasons, to the elaboration of reasons as to why one arrives late or early for an appointment, or for that matter why one arrives exactly on time. The devil knows what sexual and metaphysical interpretations are possible, but here I was nevertheless (for one moves, even through the miasma of reenforcing or contradictory interpretations) early for our meeting, anxious for our meeting. Walking up from my apartment on Jackson Street, I felt the wonder of this hot summer night, felt my youth and strength as I walked the familiar streets, dreaming love and glory, an endless panorama of these hot summer nights. Waiting on the bench, I gazed at the star-studded sky, lost in those icy distances, then heard Melanie take her place at my side. Her place at my side! I moved over silently, to embrace her, but she held me off, impersonally I thought, and that is the worst way to be held off. We sat silently for a while, and then I asked her what was wrong.

"It's about Dan," she said. "I heard from him, it's all very depressing."

"Is he sick, or in jail, or what?" I asked, not very much interested in her ex-husband.

"He's working for a company that manufactures and sells a spark-plug cleaner and tester," said Melanie. "He was all excited when he left, thought it was the greatest thing on the market, bought himself a car on time, and was given a territory in the Midwest. He disappoints very easy. He wrote from somewhere in Iowa; nobody seems to be interested in the spark-plug cleaner and tester, his car broke down, and he's plain broke and disgusted."

I too was upset, because my plans had been destroyed— I was all prepared for a little act. I had meant to tell her about the orgy of criticism I had directed against her, and to explain how this criticism was really a protection against a further involvement, a shield against love, against developing love. But she appeared with a preoccupation that excluded me, in a mood that denied my importance, almost my existence. My own mood of hope and futurity faded, I entered into her mood of glumness, helplessness, and we sat silently, the glorious summer night suddenly denuded of all its powers and promise. I was angry at the unexpected turn, angry that Melanie had come to me with problems that did not concern me (but they did concern me because of my concern for her), angry that my act had never reached the stage, angry that the power and promise of the summer night had now disappeared.

"What's his real problem?" I asked brutally, but the question apparently did not strike her as brutal, because she answered it, and not the way one answers a brutal question.

"He has a fundamental character weakness: he makes irrational decisions, is carried away by possibilities which he never deliberates on, the consequences of which he refuses to acknowledge, and so the reality most often disappoints him. He's always being disappointed—it goes back to a family situation, things promised to him as a child and then never delivered."

"I'm tired," I said, "of all this determinism about grown-up behavior. It's all right to excuse the behavior of children, even up to the ages of sixteen, seventeen, and eighteen—I don't know just what the cut-off date is—but at a certain point they must be judged as free agents, else life becomes a joyless reductive process."

"Yes," she said, "we're full of determinism for our friends and full of free will for our enemies."

"Your ex-husband is no enemy of mine," I replied. "I'm just not interested."

That wasn't very convincing, and we sat silently again, in the grip of an impasse.

It was an impasse, in the sense that it is impossible for two individuals to occupy separate worlds and, at the same time, to have any connection with one another. It is one of the most common forms of impasse, happening all the time; it is a cold and bitter thing, and it is even worse if there is a slight mutuality (meaning that the worlds have a certain connection), for what is worse than a slight connection when one's desire is for a full connection? For true distance, true individuality, is possible only when the mutuality is real, and it is only when the mutuality is real that the independence of the other can be respected.

"Let's walk," I said, and we headed north, under the star-drenched (why no longer star-studded?) sky.

"I wish it were raining," I said. It semed to be raining; the wonder of the summer night, on which I had embarked so joyously, which overflows reality (the way bubbling wine overflows the rim of a glass)—nature's fulfillment, creating man's hope of fulfillment, I must repeat that this hope was utterly destroyed, that wonder was utterly destroyed, I walked in a grey driving rain, walked in my soul's landscape.

She laughed, the gray mists began to fade.

"I'm glad we're walking," she said. "It's a lovely night."

And she made it so, by moving out of her troubles (from which I was excluded) into the wondrous present. It stopped raining, the stars appeared through the dissolving mist. What wonders a few words can accomplish, what remarkable power is in this our language, to make and unmake worlds, in a passing moment.

"I'm sorry that I bothered you with my troubles," she said, and that of course made me feel guilty, that I could not break through my own calculations and reach her, she being troubled.

"I'll send him some money," she said. "He'll get out of it quickly enough, and find something else to interest him."

She sounded as though she were talking about a child, but I naturally made no point of that.

On her way to her house (for we were clearly on our way to her house, the night was obviously coming to an end at the foot of the stoop) I told Melanie something about my critical reflections concerning her. I told her that I considered these critical reflections a barrier to other feelings, but when you overthink or overfeel a matter, it is hard to talk about it with much sense or much feeling—you find that you are reading a script that you have memorized. So my remarks didn't have much strength, they didn't too much reflect my feelings, they seemed rather unreal. I was sorry to be making these remarks, and stopped making them because they had lost their importance for me.

"Someday," I said, "I'll tell you what I really thought, when I'm off the stage."

"You've told me," she said.

We were in front of her apartment house. The great distance between us with which the evening had begun was cut down, but it had not disappeared, and the night ended on a friendly note, the kind of note I hate, for it creates a connection which I find very uninteresting.

Nevertheless, there she was, with me, at the top of the steps.

"Goodnight," she cried, smiling, "and thanks for not referring to me as *Craig's wife*."

Puzzled, I realized that her married name was Craig.

8. *"Three Days Passed"*

Now time passed. It happens in the best of fictions, the way it is written: "After three months," or "In the year that elapsed." I find such phrases very unpleasant; usually they mean to me that the author is avoiding the hard reality (he is not alone), the difficulty of everyday life, so he creates these vacuums of time, and then moves to some exciting moment, to something more *interesting*. It is what makes difficult the description of a working day or of a day-to-day married life. We seek the peaks of existence, but all dramas, revelations, epiphanies—call them what you will—require a matrix of experience, of behavior, the necessitous and not always inspiring acts and dreams of the working day, the working marriage. No essence without *materia*, if I quote the philosophers correctly. So it is easier, more *interesting* (in a way), to describe the action of characters who do not live together and whose meetings necessarily follow these time spans, these pockets of time—that is a more interesting phrase. Three days passed before I saw Melanie again; I phoned her and made an appointment for Saturday afternoon. I found that the time (between one meeting and another) passed slowly, for I was anxious to see her again. The days between were made interesting by the prospect of the meeting, the way it is under the circumstances.

9. *Something About My Plans*

I picked Melanie up on Saturday afternoon, and we decided, that is, I suggested and she agreed, to walk across town and take the Christopher Street Ferry over to Hoboken, more for the ferry ride than to get to Hoboken, but with Hoboken as a goal nevertheless. It was the time when Hoboken was losing out to Brooklyn as the place-name whose mention (with a given intonation or emphasis) was enough to cause laughter—if not gales of laughter, certainly a grin of perverse satisfaction. Brooklyn was moving ahead in this unenviable race partly because of the antics of its big-league ball team; members of this team were stealing occupied bases, passing base runners, catching high flies on their noggins, etc. As a historian (for that was my chosen field) I mentioned this curiosity of certain cities becoming butts, their very name striking people as comical.

"It's sometimes the very sound of the name," she said. "Oshkosh."

We both laughed.

"It's probably a corruption of a fine Indian name," I said. "But Brooklyn," I went on, "doesn't have a curious sound," and I told her about some of the Dodger antics. She was not interested in baseball, though it was the time in radical politics

—in which she *was* interested—of the flowering of the People's Front, when every American custom, previously excoriated as a symbol of bourgeois decadence, formalism, or escapism, was suddenly invested with a deep historical value. Roots were discovered everywhere. "If Jefferson were alive today, he'd be a member of the C.P." "If Lenin were alive, he'd be playing second base for the Brooklyn Dodgers." After a while, it was the critic rather than the adherent of the line who was making these remarks. Melanie was not much interested in the national pastime, saw it neither as a mechanism of escape nor as a flowering of our culture; she didn't think it was very important, thought there were more "serious" things to consider, was depressed by this factitious method of reaching the masses, and was only mildly impressed with my (I hoped) graphic descriptions of the behavior of some of the Dodgers.

"Hoboken sounds funny," she said, "because of the word *hobo* in it."

"I never thought of that explanation," I said. "Sounds pretty reasonable."

We passed the Cooper Union and went right down 8th Street to 6th Avenue, at which point we crossed over to Christopher Street and headed for the docks. It was a hot afternoon, we walked very much together, Melanie rather quiet, but not dissatisfied, and holding my arm, the first time she had ever done that. It was very pleasant to walk the streets that way, in a kind of free-floating manner. We seemed more together than we had ever been, and I thought to myself, selfishly, that it was better to be with her away from her apartment and associations.

"I just thought," I said, "that you seem so much more with me when you're away from your own place, when we're moving in new territory."

"We do have to get back" she said, "but why bring the matter up?"

She smiled, held my arm more firmly, and so we moved

easily down Christopher Street and found a ferry waiting for us.

The short water ride, plus Melanie's easy attitude, caused me to tell her something about the work that I was doing. She knew, of course, that I had won my master's degree in American history, and was now working toward my doctorate.

"I have a great desire to write universal history," I said, as we stood looking down toward New York Bay and sensing the ocean beyond, "but that is the most philosophical, and I'm not ready for it. I say that, but sometimes I think I'll never be more ready than I am now, because it's best to do the biggest task when you have the most energy. Yet, history is not like poetry. There *are* materials, and we *must* gain an understanding of these materials, and then a control over them. The more knowledge and control, the keener the intuitions, the more you can light up the field. At any rate, I've slowly been cutting down my work area. I was going to work on a history of New York City, I don't want to give up altogether my interest in universal history (the way it is when you deal with an entity), then I worked that down to a history of the street on which I'm now living, having considered first, naturally, a history of the neighborhood. The street I live on is Jackson Street, and I'm living there because it was the street on which my father lived when he came to America. What really happened was that I was looking around for a place, picked this place though there were others with more advantages, and *then*, having moved in, I realized that this was the street on which my father lived when he first came to this country."

"A history of Jackson Street could be a history of America," said Melanie.

"True enough," I said, "but I'm not writing a history of Jackson Street, I'm writing a history of the building in which I live. To be more precise, I'm writing a history of the apartment in which I live."

Melanie smiled at my somewhat precipitous decline from the grandiose to the minute, but it was a friendly, sympathetic smile.

I paused in this account of my intellectual autobiography, and we saw, down in the bay, the shape of a transatlantic liner moving up toward its river berth.

"It's very nice," she said, "to see the city from the water this way. Isn't it one of the ways that Whitman liked to see it?"

We looked back together at the island city in the shimmer of the afternoon sun, and then the ferry worked its way into the Hoboken slip, and we landed, as though from afar, and set our feet on the alien soil.

10. *Abroad*

"It is like being abroad," I said, as we set feet on the soil of Hoboken.

But it was because we were together in another place, that the place seemed strange; it beckoned to us in the way that a familiar place neglects to beckon.

We blinked in the Hoboken sun, we walked on the earth of Hoboken above the dead of that city, we gazed, going nowhere in particular (quite different from going somewhere in general), at the citizens of Hoboken and the visitors to Hoboken, we looked into the store windows and sized up the architecture of Hoboken, we walked along the Hoboken docks, breathed the air of Hoboken, enjoyed its hospitality and then, exhausted (outdoor museum fatigue), we sat down in a diner, in a corner fairly close to a jukebox, which was playing a song that was a couple of years old, "*The Very Thought of You.*"

"*And I forget to do the ordinary things that everyone ought to do,*" I quoted, as we ordered from a cheerful waiter, as compared to a glum waiter. It is very pleasant when tired to be greeted cheerfully in a restaurant or diner—it revives, at a time when there are eating places everywhere, the notion of an inn as a sanctuary against the elements. Tired, exhausted after driving through rain and storm for six hours, you drive into the courtyard, throw the reins to the porter, and enter the cheerful inn, warm and waiting.

"How are you getting along with your thesis?" asked Melanie, and I was surprised by her question, not so much because I didn't think she was interested, but because I thought she wouldn't find the subject interesting to talk about. That relates to a curious weakness of mine: it never strikes me that anything in which I am involved can be of any importance to others, but at the same time I will think that it is too important for them to understand.

"The building I live in," I said, "is seventy-three years old. It is now owned by a direct descendant of the original owner, who had it built as a private home. The present owner is in his eighties, he moved into the house when he was about ten and lived in it until he was thirty. The neighborhood changed, the house was converted into an apartment house. I have all the information about the original structure—the old man has all the bills and documents, which he has kindly put at my disposal. And there are the old man's remembrances about the house and the neighborhood. He is pleased to talk about those days; they must have been happy ones for him, though people talk about unhappy childhood days, too. There have been only six occupants of the apartment that I now occupy. That seems amazing, doesn't it? But Oliver Wendell Holmes's grandfather was a contemporary of Washington's, isn't that so? We live in a young country. At any rate, of the six occupants, one is dead or untraceable, one family lives out West, the other four (individuals or families) are here in the city. They represent successive waves of immigration, reflect the social and economic changes. I saw a woman last week who had lived in my apartment for seven years. She is about fifty now, married to a well-to-do merchant—that word sounds a little more respectable than a businessman. I am convinced that she was a prostitute; she was very suspicious when I came to see her, didn't cotton much to my explanation about the doctoral thesis."

Melanie laughed.

"You have a way of looking for women, and your explanations don't quite satisfy."

I was a bit miffed by her remark.

"You're making a mountain out of a *mohel*," I said, and when she looked puzzled I explained that a *mohel* was a circumcizer among the Jews.

"Of course," she said, "but you pronounced it so curiously. I remember vaguely my brother's circumcision."

"So you remember the circumcision of a younger brother to whom you are very much attached. It's obvious that you thought he was being killed, which fitted in with your own desires, and then when it turned out that he hadn't been killed you were relieved, but nevertheless it is always as though you were an accomplice in his death."

Now in those days it was a sign of affection to engage in that kind of wild psychoanalysis, and Melanie smiled it off.

"Anyway," I went on, "I've gathered a lot of information about the house and the apartment. I even have the achitect's plans. The material is piling up, and my problem already is to pare it down, to make something real of it."

We listened to the jukebox play a real old song:

Everybody loves my baby
But my baby don't love
Nobody but me

and I said that when I first heard that song I thought that the word "baby" referred to an infant, and then I went on about my thesis.

"My problem," I said, "is that I can't get close enough to

the materials. You see how little I've really told you—no names mentioned, nothing incriminating, everything quite abstract."

She put her hand on mine, and I thought that a most charming gesture. I removed my hand from under hers and put it on her hand, kept it there till the waiter came by.

"What you're doing sounds great," she said. "You have a chance to get to the heart of our society, to its class structure, to the element of fluidity in that structure; also the birth and death of neighborhoods."

These remarks pleased me; her connection with my work made the work seem more interesting.

It was coming to be evening, and we decided to have dinner in the city and then go on to a dance recital, which Melanie wanted very much to see.

11. Back on the Ferry

We were early for our ferry, found it waiting for us —like a good faithful creature—and took seats in the stateroom for the eastern crossing. On the wall were instructions about the use of the life preservers, describing their location, with pictures of a gentleman properly accoutered for the conceivable emergency. The boat rolled gently, proving that we were in water.

When the boat started, we went onto the rear deck, and I said, in the manner of the announcer at the end of the travelogues as the boat is leaving some exotic Pacific isle: "So we say farewell to Hoboken, to its smiling inhabitants, its strange customs, its curious architecture and ancient taboos. Farewell to the jukebox and all it's meant to me, and as the sun sinks over the horizon we leave (regretfully) the friends we have made and promise that, if circumstances permit, we will return again, to live once more among these friendly people, to eat their food, to drink their beverages, to join with them in their festivities, to sorrow with them in their trials and losses. Farewell Hoboken, aloha. . . ."

This travelogue was interrupted by the appearance of a man who came up to us and greeted Melanie in what I thought was a rather angry and distant manner, a little hurt and a strong personal interest underneath.

Melanie introduced us. He was about thirty-five, thin, intense. He spoke slowly, meant others to think that his words deserved special attention, no triviality here. His remarks to Melanie had a significance which was meant to exclude me. His name was Arthur.

"Haven't seen you around for a while," he said in this meaningful manner; the most commonplace remarks were given this treatment.

"That's true," said Melanie, "and you won't."

After this esoteric exchange, I was included in the conversation, and we discussed, for a few minutes, the up-coming campaign.

"Landon must be defeated at all costs," said the newcomer, which meant that he was going to vote for Roosevelt instead of Browder.

At the time we naturally did not know that Roosevelt would sweep the country, excluding Maine and Vermont, giving rise to Jim Farley's famous quip, "As Maine goes, so goes Vermont." So the slogan "Defeat Landon at all costs" turned out not to have been the most profound prognosis of an American election. But this is thinking backward; it was my intention to vote for Norman Thomas, a statement that either annoyed or upset Arthur, I couldn't tell which, but it certainly—how shall we say?—speeded up his hostility. He was every bit as angry at Melanie for being with me as he was at me for favoring the Socialist candidate. But he was angry at me before he knew that I was going to vote for the Socialist candidate.

"The Republicans will destroy all the gains of the New Deal," he said.

"*Vote your hopes, not your fears,*" I quoted, and Arthur snorted.

"Idealistic idiocy" he said, but the ferry was moving into the Christopher Street slip, and that brought our short conversation to an end.

12. *Covering Some Ground*

A narrative is selective; there is no need to tell everything that happened, or if there is such a need it cannot be fulfilled (for reasons of selectivity). Only that is chosen from the minutiae of happenings, the vast (though finite) number of minutiae, that has a bearing on what it is the story is coming to say (the absence of the unerring choice keeps you in the chaos you are trying to avoid), and much of this narrative, of what it is that happened, can be told swiftly, not because it is less important than what has to be told slowly but simply because it becomes necessary at a given time to get along with the thing, not to resist the necessary development (out of ignorance of what is going to happen or out of fear of what has to happen), and to imitate experience, to heighten and depress it. We went off the ferry without another word to Arthur, moved onto the practically earthquake-free isle, onto the crosstown bus moving (naturally) east, and rode with a group of strangers over to 8th Street—past landmarks since demolished, for we are free with our buildings on this earthquake-free isle to destroy what Lisbon or Prague would keep for centuries, past the Lafayette Hotel (may it rest in peace), past the Cooper Union and the Bible House, the latter now buried in the demolition-construction graveyard, past the Turkish Bath and many another landmark, buried or standing—till we came to the corner closest to Melanie's apartment house, and there we alighted (no fools we), having decided (Melanie had, en route) that we'd have a bite at her place, she being a bit tired and wanting the feel of home, very restful for some, which was all right with me. I was glad to have something at her apartment rather than rush through a meal on the outside, and I watched in admiration as she whipped up a fast dinner. I found it very pleasant to be in that domestic air, unusual for me outside the home of my parents. I found it difficult most of the time to realize that Melanie had been married; she didn't *look* as though she had ever been married, but watching her move with ease (and grace) at the task of preparing a meal, that ancient ritual, I saw her as a young woman recently divorced, and that put me at a certain distance, the way a lack of understanding will. Melanie changed her attire, and there we were, going out on Saturday night! I complimented her, rather gravely, on her appearance and followed her down the steps. Outside, we passed the super's wife, who was standing in front of the stoop. She said hello to Melanie and looked at me without batting an eye. We walked over to 3rd Avenue and then up to 18th Street, coming to the recital hall twenty minutes early.

13. *The Moment Before the Recital, the Recital*

I have a tendency, much criticized (by myself and by others), to stand before an object, or to circle round it, or to consider irrelevancies—all ways, I am told (or tell myself), of avoiding the object, ways of not coming to grip with the object. So, if I am sitting in an auditorium, when, as now, I am sitting in an auditorium—benches for seats, lack of decoration everywhere—early as we were for the dance recital, I become preoccupied with the moment before the opening, with the concept of the moment before the opening. I find that moment very interesting—the build-up of hum, the slow gathering of strangers, the expectancy, and when the curtain opens, the moment we are all awaiting, I feel that the best part of the evening is gone, just when the first line is spoken, or the first move made, just when it becomes necessary to come to grips with the prepared reality, the words or the movement calculated to please, to electrify or improve, to bore us to tears (I have never been bored to tears, only to stupefaction), to anger or exalt us, or having these effects without calculation. Though the curtain is up, and the first movements made, I find myself still preoccupied with the moment before the opening, and then it is an effort to come to grips with the prepared reality, but come to grips with it we must, and do, and so watch the movements on the bare stage, designed in the mid-depression style, as compared to early-depression and late-depression.

This dance group, to which Melanie belonged—more as an advanced student than as a performer, though on an occasion she might fill in—was one of the splits from the Martha Graham group. It was the time of splits, in politics and in art. This particular group moved towards the social protest —Graham in form, radical in content. The slogan "Art Is a Weapon" was now popular, and the most violent attacks were being made on the Ivory Tower; art was to point up the evils of the time and to impel the reader, or listener, or observer, to an action calculated to remedy these evils. This is not an ignoble theory of art—why very little of greatness came out of this movement is an interesting puzzle. Little of greatness comes from any art theory. There are no doubt special problems relating to art and immediacy, there is a danger of rawness, the nice balance between movement and message is blurred, or lost; with a more philosophic, and so more timely message, Martha Graham continues to move towards the heart of reality. The Great Depression did not bring suffering into the world, it brought more of an old form of it into our world, and these girls moved toward us, accused us of indolence, of participating in monstrous crimes—*our* hands were on the throat of China, *we* brought Hitler into power—as though they had suddenly discovered suffering and injustice, knew the cause, and where to put the blame. After a while the audience became restive, including even those who agreed with the dancers' analysis of the situation. We were being told what we pretty much knew, the content was swallowing the form, a man in front of me was feeling his head as though he had been pounded by a rolled-up newspaper. Now and then there were flashes of genuine feeling, even illuminations of the sordid reality, hints of the Utopia which all honest critiques of social injustice must reveal.

14. *Claw and Conscience*

During the intermission (whose psycho-formal attributes I neglect to chronicle) I saw Horace Dow, a biology instructor at Columbia, and his wife, Mathilda. I had been to their apartment for dinner, and asked them to join us for coffee after the recital, not so much in payment for the dinner—what sort of repayment would it be for dinner?—but because I rather liked them, and particularly liked Horace, though we were by no means on close terms. He is the most genuinely *nice* person that I know. "Nice" is of course a catchall word, said out of guilt, ignorance, lack of knowledge, lack of interest, or plain laziness in the face of having to characterize a person (as though a person were incomplete unless he were characterized). But there is a purity at the heart of every word, and Horace was nice because he was without airs, because his envy was at the irreducible minimum, because he did things for people without making a big deal of it, and because he had an interesting way of looking at things as facts of nature or society (one can be nice with the opposites of these qualities, the niceness being an amalgam). Now this last-mentioned quality could be described as *aloofness;* it has the elements of aloofness, in another person it could easily *be* aloofness.

But Horace was not aloof; he observed with thought, with interest, if not with a partisan involvement, the way, I suppose, a scientist watches a specimen in growth or decline—some scientists, that is, because there is a breaking point of involvement for all. If I knew Horace better, I would surely find a bias, a morality buried deep in his attitude. But that morality (I was convinced) would be in the area of tolerance, fairness, the old virtues we are sometimes ashamed to acknowledge when partisanship is so much called for (but partisanship and fairness can go together). Mathilda (whom I knew not so well) was a spirited girl with a New England background who loved the arts and was full of enthusiasm for the new and for the good cause. She was a mid-thirties liberal (I am talking of the time and not of her age), the word "liberal" of course demanding the most scrupulous definition from period to period. The Dows agreed to meet us after the recital. Melanie brushed off my late realization that she might want to see some of the girls in the troupe afterwards. The four of us walked to a cafeteria a few blocks off.

Taking everything into account (undoubtedly a phrase from the commercial world—figuring the profit and the loss) we had a pleasant, even an interesting time. Now a typical conversation among four reasonably articulate adults over a period of two hours would run to something like twenty-five or thirty thousand words, most of which are clearly not worth repeating—I mean the fatuities, politenesses, insincerities, witless pleasantries, and factual materials of an uninteresting sort. Some conversation, in the form of meetings of generals, conspirators, executives, is meant to push forward a plan of action; it is not conversation at all, for conversation has an ease, a largeness, it is not predetermined, it gives each individual a chance to express himself on a subject that all choose together. It is the triumph of society, and one of its abiding pleasures; combining intelligence, morality, and wit, it can even be a supreme pleasure.

Our conversation dawdled; we discussed the recital, I asked the Dows about their five-year-old daughter, gossiped about the University, we asked and answered polite questions about one another's activities, moved back to the recital, and then got onto the question of egotism and altruism (via the problem of Marxism and morality, the prophetic strain in Marx, if Isaiah were alive today, etc.).

This area of the conversation was carried on mostly between Horace and myself, the women having deferred from the discussion of "serious" matters as they will do sometimes —I put the word *serious* in quotes not to run down the seriousness of the subject but only to suggest that most any subject may be treated seriously. Horace, with his usual restraint, upheld the importance of egotistical behavior in natural advance and therefore in social advance as well. He used the classic Darwinian arguments, pointed to the disappearance of species that were too weak to survive, and suggested the value of strength, the aggressive instincts, in the evolutionary scheme.

"But what about that chapter in the *Descent of Man?*" I asked. "Doesn't he give examples of sympathetic, even sacrificial behavior—of the mother bird for the fledgling, and so on? And don't we see examples of mutuality in the primitive tribes, examples of help towards the weak and helpless in one's own tribe?"

These thoughts (as I pointed out) I had found reenforced by a recent reading of Kropotkin. I was tired of the argument (which Horace had hinted at) that sympathy for the oppressed was a kind of self-indulgence if it was not followed by dramatic action on their behalf, and argued that if it were not for this original sympathy (which so many radicals were ashamed of) there would be no consequent action, and egotism would triumph everywhere. I threw in some swift blows at Hobbes, and pointed up the Nietzschian elements in this argument for egotism.

As the argument proceeded, I became quite excited, even furious with Horace, who maintained his position (involving, as it did, the priority of the aggressive instincts) in that manner of his that did not claim that his position was right, but simply described how natural, individual, and social life developed. I accused him of Hegelianism and reminded him that Hegel's position brought the philosopher to a deification of the Prussian state—what is, is right, etc. But Horace denied holding such a view, maintained his stubborn spectatorial attitude towards the processes of natural and social selection. So there he was—arguing urbanely, politely, on the side (as I saw it) of egotism, while I, angrily, full of hostility, argued for sympathy, mutuality. Then the discussion tapered off, became desultory, and so we left one another.

"Try to be sympathetic to my point of view," said Horace, with an unaccustomed ring of acerbity. I answered that I was sympathetic to him but not to his point of view, but the remark had a hollow ring to it. I was *fundamentally* sympathetic to him but not sympathetic at the moment, though somehow I didn't get around to making that point to him.

15. *We Discuss the Situation*

I am not a statistician, but I know that in a city of eight million, the odds against meeting anyone who does not live in your neighborhood or work near where you work (or near where you live) are very high. I am acquainted with many hundreds of people on the island of Manhattan, people I have not met in the streets for ten, twenty years, in some cases never met at all. However, if you know where a person lives, or works, and make it a point to walk into that area or onto that street, the odds against meeting (statistician or not) are obviously going to be cut down considerably. And if you should stand in front of a building, at a time when the working day is ended, waiting for a person who works in that building, the odds for the meeting will obviously turn sharply in your favor. So I wasn't surprised when Melanie came out of the Con Edison building, though she was surprised, because the odds against two people meeting one another in a city of eight million are staggering. But when she came to realize that I was waiting for her in front of the place where she worked, and precisely at the time when she was due to finish her work, she was less surprised than she had been at the moment of meeting. The odds against our meeting, under the circumstances, would not have interested the cagey gambler.

She was surprised but not displeased to see me, to find me waiting for her. She was not overwhelmed with joy; she felt my presence as a kind of intrusion, a taking-for-granted of a situation that she did not altogether take for granted. But she was not seriously displeased at seeing me, had no appointment for the evening, and accepted my invitation for dinner.

We went to one of those Russian restaurants with native music (though it is not easy to say what the native country is —there is always a little gypsy mixed in) and a tall chap in front—more of a come-on man than a doorman—with a Cossack hat and a definite Czarist, White Guard appearance. "Comes the Revolution," I said to him, "we'll *all* eat strawberries and cream," and he grinned, for the place was frequented by radicals of every shade of opinion, and he was prepared for most any remark.

Melanie spoke to me about her political life. I mentioned Arthur's name; she said that she knew him from the Party, knew him by two names, and could never remember which was his real and which his assumed name, his Party name, and that was why she introduced him by his first name. She had been a Party member for about a year, but had quit—she didn't like the concentration of power in the Soviet Union, she felt that she had no real access to what was going on there, she had heard disquieting news about the forced collectivization, the famine of 1932, the beginning of political purges, the steady cultural deterioration, and felt keenly the inability to get reasonable answers to questions she raised. It was as though the raising of the question was in itself a sign of disloyalty; the information given out seemed to be screened, in line with what the leaders thought ought to be given out, and sometimes it seemed as though the leaders themselves were being fed screened information.

She was troubled and felt that something ought to be done. She was activist by nature or inclination, she didn't like to be on the outside as a critic, spoke about Fascism, the unemployed, the war danger. She was not neurotic about her political allegiances, showed a sober interest in what we called, in those days, "the objective situation." She had a strong sense of injustice, and wanted to be involved in the remedying of these glaring social evils, but was now in an impasse. She felt that the Party was doing a certain amount of important work, particularly in the unionizing of the mass industries, but feared the mindless totalitarian drift.

"It is no accident," I said, using the famed introductory cliche, "that you are telling me all this here in this fortress of counterrevolution, in this White Guard cesspool."

She didn't take to my badinage; she was upset by her position, or lack of a position, and was seeking a way out, a way of using her moral energy and strength to improve the situation.

16. Back in the Street

We went out into the street and walked aimlessly, the way people who are interested in one another can walk aimlessly, up Irving Place, back and around and so to Union Square. There was a great deal of activity on the Square. Dozens of groups filled the park (it has no playground equipment of any sort). There were political speakers ranging from Oehlerites to Liberty Leaguers; there were vegetarians, naturopaths, experts in evolution, statistical demographers, Malthusians, evangelists, meliorists, Manicheans, deep breathers, necromancers, milleniards, maybe a guilt-ridden millionaire, antivivisectionists (but no vivisectionists), militant pacifists, Single Taxers, a weird spectrum of those who felt they had something of interest to say, and said it, in varying degrees of sincerity and conviction. A gray and sexless scene. The pathos and helplessness of it! the lumpen drabness of it! the struggle against forces so powerful, so distant, so mysterious! We walked from group to group, lingering according to the relationship between the interest of the subject and the ability of the speaker. Curious how the sexual distinctions were blurred here, the women losing their sex in this welter of discourse and harangue. The men theirs! Lightning flashes lit up the scene—the circles of discussants, the open stretches of pavement, the stone horse and rider, the trees desperately staying alive, we all hungrily reaching out to one another, to create a sense of individual value, a sense of communion. Then the rain began to fall—those big, soft, slow drops that presage a downpour. We scampered across 14th Street to the protection of Ohrbach's awning, and then to the cafeteria near the Academy of Music. We sat by the window and watched the rain come down, solid summer rain with its accessories, growling thunder and the zig and the zag of lightning. It was the kind of rain that brought you together, in the sense that you couldn't possibly go out, and because the rain, not being a menace, constituted a protective sheath against the horrors beyond. The situation in which we found ourself was quite different from that of our aimless wandering.

17. *Out of the Rain*

"Our house was unusually orderly," said Melanie, "and it was all my mother's character, her doing. The house was an intricate web of order, I can't put it any other way, and my mother was acutely sensitive to the slightest break. If a little mud was tracked onto the carpet, or a coat wasn't promptly hung up in the closet, or a desk wasn't tidied up after use, that kind of thing, she would become very annoyed, read us all sorts of lectures about neatness, order, discipline. It was a way of warding off the uncontrolled outside forces, to keep out the winds forever howling at the door, to create a self-contained system, a shield against chance and fortune. And then my father killed senselessly, in a moment. . . ."

Her eyes clouded; she paused and went on: "So you see I've reacted against that kind of artificial order, where it is meant to keep down the forces of life, to take a stranglehold on growing reality; you see there is a basis for the disorder which seemed to upset you."

I side-stepped the criticism which was being tossed back at me.

"Your life doesn't seem too unusually disorganized," I said. "You have a regular job."

I smiled, in order to disguise the fatuousness of this remark.

"No, I don't," she corrected me, "it's a temporary job. I was on Relief before, and I hope to be getting on the Writer's Project in the autumn."

She was perhaps waiting for me to criticize her for her occupational irregularity, but I wasn't at all in the mood for that; I picked up the general thread of the conversation.

"The kind of order which you speak of is very common in our society—what you said about this order as a technique to ward off the unexpected, the horrible, to propitiate the forces of evil and accident, is quite true. Look how we're insulated from poverty, from sickness and death. I remember standing in front of an apartment house one evening, and suddenly two men came through the door swiftly, carrying a green bag. A dead person was in that bag. You'd think that person had done something shameful by dying, to have to be spirited off that way in the evening."

"Let's skip that part," she said, and we looked out at the rain, which had lost its torrential character and was coming down steadily.

"The elements are disorderly," she said, "but we had enough sense to come in out of the rain."

"That's true," I said, "but we're not denying that the rain exists, the way some deny the existence of poverty, disease, and death."

We looked out at the rain, which had lost its steadiness and was now coming down slowly. "Let's make a run for it," I said, but when we got into the street we discovered that it wasn't raining at all, and we breathed in all the freshness of the recently departed summer rain.

18. *Happiness*

"But my parents were happy together," said Melanie, and it wasn't clear to me whether she believed that or said it out of guilt (carrying the guilt for her mother, as though her mother's habits of domestic order could have caused an accident outside the house, in an automobile!) or said it out of a sudden rush of loyalty, to protect the identity of her family, the merits of her family, against a stranger.

"I mean," she said, "that their marriage was not one of those patch jobs forever breaking open at the point of weakness; it had a kind of boring solidity. I remember how they'd come back at night, after a visit to friends or some social function, and sit up late, over coffee, discussing the events of the evening, laughing over this one's behavior or that one's remark. When people return silent from an evening out —that's a bad sign."

It was not late—we walked slowly, if not aimlessly, hesitated on 2nd Avenue, and then (it was only ten o'clock, the streets were so cool) continued on towards the river.

"I guess there is a certain element of boredom in happiness, I said. "At least the novelists seem to think so—people's trials and difficulties interest them most. A description of a happy marriage is a literary rarity, probably something to do with the absence of conflict."

"There could be no happiness without the conflict," she said. "Happiness is an accomplishment over odds, it is something won, or lost."

"Look at the ending of fairy tales," I said, *"and they lived happily ever after.* When the trials end, and the happiness begins, the author ends his tale, begs off."

"That's a particular kind of adventure story" she said, "that tends to end when the marriage begins. The harder task, and I imagine the truer happiness, is the life you make together against the outer world, rather than the one that is forced on you. Marriage is a difficult institution—daily habitual life easily turns boring, then violent."

"The happy marriages I've seen," I said, "depend a good deal on the man's accomplishments outside the house."

"That's a factor," she said.

"It seems as though happiness is an ideal," I said, "and that the novelist is more interested in the unfinished situation."

"No no," she said, "happiness is not an ideal, it is an actuality struggling with other actualities; once you look upon it as a goal, you're in trouble. It is what Flaubert said about success, that it is not a goal but a result."

"That's true," I said, "and yet we say 'seeking happiness.' It's a common expression."

"Well," she said, "you cannot have too much of a good thing."

We had come to the river; having reached it, saw that it was somewhat a goal, and sat down. We took our fill of the scene, for the moon had appeared after the storm and lit up the scene for us. We silently watched and silently kissed, silently followed the harbor boats and the passage of the moon.

19. *Night at the Stadium*

The very next day (after our dinner in the Russian restaurant, our aimless walk, our discussion—in the cafeteria, during the rain—about order and—over the river, after the rain—about happiness) Melanie called me and said that her brother was in from his summer camp in Massachusetts (he was a counselor) on an unexpected day off and asked whether I could go with them that evening up to Lewisohn Stadium.

"I sure can," I replied, particularly pleased that she had asked me because I knew how close she was to her brother; that feeling was cut back a little when she told me that Frank —her brother—was bringing a girl.

A series of complexities ruled out dinner together, and we met in front of the Liberty Restaurant on Broadway and 137th Street. Frank was with a girl he knew from Ohio State, where he had finished his junior year. The girl's name was Jill, I didn't quite catch the second name. She was a pretty, dark-haired girl of nineteen; Frank was a good-looking boy, and they made a nice couple, whatever that means. Melanie was flushed, happy, she hadn't seen her brother for a year, and as we walked up the steep blocks towards the Stadium she told me that this was the first time that she had been on a double-date with her brother. Frank was a waterfront counselor at camp, and Jill was working in the city for her father, who was a lawyer specializing in real estate.

I found Melanie's happiness somewhat irritating, found it annoying that another person (even a brother) should bring her happiness, or more exactly that *much* happiness, for she was unusually elated. It meant, of course, that I had no confidence in my own ability along these lines, I mean of making her happy, or creating the preconditions for her happiness. But I noted the canker on the rose—if Frank were not her brother, he'd have been the kind of young man she would not be interested in at all. There was—how shall we say—an absence of seriousness in her brother; he seemed not at all preoccupied with the problems that disturbed her, problems of justice and choice, all the strange moralities tied to the burning social issues of the day. He was very much interested in swimming, thought that he might make a career in the field of physical education; there was nothing wrong in that, but brother and sister looked at the world so differently —he was interested in making his way, his approach was conventional, he lacked his sister's awareness of suffering, of the historic process, he looked away from the horrors of the time. He and Jill were walking ahead of us up the hill, and Melanie said to me:

"They're going to a fraternity dance afterwards."

She said it somewhat defensively; my reply was perverse.

"What's wrong with that?" I asked. "Isn't it fun to dance?"

I realized that I had never danced with Melanie.

"I didn't say there was anything wrong with it," she said, "just an objective statement."

Then she added: "Well, maybe not so objective."

"They're a very nice couple," I said, and hearing the remark wasn't quite sure whether it was flat or ironical.

But she didn't want to make judgments of that sort about her brother and his friend—she was holding on to something very important in her childhood, and did not want to destroy that. She objected, however, to what she considered to be the blandness of my remark. The fact is, though, that I tend to be rather less judging of those I do not know well, particularly strangers, than I am of friends or those I know well (for it is not the friends we necessarily know well), and was rather interested in Frank and Jill, in their "frame of reference," so to speak. And Jill was very attractive. Melanie was rather reserved with her, found conversation difficult, but I talked easily—about college life, curriculum, sports, faculty, etc. I was part of that life myself, and was not too bored by the institutional small talk. My ease with them annoyed Melanie; that is, she was pleased that I got along with them (for that made the evening so much easier, if not more pleasurable), but suspected a certain condescension on my part, maybe even thought that I was scornful of the couple and putting on an act. But she was happy to be with her brother.

"Sandy Warren is having a few friends over tonight," she said. "Would you like to come?"

"Certainly," I replied, piqued at the formality of the invitation. Why couldn't she have said:

"Sandy Warren is having a few friends over tonight, and he's expecting us?"

But she invited me; I knew she was disturbed by the way her brother was growing up and perhaps angry at me because I understood her feelings. Would she rather have me obtuse?

Now we were in front of the Stadium, early enough to get seats without any trouble (Frank insisted on buying the tickets for himself and his date, over my remonstrances). Then the night slowly fell, and we were part of the great crowd listening to the concert. Frank was pleased to be with his sister, but was uneasy about her lack of connection with Jill, who seemed less concerned than the rest of us and more involved in the social and natural scene. She didn't act annoyed, I don't think that she was much interested in Melanie or in me—we weren't her "type"—but she wasn't em-

barrassed the way others might have been under the circumstances. We were not the most homogeneous group. Then the
music came, mostly Beethoven and Tchaikovsky, and that
carried us off into our separate reveries, according to our
needs and inclinations, according to the content, style, and
tempo of the music.

20. *We Break It Up*

After the last note had died away and the last of the
listeners was out of the Stadium (though before the last star
had faded), we stood together on the Amsterdam Avenue
corner, at rather unpleasant crosspurposes. Frank and Jill were
headed for the West Side (it was not a fraternity dance; one
of Jill's sorority sisters was having an engagement party. How
could Melanie, who was so scrupulously honest in her personal reportage, have thought it was a fraternity dance?
Because she could not have it that Jill was leading her brother,
she was antagonistic to the direction in which he was moving.
Better his fraternity dance than her sorority party. So does
personal predilection, the soul's bias, distort the mind's objectivity), and we of course were going down to St. Mark's
Place for Sandy Warren's party. We were bored as couples
but tied as a group by the intense consanguinity of Frank and
Melanie. They found it difficult to go downtown separately,
though it was what they wanted as individuals in the separate
couples. So we carried on an absurd conversation about
transportation routes, trying to bridge the East Side and the
West Side by means of crosstown buses, etc. But all the time
the two couples wanted to separate, go their own ways. "My
friend is on Riverside Drive and 77th Street," said Jill, and
one suddenly saw the width of the island as a vast no-man's
land. I was quiet, for it was one of those moments when
anything you say will be wrong, and then Melanie said:

"We'll take the Independent down, and we'll see you later, Frank," as though the later meeting would cancel out the deviate routes. Then we said good-bye all around and moved off, relieved at the disjunction.

21. *The Party and Its Progress*

There were about fifteen people at the party when we arrived at a quarter past eleven. Of this company, I'd say that four were on relief, two were Relief Investigators, three were on one or another of the Arts Projects, and six were in the private sector of the economy. People came and went, but the proportion remained roughly the same, a proportion true to the milieu, if not to the society.

Sandy greeted us warmly; that is, he greeted Melanie warmly and included me in because he was too polite to greet us separately, and according to his feelings, but at the same time he was unable to hide his strong feelings for Melanie or to disguise the rather suspicious attitude toward me which abided from the time of our first meeting. Added to the lingering suspicion was the normal hostility to be expected under the circumstances.

"How was the concert?" he asked, and I let Melanie answer, for I wasn't pleased that he knew where we had spent the evening. How far did her confidences go? She answered in a noncommital manner. She hadn't enjoyed the concert, but that had nothing to do with the music, and she wasn't prepared to go into the real reasons (was that the extent of her confidences, or would she tell him privately?) Then Sandy darted off on a hostlike errand; we chose beer over whisky and took seats in a corner of the room (high ceilings, little furniture). Some couples come to a party and sit together all evening, out of shyness, anxiety, pride, or because they enjoy being together in a crowd, they somehow come closer in the social surroundings. That was how we started out—Melanie knew a number of people in the room, maybe half of them, and told me what she knew of them. That is always fun; you get a swift, rather dramatic view of the characters, and Melanie's vignettes were sharp, clear, witty, memorable.

Three contemporary European figures—Adolf Hitler, Joseph Stalin, and Leon Trotsky—were key figures at the party. The German dictator, of course, had no adherents in this room. It was before the time when he was described in some leftist circles as a diabolical genius. But he was making his impress on world affairs. He was currently threatening the Rhineland; at home (whose home?) the Nuremberg Laws were in effect. The Russian dictator and the Russian exile had their adherents, the Stalinist supporters and sympathizers greatly outnumbering the Trotskyite supporters and sympathizers. It was about this time that the Communist Party had issued a directive that made impermissible any personal contact between its members and those of the Trotskyite persuasion. This created odd, if not world-shaking, situations in the social life of the individuals so involved.

Melanie, in talking of this directive, pointed out two individuals in the room—a Stalinist youth and a Trotskyist girl. They had gone together for a while, lived together for a while, and then drifted apart, for a combination of reasons and not on a particularly unfriendly basis. But now he was avoiding her studiously—she thought the situation most comical and absurd and made a point of talking to him, idly joining a conversational group of which he was a member. He refused to talk to her and left the group when she joined it.

"He is very strong on the directive," Melanie explained to me. "For him it is no contact all the way down the line— if a Trotskyite crosses his line of vision, he acts as though that person did not exist."

And so this youth was behaving now because of a directive, but not all took so strong a stand. The keenest psychologist would not have been able to explain the youth's behavior without this bit of political information. Passing him in the room, the Trotskyist girl smiled sweetly at the Stalinist youth; he looked past her as though she were not there.

"The danger in acting as though the other does not exist," said Melanie, "is that after a while you do not want them to exist."

"Hello," said a voice which turned out to be a familiar voice.

"Hello Eric," I said. After I made the introductions, we asked one another what we were doing.

I had known Eric at college when he was a member of the Young People's Socialist League. He was now a public school teacher out in Queens. He was, the way so many of us were, a serious chap, with an edge of bitterness which I never quite understood. But I knew very little of his private life—I think his father was a cutter in the garment industry—and we enjoyed one another's company, a kind of distant friendship without responsibility.

"What brings you to this neck of the woods?" I asked.

"I come as a shlepper-along," he said. "The Kings (he pointed to a couple in the corner) saved me from myself—my engagement book showed a significant blank for the evening."

We spoke of college days, and then got into a discussion of the recent rebellion of the generals against the Spanish Republic, an event that was to shape profoundly the lives of many of us. He expressed confidence in the policies of Leon Blum.

Then we spoke of the "no-contact" directive, and he told us of a man who had stopped talking to his wife because he suspected her of Trotskyite leanings.

"But I think it was more of an excuse than a political

attitude," said Eric. "He was really interested in another woman."

Then we spoke of the "French Turn," which signified the entry of Trotskyites as individuals into the world Socialist parties. Eric feared the consequences for the S.P.

"Their view is as monolithic as that of the Stalinists," he said. "Trotsky's exile, his dramatic situation, his polemical wizardry, do not alter that fundamental fact. Remember Kronstadt."

The role of Trotsky in the bloody repression of the Kronstadt sailors was invariably brought up when the question arose as to the course of the revolution had Trotsky triumphed in the Soviet Union.

The girl who had been needling the Stalinist youth joined us because she overheard part of the conversation, and it interested her.

"No question about the need for the dictatorship of the proletariat," she said, "else the revolution would have been destroyed, the way it is being destroyed now by the Soviet bureaucracy, which is strangling production, hardening the political forms, and not permitting intraparty dissent."

"Why not other parties?" said Eric. "How can you criticize 'hardening of the political forms' and support the dictatorship?"

"Because the revolution is not firmly established," she said, "the bourgeois forces, under the guise of parliamentary democracy, would restore the old property relations, destroying the social gains of the revolution. These gains must be maintained at all costs. Think what would have happened to European development had the social gains of the French Revolution been destroyed by the Thermidorians."

"You're arguing that history can develop in only one way," said Melanie, "as though the book has already been written, a kind of secular predestination. Isn't it possible, that with other policies, the social gains could have been maintained *and* the Reign of Terror avoided, or minimized? And now the Moscow Trials—you underestimate the value of political freedom."

"And you," said the Trotskyite girl, turning to her new adversary, "are making a fetish of it. Had the revolution triumphed in Germany, spread to the other industrially advanced countries, you would have seen a loosening of the political forms inside the Soviet Union. Political freedom is a reflex of the economic organization. It does not exist in a vacuum."

At this point we got into a discussion of Means and Ends, whether dictatorship and repression were justifiable in the name of future freedom.

"You talk of the Reign of Terror," said the Trotskyite girl, "but think of the French people killed and maimed and impoverished through endless wars and crises, wars and crises that could have been avoided under a just social system. There is a Reign of Terror being carried on against the masses all the time, and only the establishment of worldwide socialism will put an end to that."

"Your own Soviet state," I said, "is conducting a terroristic policy against its own people, in the name of Socialism. Do you really think it is possible to keep the power by terror and to build a just society at the same time? The content of freedom has to be kept alive, else it will be buried beyond reach, no matter what the economic organization. I am not denying the relation of political freedom to economics. But you must grant this freedom a certain independence: it is a function that can be lost, and the most rational society will be hollow without it."

"Political freedom," said the Trotskyite girl, "will develop naturally only as the class structure is dissolved, as the productive relations are strengthened, but the capitalist world is only too anxious to destroy the Soviet state precisely because it is establishing these new social relations, because it is creating the conditions for its own withering away."

"But meanwhile," said Eric, "your own group is being destroyed. How will the Soviet people come to understand the nature of the repression unless there are other communication organs beside the government ones, unless there is some kind of political flexibility?"

22. *An Interruption, an Attack on Formalism*

The conversation was interrupted by the appearance of a rude stranger who made his presence immediately and heavily known. He bore down on the company. He was a stranger in the sense that nobody in the circle knew him, and he was rude in the sense that he imposed his own self (his self was his weapon) to the detriment of the existent sociality. He introduced himself as though he had stepped into a room of people silently awaiting him, expectantly awaiting him. He destroyed the discussion as though he had cried "Fire," and asked me (for no other reason, as it turned out, than that I was standing next to Melanie) what I did. Like anyone who is not perhaps sure of his goal in life, I was sensitive to this question and replied, without a moment's hesitation:

"I live from sand to drought."

"What's that?"

"I said I live from sand to drought."

"What does that mean?"

"It's a play on words," I explained (and I realized as I said it that I was using the rhythm of the fellow in the Lardner story who was explaining to a busher that a hurricane is a "kind of a storm"), "a play on the expression *from hand to mouth*. For *hand* I substitute *sand* and for *mouth* I substitute *drought*. It is a description of a situation of paucity—all sand, those vast desert spaces, and no oasis in sight, only the endless flow of sand, no water. *From sand to drought*."

"I suppose you think that's very funny."

"It's not the worst play on words."

Thereupon, the intruder launched into a vigorous attack on puns, plays on words, verbal displacements (from above and below), the revolution of the word, surrealism, dadaism, and James Joyce.

"It's all escapism," he said, "just flight from content, to the Ivory Tower, a kind of idiot art for art's sake, an attempt to avoid the crucial issues of the day. You are building systems of fantasy, taking the minds of the people from their real concerns by creating these formalistic objects, time-obsessed and all that. Joyce is a reactionary necrophile, living off the putrefying corpse of capitalism."

"How do you explain Marx's respect for Balzac?" asked Eric, "that political reactionary."

"Because Balzac realistically portrayed the society of his time," said the intruder. "He knew that society at every level, and laid bare, if from a reactionary angle, the class structure of that society, and one could learn from that."

"Doesn't Joyce do the same for twentieth-century society?" asked Eric. "He lays bare the life of a city of the West, at every level you can think of."

"All tricks and word play," said the intruder, who was angry because Melanie was paying no attention to him (he kept looking at her and she kept paying no attention to him). "How can you compare all that trickiness and narcissism to Balzac's honest and painstaking analysis, his extraordinary knowledge and sober description of the life of his time?"

"How was he able to avoid his own class bias in this comprehensive analysis?" I asked.

"He was an honest reactionary," said the stranger, stubbornly, "that's all Marx meant. None of those ridiculous puns, in all *sorts* of languages, none of this deification of form as hero, none of this sanctification of the word. A word is a tool, not a fetish."

"What kind of a tool?" asked Melanie, "a hammer, a buzz saw?" This question upset the stranger a good deal; he was silent, Melanie went over to Sandy, I went for another drink, and then got into a discussion on

23. *An Aspect of the Artist's Relation to Great Historical Movements*

This was not so much a discussion as a kind of lecture by a rather short chap, with those burning, luminous eyes that characterize some of the immigrant youths from the lower East Side (this lad was in fact not from the lower East Side, and he was the grandson of an immigrant).

"There is a good and sufficient reason" he said, "why the artist type is drawn to great historical movements. As a creator of objects, objects of a given harmony and beauty (for no one in his right mind will try to create what is unharmonious and unbeautiful), he must be appalled by the formless nature of the social structure, this social chaos cries for form, the way the original chaos called for a world, appealed, so to say, to the creative spirit in God. So the true artist (for there are false artists, or nonartists, who do not achieve the harmonious and the beautiful), far from retreating to an Ivory Tower, is deeply impressed by the doctrines of an Isaiah, a Christ, a Marx, and will want to do his part in the making of a world without poverty, without injustice, without greed. The creation of beauty involves the destruction of ugliness, both processes go on at once, and the creation of a harmonious society involves the destruction of the social imperfections I have mentioned. There are, of course, many other imperfections. The incomplete artist may retreat from these horrors and may also be drawn to them for the wrong reasons, but the true artist will be drawn to these great movements of social change because he is appalled by the social chaos and drawn toward the creation of a harmonious society, an object far more sublime than any novel or painting, or even musical composition."

"That's an old theory," someone said, "the theory of the state as a work of art."

"But only as an ideal," said the speaker, "for no art work is perfect, it can only approach perfection, and that is true of the state too. If God made an imperfect world, how can man make a perfect state, or society?"

"The perfection of the state," I said (and in this sense I was involved in a discussion of "An Aspect of the Artist's Relation to Great Historical Movements"), "is related to its disappearance, the famous 'withering away.' "

"Yes, yes," said the luminous-eyed youth (the intense type), "it was Kafka's thought that 'the story . . . perishes thus from its own elements. . . . There is no more beautiful fate for a story than for it to disappear.' But the disappearance of true form means its dying into a new and superior form, forever, world without end."

24. *Separation*

Standing in this group—mostly strangers, and they constantly changing—I looked across the room, from time to time I looked across the room and saw Melanie, in conversation with Sandy, as part of a group that included Sandy (The Theory of Groups), and felt keenly the pathos of separation. It is not necessarily the extent of the separating distance that creates the pathos, there is no ratio here ("distance lends enchantment," "out of sight, out of mind"), and the width of a room is enough to create the sense of separation and loss which is forever crowding us. Yes, I saw her dear face across the room, that dear serious face which I can never forget, saw her as she spoke, as she listened, as she sat buried in self and silence. I had only to walk across the room in order to be at her side. A likely solution! That move, that maneuver, would not destroy the separation; any fool knows that proximity does not necessarily destroy the separation, and may even sharpen it. The fact is that I thought Melanie ought to come over to me, over to my side of the room. I had left her side out of guilt and consideration, and it was her move now. She rarely moved in my direction. Wasn't yesterday the first time she had ever called me, and hadn't she called me because she was not at ease with her brother and his girl friend? And mightn't she first have called others and found those un-available? It was clearly her turn to make a move in my direction, a move that would indicate that she wanted to be at my side. And what is more indicative that one wants to be at your side than a movement bringing one to your side? But it wasn't only guilt and consideration that had taken me from her side, there was also an element of mutual boredom, of an overmuchness of contact (the way married couples spend an evening at a party away from one another and joyfully leave together), there was a pause, maybe a halt, in that mutual discovery that is so much of the joy of early friendship, early love. So, I did not want her to cross the room and come to my side, but preferred this separation, that I might look at her longingly across a crowded room, having left her side out of guilt, consideration, boredom (really the fear of boredom) so that she could be alone with one who desired her and had been rejected by her. I would not have been so guilty/con-siderate, I would not have been so bored, had I thought there was any chance she might accept this man (the one of whom I had been so absurdly jealous), or was I bringing them together, to invite jealousy, as a more *interesting* emotion than loss? But I was in love with Melanie, and looked at her longingly across a room crowded with strangers. She made no move in my direction.

25. *Sitting Alone, the Spectator*

In the middle of that room, Fabricant, one knee on the chair facing him, surrounded by a half dozen viewers and listeners, was holding forth. I was out of range, or just not listening, sitting alone and watching this scene, with all its minglings and changes. I was sitting as a viewer, a spectator (though not passive), an attitude toward which I am prone and one which some of my best friends find distasteful. It was certainly an attitude that Melanie did not much favor. To some my behavior was typical of a tenant in the Ivory Tower —for some saw this edifice in the mind's eye as an apartment house—the last refuge of the antisocial intellectual, the looking for looking's sake; Melanie (who resisted the polemical cliches of the day) saw my behavior as a withdrawal, an attempt at an objectivity which she considered impossible to achieve. "There is no such thing as pure objectivity," she had once said to me, "one must take a stand, even if it turns out to be wrong." I did not disagree with that statement, but neither did I consider that the search for objectivity was in itself wrong. "Just as a position we take can be wrong," I had said, "so an objectivity can be impure, but that doesn't deny the need for the philosophic search." She somehow distrusted the word "philosophic" in this context; it had an "above the battle" feel which ran counter to her more pragmatic approach. "You must take a stand," "If you're not with us, you're against us," "There is no neutrality in the class struggle," "Objectivity is a form of escape"—one heard phrases of this sort all the time.

Nevertheless, for the temperamental bias is not easily sidetracked, I looked around the room with interest, observing the details, trying to bring them together into some kind of a meaning (the meaning of a random, one-shot collectivity). As a historian I find it necessary to stand aside from the materials; how else, I thought, can the mind grasp this ever changing flux, transform it into guidelines, directions, perhaps laws? Even the most immediate kind of propagandistic pamphlet required that element of disinterest (not aloofness). So I looked around me (always with interest, rarely bored), caught Melanie's somewhat disapproving eye (though she was sitting alone at the moment, too, and of necessity looking around). I thought of the fine word "disinterest" and how it was slowly losing its meaning, being used most often in the sense of *uninterested, lack of interest,* and at the same time heard discussion of other issues of the day—Scottsboro, the struggle between the industrial and the craft unions, terror in the mines and on the picket lines—and was somewhat ashamed of my search for the objectivity which I thought so necessary, criticized my temperamental bias, and thought of a successful conjunction of action and disinterest.

26. *Story of an Early Injury*

On my way across the room, for a reason I have forgotten or which is not quite clear to me now, I ran into Melanie, and we both, seeing a familiar face, paused. I bowed, ceremoniously, and asked her something I had often meant to ask her, but had never gotten around to asking her:

"That scar over your eye, how did you get that?"

It was the scar that I have already mentioned in an early description: a thin line, maybe one-and-a-half-inches long, above her eyebrow.

"Oh that one," she replied. "When I was a girl of eight, I loved horseback riding and used to ride whenever I could, particularly with my older brother."

I looked at her in surprise, for this was the first mention of an older brother.

"He was three years older than I was, died very young

after an attack of paralytic polio." She paused during my confusion, and then went on: "We were riding together one day; he was carrying a branch, or a stick, which I wanted very much, and I rode after him, furiously, for he said that he would give me that stick if I caught up with him. In my excitement, I lost balance, fell off the horse, and hit my head against a rock." She rubbed the scar.

"That's the most primitive Freudian fable I've ever heard," I said.

She looked puzzled.

"Your older brother," I went on, "he had a long stick, something that you wanted."

"Isn't that strange?" she asked. "I never thought of it that way at all."

And then we went our ways across the room. I stopped to hear Fabricant, the way one stops at a carnival booth, an interesting place, to hear this somewhat mad monologist, who held a leading position amongst the incessant talkers of the day. He was indeed, considered by many to be King of the Ear-Benders.

27. *Fabricant Discourses, Frank Appears*

Of course I listened to Fabricant. Under the circumstances (and the circumstances were that I had nobody in particular to talk to at the moment and was tired of solitude) why shouldn't I have listened to Fabricant? He put you under no compulsion, you could come and go as you pleased, stay, leave, and return. And there was no charge—Fabricant was not singing for his supper, making no kind of pitch at all. It was just that he liked to discourse in company, loved to be surrounded by a number of individuals—in a room that contained other individuals as background and as a source of replenishment for those who might tire, or find more congenial company, or leave—who listened to what it was he had to communicate. He ranged widely in his subject matter, more in the free-associational than in the arbitrary style, and if the going got rough, was not averse to picking up a book from a nearby shelf or a letter from a nearby pocket (his own) and reading aloud from these documents. But he was rarely forced to these extreme acts, depended mainly on his powers of recollection and the exigencies of his unconscious promptings. Nor did he fail to take advantage of the comments of his listeners—he had a remarkable way of picking up these comments and somehow absorbing them in the ongoing flow; everything seemed to be pertinent to what he happened to be saying, so that he could not be deflected from the course which he was creating as he went along. He was at the moment discussing sanitation measures in the cities of antiquity, this stemming from his encounter earlier in the day with one of our municipal street cleaners, and I listened with great interest, for Fabricant was in one of his great moods, full of wit and dramatic circumlocution, using his knowledge to form the most elaborate historical arabesques, recreating and making familiar a world I dimly knew. Then, across the smoky room, through the fumes of this discourse, I saw Melanie, and she was seated with a familiar figure. Her brother Frank! And his friend Jill nowhere around. Melanie looked very happy seated with her brother, who had the worn and interested look of the latecomer to the party, whose night, ended once, now seemed to be starting again, though the hour was late and the party past its peak. He was the only male member of Melanie's family alive. Her father killed in an accident, her older brother early dead—no wonder she clung in guilt and passion to Frank. And so much more at ease with him when they were alone— she was describing, characterizing, some of the people in the room, and had to pass me in moving from one person to another. I became as if absorbed in the sanitation problems of ancient Athens (problems that had genuinely interested me only a minute before), but by a process difficult to describe, if not hard to understand, I became somewhat morose and very critical of this society in which I found myself.

28. . . . *that I am not inferior to those I despise*
—BAUDELAIRE

The party was old, it was tired, everything began to feel stale—people and drinks, everyone seemed to be going through the motions, repeating without adding. A number of people left, and of those who remained most gave the impression that they stayed on because the prospect of home was less interesting than the prospect of a party coming to its end. I was tired, and was angry at what I saw around me, angry at the bareness of this life (there wasn't a handsome, colorful object in the room), at the absence of charm (of this life), angry at a certain sardonic grimness, a loveless cynicism. In criticizing a group, one naturally extends the feeling to the individuals who make up that group, and I felt contempt for those who surrounded me because they were not living up to some ideal I secretly cherished but could not easily explicate. Then I thought of what the French poet had written—was I superior to those I criticized, or was this merely envy for those whose accomplishments (or possibility of accomplishments) were greater than mine? So I criticized myself for not living up to my secret ideal and felt that I must despise myself if I were inferior to my own ideal. So the criticism you make of others is not objective; you blame them for your own lack of achievement—you have not lived the heroic life, not shown the courage inherent in all ideals and particularly youthful ideals in a time of suffering, social injustice. These others are in your way! Therefore you despise them. And not only here at this party, but in your everyday life, in your everyday contacts, so much energy, time, consumed in despising others, running down their lives, their goals, their achievements. What a pointless way to use up the psychic energy. How effective that energy could be against the real difficulties and hazards of life, against the true outside enemy, against the weakness and indecision within! The fact is that you are in your own way, and so you must despise yourself for being in your own way. So I despised myself for being inferior to my own best self, though it was easier (in some ways) to despise Eric, or Fabricant, or the rude fellow who had tried to impress Melanie, or whomever—easier to blame the others for my own insufficiencies, but in other ways easier to blame myself, the self-criticism obviously answering an old and deep need, response to all the dark deeds of the soul. Nevertheless I was angry at what I saw around me—all that waste, and of idealism—and the anger spilled over, became indiscriminate. Not to be inferior to those you despise, for if you come to realize that you are inferior, then your criticism becomes maddeningly pointless. And if in your everyday life you are inferior to what you despise in yourself, then your self-criticism *is* maddeningly pointless.

29. *Meanwhile, Around Me*

Meanwhile, around me I heard conversational fragments of what was being discussed at the moment: "Lenin did *not* say that sex should be like a drink of water. He was arguing against this matter-of-fact, this sanitary position, he favored a greater admixture of the romantic element in the sexual situation, without, of course, going to sentimental extremes." "I don't go along with Descartes' formulation, it has seized philosophy and everyday thought, shakes them with an icy, rationalist hand. Not *I think,* but *I hope* and *therefore I am*— that is the human way of putting it." "No, you've got it all wrong, we're supposed to go to their house, and then we're all going to pick up the Michaelsons." "Joyce said that he never used such words in conversation, only in his writing. Lady Chatterbox is the way he referred to the Lawrence heroine." "We need the collaboration of all the progressive forces, brought together into a Peoples' Front." "What non-intervention? You think that Germany and Italy will stay out of Spain?" "So when the man came back after thirty years of reflection on life's meaning with the conclusion that 'life is like a fountain and was questioned as to *why* life was like a fountain, he immediately replied, '*So it's not like a fountain.'* "

A stranger, retired from the dying party, was playing records in the corner, and I heard "The Music Goes 'Round and 'Round," "Summertime," "These Foolish Things," and "Until the Real Thing Comes Along."

A small group was singing a parody of the Communist critique of the Social Democracy (for we were just out of the Third Period, the hard line when the international Social Democracy was characterized as the other side of the Fascist coin. It was the theory of Social Fascism) :

> *The Hillquits, the Cahans, and the Thomases*
> *They make by the workers false promises*
> *They preach Socialism, they practice Fascism*
> *In the third capitalist party of the bosses.*

Melanie came over and asked if I'd like to come up for coffee; then the three of us (Frank the third) moved toward the door. We no longer had to thread our way, as we were leaving a dying party.

30. *Party Post Mortems*

It was pleasant to sit in Melanie's apartment—how orderly it was, compared to the chaos downstairs, all those random incompletions—and to drink coffee on a table, near a window overlooking court and roof. We ate and drank on

the familiar red and white oilcloth (familiar because I had
seen it a number of times here and because it was very
popular—that color, texture, and design found in thousands
of restaurants and bars throughout the city). There was a
knock on the door; Melanie, going to answer it, said that she
had asked Sandy to "drop up" (yes, yes, it is still a common
phrase) and such was my euphoric state—I can think of no
word more accurately describing the way I felt—that I was
not at all disturbed by the prospect of his presence, and then
by his presence, welcomed it in fact, for if I were to be alone
with Melanie and her brother (is it possible to be alone with
two people?) better, far better, that Sandy Warren should be
alone with us too. He joined us at the table—downstairs only
the mute evidence remained and the awful silence that follows
conviviality—and we discussed the events of the evening, the
way most of the others, on their way home from the party, or
home from the party, were discussing the events of the
evening—with interest, malice, indifference verging on boredom, or in the drowsy euphoric state that characterized our
conversation. Just another party (or was Fabricant still holding
forth downstairs, the auditors further reduced, maybe nonexistent?) which, in the telescoping of the years, would
coalesce with a hundred others, so that, enough time elapsing,
the features of no one of them would be distinguishable. And
though the remembrance of who said what to whom (at the
party just ended) was already beginning to fade, who knows
the importance of the contacts here made. Flirtations leading
to marriages! Beginnings of lifelong friendships! of political
associations utterly transforming the direction of a life! But
our conversation gleamed on the surface of what we were
beginning to forget; it was as if we were speaking about a
play, a carnival, a masquerade we had just witnessed. "Like a
masquerade," said Sandy, "each one wearing the face and the
manner he thinks appropriate for the occasion, to attract or
repel." We passed lightly over the names of the guests. Then

we went a little deeper. By a reductive process we laid bare the material or sexual nexus underlying given behavior. Then, forsaking analysis, we prophesied future developments, future failures, and future successes. We noted rudeness, gaucheries, and repeated the more impressive pleasantries. We laughed over the comical moments, pilloried this one, praised that one, expressed doubt over the other, repeated witticisms, criticized certain comments, wondered about this one's future and that one's past, roared in remembrance (in flight from the euphoria), passed over the unpleasant moments, filled in the unknown details (for there is always someone who has something to add), babbled to fill in the time, hexed and huzzaed (as we were repelled or drawn to). Then I rose to leave, and Sandy rose a split second afterward, just as I would have risen a split second afterward had he made the first move. But we did not nod to one another the way friends do when they feel it is time to go, so we left together only in a formal sense. We said our good-byes. Then Sandy and I walked down the four flights and shook hands in front of his apartment. "Thanks again," I said, "it was a great party," and he went into the apartment to face at least forty unwashed glasses, some of them ashy or with floating cigarette butts, many with "lipstick traces," and I went into the 3 A.M. streets, to walk home slowly in that dear quiet, under a star-studded sky, the end of an imperfect day.

31. *Not Only to Help Her Out of a Difficult Situation!*

I heard from Melanie that Monday afternoon. She said, in that serious yearning voice which never failed to touch me, that she'd like me to come over that evening, because she didn't want me to think that she'd asked me on Friday night only to help her out of a difficult situation! As I walked down to her apartment (my uncle's printing plant being in the 30's) I continued to think of the devious connection between guilt and love—continued in the sense that I had been thinking of it before I started to walk downtown and also because it is a problem about which one continually thinks. First she had called me to accompany her on a difficult double-date, now she called me to see her because she was guilty about having invited me to accompany her on a difficult double-date. So when would she want to see me because she wanted to see me? It is pleasant, I thought, to be seen for one's own sake, not for instrumental purposes. But did I always go to see *her* for so pure a reason? Didn't I sometimes go to see her because it seemed the best of all conceivable possibilities at the time, in short, because there was nothing better to do, and then, guilty of having gone to see her because there was nothing better to do, act as though I had come only to see her? But very often I did want only to see her; one suffers and enjoys the ache of desire (the way it was this evening), one moves as in a trance toward the one he most wants to see (also known as the object of desire), there are no other possibilities, you are on a field where two figures are playing, and no spectators. I found a note in the hallway of Melanie's apartment, saying that she had left the keys with the super and would be back in half an hour. I went downstairs and knocked on the super's door. Far from the super's wife answering, it was the super who answered, a rather thin man, of obvious Scandinavian descent, who reminded me (as he did others) of a character actor in a Hollywood movie whose name—both movie and man—I continually forgot; what happened was that I'd remember his name and then it would skip my mind, year after year.

"Mrs. Craig asked me to pick up her keys."

"Sure," he said, "she said you'd be along soon."

He fished the keys out of his pocket and handed them to me. There was the downstairs key, the apartment key, and the letterbox key, ringed. He gazed at me in a friendly manner.

"How is the weather outside?" he asked.

He was not making conversation, he had a particular interest, and it was pleasant to be asked about the weather that way.

"Pretty warm," I replied, "I'd say about 83, not too humid."

"Fine," he said, as though this information would help in the formulation of his plans for the evening, and he withdrew into the fastness of his basement home. On the way upstairs I caught up with Miss Wankowitz, then passed her on the landing where she lived. She opened the door to her apartment rather swiftly and slid inside, the door closing right behind her, the movement performed very gracefully. It is the kind of movement you learn to make swiftly if you fear being followed into your apartment. Then I reached Melanie's apartment and made myself as much as home as was possible under the circumstances, those being that I was waiting in another's apartment for the arrival of that other. I thought—very idly indeed—that having me pick up the keys betokened a certain trust. Why couldn't I go down and have a duplicate set made? A completely meaningless thought—why would I need a set of duplicate keys? Then, out of tiredness or excess of comfort, for I felt very much at home here, I dozed off, and was awakened by a knocking at the door. "Who is knocking at my chamber door?" I thought, and half out of my sleep I felt ashamed of having remembered this line from the poem which we memorized in the seventh grade. Then I was wide awake and realized that it must be Melanie, without her keys, knocking at her own chamber door. I opened the door. "My little dove," I exclaimed, "Marya Timofyevna, Yulia Mihailovna." She missed the W. C. Fields, but picked up the Dostoevsky, and we talked about the Russian novelist, and while she prepared dinner (for it was a dinner invitation I had accepted) I delivered a kind of monologue, entitled:

32. *A Disquisition on the Form of Dostoevsky's Novel*

"The absence of the telephone," I said, "made possible the frame of Dostoevsky's novel. There are some dozen people who live in various parts of the city (St. Petersburg). They know one another when the story starts, or they meet one another, and immediately become incredibly familiar and intimate, whether drawn or repelled. They call on one another, sometimes by plan but most often when the desire is present, because they have something very important or nonsensical to say to that person, or feeling that they must be near and close to that person. All these people are involved with one another in various ways—in the fields of love, conspiracy, friendship, etc.—and these meetings, conversations, monologues, diatribes, all create new disturbances in an already troubled area. This conversation does not much have the effect of gossip because it is self-revelatory more than revelatory of the one discussed, and in any case it is all meant to hasten the action. The action hastens on, more and more is understood, more and more is uncovered (even dreadful secrets come to light), everything moves towards a future swarming with new complexities, new disturbances and unravelings, new dreams and disclosures. But I was making a point about the spontaneous nature of these calls. Today we call a person on the phone and make an appointment (the same word we use to see a doctor or a dentist)—for the same day, the next day, a week off. But we are interested in seeing the person at the time we make the call—in many cases the call takes the place of the visit. 'Have you seen him?' 'No, but I spoke to him on the phone'—and by the time we make the visit that interest is gone, or declined, or transformed. The one we want to see expects us; he makes his preparations, puts on his mask, prepares a drink—an element of formality is introduced. But in this novel you call on the person at the moment you are interested in calling. Your host is not expecting you (though he may not be surprised). He has had no chance to prepare his defenses, and if he is not interested in seeing you, or even angry at you for coming, well, he can either do nothing about it or express his anger, his lack of interest. The visit is more of a confrontation—there is a personal or dramatic purpose behind it, not merely because you have nothing to do, though that too can be a purpose, the visit being an escape from boredom, from the gnawing sense of the unimportance of your life, a need to make something of your time, and so you proceed to the house of the one whose presence may give some meaning, or even forgetfulness, to your life. But generally the purpose is more specific, more *personal*—to explain something or have something explained, something that's been eating you and you want to get to the bottom of it, to apologize for something done, or said, or thought, to discover the meaning of a remark that puzzled or infuriated you, to declare love or condemn cowardice, to find out whether a third party has been there, and for what reason, to burst out into a tirade on the state of society, on the crying need for change in people and institutions, to point out that you have been misunderstood, that what you have said was taken in a wrong context, that wasn't what you meant at all, that it was taken in vain, that your deed had an altogether different character, another (even incomprehensible) motive, to remind the one you are calling on of a promise made and that the time has come to fulfill that promise, to add to the confusion and uncertainty in which these dozen people are living, to give a rough shape to the reality constantly being described and constantly changing its conformations, to create a sense of your own value as a thinking, feeling, person, to make (as we say) contact, and that, of course, is an electrical term, the power is on, the sparks jump."

33. *Anger and Guilt*

It goes without saying that my remarks were interrupted by the insolent ring of the telephone; Melaine picked up the receiver and after a moment's conversation turned to me, her hand cupped over the mouthpiece in a gesture so typical of our time and place that no painter has yet shown it back to us with the elegance and mystery that it deserves.

"A friend of mine," she said, "wants us to see *Storm over Asia* with her. It's at the Acme."

I knew there was something wrong with this request, and it was not that I had seen the picture once before (I often preferred to see a film twice), nor was it the curious use of the word "us"—as though the three of us were all friends—but at the moment I did not know exactly what was wrong with the question. I therefore said, "Why not?" so expressing my puzzlement and acquiescence at the same time. Whereupon Melanie uncovered the mouthpiece, made the arrangements, and then we sat down to eat the dinner that Melanie had prepared during my interrupted disquisition.

"She's a member of the dance group," explained Melanie. "Her name is Nora Worth and she comes from out West, I think Oregon. She's very pretty and very confused, torn between the art dance and the popular dance, and confused in other ways, too."

As she spoke on, I realized what was wrong with her request—she had asked me to come to see her and without any hesitation was bringing a friend along, and this after inviting me down to make up for the double-date situation. Did she find it unpleasant, or boring, to be alone with me? I asked her that question, and she said, as she went in to dress, "Don't be absurd; if you had wanted to be alone with me, you could have said so." That was true, but she could have told Nora that she was busy, without having to turn to me at all. Waiting for her to come out of the bedroom, I picked up a poem, in Sandy's handwriting, which I had not noticed before. I make it a habit to read all open documents, postcards (but not letters in envelopes, even though the envelopes are open).

NIGHTTIME POEM

She comes lightly, through the night, into my waiting bed
She comes slowly, through the night, down time's corridors into my
    waiting bed.
Who comes into my waiting bed, most amorous and expectant?
Who comes lightly into my bed, down time's long corridors in the
    night?
She comes, in the night, most lovingly, into my waiting bed.
I am overwhelmed with joy, my expectancy is gratified,
For she comes lightly into my bed, in the waiting night,
Enters noiselessly and anxiously into my nighttime bed.
I am most joyous at her coming, she is a joy to the loveliness of
    the night,
She is my bride, my companion, in the sublimities of the night,
She brings nighttime joy, tender greeting for the morning,
She is bride of the night, and the dawn's companion,
She steals noiselessly down the corridors of time, in the early hours,
She is fair and noiseless, brings joy and expectancy
In the early hours, in the nighttime hush, in the joys and expectancies
    of the night.
Who comes lightly into my bed, breathing dawn and expectancies.

Having started to read this poem, I was sorry that I had started to read it, and, having finished reading it, I was sorry that I had read it. But I had really gotten the sense of it at the first glance—my eye immediately took the page in, and to finish reading it was a kind of formality. It was obviously not meant for my eyes, or the eyes of any stranger, but there it was in the open, and I had the keys to the apartment (though the occupant had returned), which put me in a somewhat "personal" position. But I felt guilty about reading this communication, and this guilt canceled out my anger at Melanie for including Nora Worth in the life of the evening, so that when Melanie came out, prepared to go, I was in an equable mood. I locked the door behind us and returned the keys. But then it turned out that my guilt was stronger than my anger, and as we walked towards the movie I wondered whether or not I ought to tell her that I had read the poem. But it was a no-decision bout, and then we came to the Acme, where we found Nora waiting. We were hastily introduced, for the movie was about to start, and entered swiftly into the familiar darkness.

34. *In Memory of Otto Rank*

As an admirer of the work of Otto Rank, one of the members of the Original Big Five of psychoanalysis, I'd like to say something about the inside of a movie house, in relation, of course, to Rank's notion of "the birth trauma," the curiosities of later regress (if not infinite), the pleasures of sleep and other dark places, the secure joy of watching rain from an open window (preferably in a northern city), the artificial creation of darkness by the pulling down of shades, the adjusting of blinds, and many other activities of the sort, formerly characterized by the slogan: *Back to the Womb!* Among these joys and securities the inside of a movie house holds an honorable place—as kids we would go into the movie not so much for what was playing there as for the fun of sitting in that dark place, friends at your side, strangers and enemies all around. "Let's go to the movies," someone would say, but now we hesitate to say it just that way, being older and conceivably full of judgment, and the movies having become more pretentiously rotten. But the yearning overcomes us nevertheless; someone says, "Let's go to the movies," and we pick and choose among the lesser evils rather than simply going to the movie around the corner, for whatever happened to be playing (even among the lesser evils) was bound to be enjoyable, dark and enjoyable. Here I was now, seated between the girl I loved and a friend of that girl, angry and guilty for reasons I have described (I certainly could have stopped after reading the first line of Sandy's poem—what nonsense about that total prefigured image!), slumped in the dry, unmoving darkness, peering at the moving configurations, judging what was being said and done, analyzing motive and message, for I was of an age, involved in the dialectics of form and content, no longer went to the movie *absolutely* without regard to what was playing (not even if that movie house were small, wet, and slowly swaying).

35. *Discussion After the Movie*

After the movie, we walked Nora home. She lived in the northwest part of Greenwich Village; we walked crosstown, stopping for coffee in the cafeteria on 7th Avenue just below 14th Street. Nora was, as Melanie had said, an attractive girl, rather tall, blonde, and unusually graceful. She was not, as the saying goes, "my type," so it was that much easier for me to judge her objectively. She had already been approached by a Broadway musical-comedy producer who wanted to add "class" to his popular entertainment, and Nora was undecided as to whether she ought to answer this siren song of money and maybe fame or stay with the dance, which required so much more of her and whose rewards were more real, if less tangible. She thought that she might be able to keep a foot in each world, but in her heart of hearts recognized that that was impossible, that the meretricious, or merely mediocre, would surely destroy the rare and the difficult. This problem, as I learned from bits of the conversation (for naturally she wouldn't talk intimately of these matters in my presence), was one of the elements in her confusion. I later learned that she was in the process of choosing between two suitors, somewhat opposed in life interests, and that added up to a good beginning on the way to a confused state.

We discussed the film, a powerful movie set in far-off Mongolia describing the rapacity and cruelty of Western imperialism and ending on a note of colonial struggle, the hero refusing to be used by his archenemies and leading his people against these enemies. The screen was filled with men speeding on horses, men with clenched fists, determined to undo, once and for all, these ancient wrongs and oppressions and to win a final freedom. "What freedom?" I asked (without denying the power of the film), and we got into a discussion of what was then called the "nationalities question."

I took a somewhat dim view of Soviet behavior toward its own nationalities. Nora had much genuine feeling against injustice, but her knowledge was not extensive, and she was often amazed by facts of which she had never heard or heard about from another point of view. She had no knowledge of the Soviet famine of 1932, the trials she saw as necessary retaliation against enemies of the state; she had the haziest notions of the cultural freeze in the Soviet Union, the suicides of Essenin and Mayakovsky, the difficulties certain movie and theatre directors were experiencing, the steady decline of the film art, the reason for the absence of strikes, the zigzags in the party line.

"All that may be so," said the pretty fellow traveler, "but they started with so little, and the government is fundamentally interested in the welfare of the people."

That brought us to a discussion of the virtues and dangers of centralized state power; Melanie said that she was opposed to the idea of an elite ruling "for" the people, and we spoke of democratic participation, the Athenian democracy, multiparty systems, Acton's comment on power and its corruptions (one of the most quoted phrases in all political history). Melanie, arguing against the uses of uncontrolled power, told the joke about the Soviet directive that all elephants were to be killed as enemies of the state, whereupon a rabbit rounded up his family and they all scampered across the border. "Why did you run away?" asked a puzzled citizen of the neighboring country, "you're not an elephant." "First they'll kill you," said the rabbit, "and then they'll ask if you're an elephant." Nora thought that was unfair and anti-Soviet. It was a typical discussion of the times, not in itself convincing but influential nevertheless, because people changed their views, slowly, under the impress of hundreds of such discussions, for most of us were willing to learn, prepared to change our views, to listen, to compare, to allow the play of the critical reason, to break up the emotional investment.

36. *Loth*

I am loth to leave this night, to exile it to time's own Siberia (if you will excuse so extreme a metaphor), and so must hold on to it a bit longer, for let go of it I must. We walked Nora to her apartment house on Charles Street (confirming my previous statement that she lived in the northwest part of the Village), bade her good-bye, then waited in the vestibule downstairs till we heard the door shut upstairs, and so I assured myself that I was not an accessory to rape, robbery, or any type of molestation between the beginning of her climb and the peaceable achievement of her apartment, at which point I felt that my responsibility ended. We turned away from her apartment house, went over to Greenwich Avenue, down to where it meets 6th Avenue, over 9th Street to University Place, then down to 8th Street and eastward again. Yes, yes, it is the time between events that we must not scorn, for in retrospect they very often turn out to be events in themselves. I am loth to leave this night, of which more can be said (or of any other night) than I am able to say. The buildings in the shadow! the crackle of neon! the moon aglow in its routine glory as we walked slowly through the streets which seemed cooler because emptier. Yes yes, we walked slowly through the deserted streets, in the living present, treating this passing moment as no intermediate reality but as the reality itself, through which we walked together, hand in hand, talking or silent, gazing at one another with love and interest, walking slowly through the quite deserted streets, for we were not alone, nothing exactly happening, the way nothing is exactly happening most of the time, though it is all moving toward one stress or configuration, something we call an event, such as my kissing Melanie—that would constitute a kind of event—but nothing planned or anxiously looked forward to or pleasurably looked forward to, something flowing out of the reality no longer intermediate. How good to be away from the perpetual waiting, the perpetual marking time, the way some children seem to await the future, thinking it holds out unlimited joys and possibilities. It does, and one can swim in these unlimited possibilities, in the living passing present, the future joy moving out of the present joy and present understanding, we moving in a continuum in which the time periods do not lie side by side but are interwoven. So we moved in this lively and interesting moment, slowly through the night I am loth to surrender, down past the Sagamore Cafeteria, where a peremptory knocking on the window attracted our attention.

37. *Nightcap with Fabricant*

It was Fabricant knocking on the cafeteria window and then beckoning us in. We hesitated, for it was late, getting to be later, and the image of Fabricant, gesturing through the plate-glass window, conjured up hours of conversation, and the first rays of dawn gleaming through this very window.

"Let's go in for a few minutes," said Melanie, and that was all right with me, particularly since Fabricant was her friend. "He looks kind of sad and all alone in there," said Melanie. "Let's keep him company for a while."

So I plucked two checks from the issuing machine, and we joined the voluble man at his window post, from which he could more easily observe the passers-by and seek the familiar among the multitude of strangers. Fabricant greeted us warmly, gathered up his newspapers, pamphlets, and documents, which were spread over the table.

"What are you doing in this part of the world?" asked Melanie, for Fabricant lived in the west, past Hudson Street.

"I was at the Cooper Union," he said, "and then came over here with some people, but they left." He said this in a rather aggrieved and disappointed tone, and as a warning to us.

"We can't stay too long," said Melanie, but Fabricant waved her off, and started off on the Cooper Union—how Peter Cooper had provided space for the as yet uninvented elevator, Lincoln's famous speech, a list of other illustrious speeches. Fabricant was the historian of whatever it was he happened to be talking about. He told us a humorous story about a poetry reading he had attended there the previous winter.

"It was a bitter cold night," he said, "and the first four or five rows were filled by Bowery gents who never missed readings, lectures, or debates when the weather was inclement. The auditorium was pleasantly warm, and the bums thawed out, lifted their heads, breathed in the surrounding warmth. Meanwhile the poets took their turns on the podium, reading from their own works. Then there was a discussion, and the moderator was beginning to thank the poets and wind up the evening when one of the bums raised his hand. 'Mr. Tate,' he said, 'would you mind reading that Civil War poem again?' The poet obliged, and another of the Bowery chaps asked Mr. Schwartz to read the poem about Plato, and he obliged, and so it went. All grew quite restive—poets, moderator, audience—but the down-and-outers were relentless, fearful of the whistling winds without, fearful of losing this delightful

warmth, and how could the poets decline, being practicioners
of an art with the slimmest audience? There we have an
example of the weird dialectical interplay between economics
and art."

Then Fabricant questioned me about what I did—a
difficult question in those days of unemployment, relief,
unpleasant jobs—but his manner was very direct, with no
unpleasant undertones; when I told him that I was working in
the field of American history he showed great interest, but he
would have shown the same amount of interest no matter
what field I had mentioned. Somehow we got onto the subject
of the idolatry of historical figures, of Weems on Washington,
etc.

"I think," I said, "that the episode of the cherry tree
is quite accurate, but has come down to us with the wrong
emphasis. Washington's father noticed that the cherry tree
was down—how could one not notice it?—and asked his kid
about it. George saw that there was no way out of it, and he
replied, 'I chopped it down, Pa, I have a small axe, and that's
what happened.' He said what thousands of kids say every
day when they are caught in some mischief around the house.
They don't volunteer the information, but when questioned
they'll admit the truth. This business of 'I did it father, I
cannot tell a lie' is falsification by emphasis, growing out of an
ancestor worship run wild."

Whereupon Melanie told the story about the two people
who were asked how they spent their days. They spent their
days pretty much the same way, but one told the story fast
and the other told it slow, creating the effect of a dynamo and
a sloth, a speed-up and a slow-down on the identical content. Then Fabricant told the joke about the telegram that
Trotsky, in exile, sent to Stalin at a meeting of the Third
International. The telegram read: COMMUNISM CAN BE BUILT
IN ONE COUNTRY. EXCUSE ME. TROTSKY. This created great
puzzlement among the delegates, until one of them got up and

said, "Let me read the telegram." Then he read: COMMUNISM CAN BE BUILT IN ONE COUNTRY? EXCUSE ME! TROTSKY. Fabricant was struck by my notion of the eccentric historical emphasis, and his fertile mind ranged over the domain of history in search of examples, confirmations, and contradictions. He found many an example and expounded at length, because he was genuinely interested and because he liked company, liked to communicate, and so he held us back, making us feel like the wedding guests in the poem (though the Mariner stopped one of three). He created a sense of betrayal if you started to leave, pulled you back by stratagems childish and devious. But leave him we finally did, and waved as we passed by. He waved back cheerfully through the window. His papers and pamphlets were once more spread over the table; he looked out at the passing strangers, seeking the familiar face, as we walked down the street to Melanie's house.

38. *Waiting; An Unexpected Call*

The next day I was restless, and the day after, too. Life lagged inbetween the times that I saw Melanie, all manner of things seemed less interesting, less important, and I found myself waiting anxiously for the next meeting. Absolutely in conflict with my feelings a few nights back about the *living present*! Here I was—waiting, looking forward anxiously, marking time. Apparently one thing is more important than another thing, you must discriminate and choose among the grades of reality, you cannot move so easily through the undifferentiated chaos but must be at the side of a friend, at the side of the one you love, you must move in circumstances that interest and stimulate you. Who are you to bring interest and stimulation to everything around you? You are not that powerful, you do not have such powers of absorption, to live

freely in a world apart from the ones surrounding you. I was
bored with my research, bored with the work in my uncle's
printing shop, avoided the living present, or strangled it, was
certainly not moving through it freely, and was anxious for
it to disappear and make way for the time when I'd be with
Melanie again. In *that* living present life would be interesting,
things would take on color, value, future and past would be
swallowed up in what happened to be happening.

I thought about Melanie most of the time, and if I were
not thinking about her whatever it was that I was thinking
about was colored by the absence of Melanie. I wondered
what she wanted. She was a serious girl, she was seeking the
meaningful. It is not true of all of us. I mean, after a while it
is not true of all of us. Disappointed in her early political
experience (it was really an experience that ranged beyond
the political, encompassed the overall meaningful), she was
seeking a new point of departure; disappointed in the dance,
she was seeking another way of expressing herself, of making
contact with the significant reality, through the form of
reportage, coming close to those who were suffering, the way
it was that the Russian intelligentsia, sixty and seventy years
back, went "to the people"; disappointed in her first marriage,
she was seeking—what? Another marriage? And was I the
one she wanted to marry? Was I that one? I didn't think so,
I wasn't thinking in terms of marriage, wasn't as the saying
goes, "in a position" to marry (but that wouldn't affect what
it was that she had in mind, or in the depths). And, to return
to me, position is everything in life (that much, at least, I
had learned in the pool parlors). I was a student (not bad,
nothing to be ashamed of), not earning any real money; that
is, the money was real, but there wasn't much of it, and of
course that is a way of not thinking about marriage. Was she
ready to marry again, after a recent unsuccessful marriage?
We knew one another only for a few weeks, and here, after
two days of absence, I was anxious to see her, violating the

living present, living prospectively, restless and bored without her, unhappy with my old friends, short with my parents. So, on that second night, I walked onto St. Mark's Place, deciding to drop in on her unexpectedly, bypassing the mail and the telephone. I thought we were close enough to one another for me to make such an unannounced visit (I hoped that it would not be altogether unexpected); that was perhaps assuming too much, and I was certainly not of one mind about visiting her this way, but rang the downstairs bell in her apartment house nevertheless (hers! not Wanda Wankowitz's!, not Warren's!), and when the answering signal came my heart jumped in the close expectancy of being with her again.

39. *An Interruption, a Discussion*

Upstairs, I found Arthur in Melanie's apartment, the same who had come up to her on the Hoboken Ferry, on our way back. Melanie and her caller were not in easeful postures: Arthur was silent, in the way one is silent at an unexpected interruption just when he is getting to the heart of the matter. Melanie was not displeased to see me, and asked me in.

"I'm sorry," I said, "if I'm interrupting." Could that sound anything but fatuous?

"That's all right," said Melanie. She asked me to sit down, and then said, "We were discussing political matters."

It was clear that Arthur was there to convince her that she had made a mistake in leaving the Party. He had an obviously personal interest; that was a special motive for his effort to convince her of her errors. He was now silent, angry at the interruption, and I couldn't blame him, considering that I could have phoned, but had chosen not to. He was angry also because of the obvious sense of familiarity which my unexpected call betrayed. How was he to know that this was that first time that I had made such an unexpected call?

"We were talking about the encirclement of the Soviets," said Melanie, "and the need for the necessary measures of internal security."

"The question is," I said, "whether such measures are meant to strengthen the state or to consolidate the ruling power."

Arthur looked at me in the way you do when you would prefer not to talk to a person but are forced to by the circumstances. I am sure that he had warned Melanie against me. There are those who warn you against others. I myself had been warned against others; the effort was made to protect me against political and cultural contamination. But my presence and my words made it necessary for Arthur to speak.

"The Soviet Union," he said, "has been surrounded by enemies, faced invasion and threats of invasion from the early days of the Revolution—by Denikin and other White Guardists, by the Americans and British in Siberia. There are other examples, and the encirclement continues. Western imperialism would like nothing better than to destroy the gains of the Revolution, to prevent its spread (indeed, to strangle it, though that becomes increasingly more difficult), but today Hitler is the main enemy, and it is necessary to destroy his agents in the Soviet Union."

"Do you really think that these old Revolutionists are agents of Fascism?" I asked incredulously.

"Why not?" he shrugged. "We are talking about confessions in open court."

"But these confessions are fantastic," I said. "How could people who devoted their lives, risked their lives for this Revolution, suddenly turn to their bitterest enemies and seek to destroy what they had helped build up?"

"I don't know anything about their psychological motivations," said Arthur. "The fact is that they are creating unrest, jeopardizing the Soviet power."

"You mean the ruling class," I said, "which is consolidating its power against the masses, and destroying more and more the freedom of those masses."

"There is no ruling class in the Soviet Union." said Arthur, "That is slander, and what you call the curtailing of freedom is in fact the strengthening of the state against internal and external enemies. As the Soviets reach higher levels of Socialism, these so-called restraints will slowly dissolve."

"What you are doing," I replied, "is adopting a kind of supernatural attitude in regard to the Soviet people. Their children, or their children's children, will reap the benefits, secular pie in the sky. But the habit of freedom is lost, and will not be easily returned by those who stand to gain by that loss of freedom."

"The metaphysics of Means and Ends," said Arthur. "For the sake of the future we all sometimes do what is unpleasant. Punishing a child, for example."

"But a decent parent will punish a child," I replied, "in an overall situation of love and concern. You are talking about imprisonment and death for an ulterior reason."

"The reason," said Arthur, "is to preserve the gains of the Revolution, and that shows a concern for present and future generations, not only of the Soviet Union, but of the whole world."

"There are dangers in freedom," I replied, "but they must be faced, and this continuing exclusion of the people from free participation and free expression drives freedom into a hole where it may die."

"By *facing the dangers*," said Arthur, "I suppose you are looking forward to the destruction of the October Revolution."

"I welcome social gains anywhere," I said, "but they cannot be divorced from the institutions and habits of freedom. These areas are not sharply separated, they penetrate one another."

"Freedom," repeated Arthur, "freedom to starve, to sell apples on street corners, to die of silicosis."

"You don't have a vested interest," I said, "in the suffering of the people, and it's possible to be opposed to injustice wherever it appears, and in whatever form."

"You are supporting a dying system," he said, "all you can do is give it shots in the arm to prolong its life, but the Soviet Union shows the way to the society of the future."

"You are prepared to destroy the living generations in the name of Millenium," I said, "but I say that we must build on whatever we happen to have of good, in people or institutions, and transform the outworn."

"That kind of moralizing," said Arthur, "is only an escape from the day-to-day struggle."

We spoke on these matters for about an hour, both growing more excited, and Melanie listened, hardly participating. Then, since I was the intruder, I felt that I ought to leave, and rose. Somewhat to my surprise, Arthur rose with me, and we went downstairs together, silently, nodded to one another distantly, and went off in different directions.

40. *No Familiar Figures*

That night (I have said very little of the nights) I had a troubled sleep, full of dreams portentous and inconsequential. Great armies formed and dissolved on shadowy plains, turned into forbidding figures; then appeared the grey void, threatening and serene in turn. Then the figure of a most beautiful woman, smiling and distant, or lecherously advancing towards me. Then a figure pedagogical and stern, shaking a finger, turning to the blackboard, warning and counseling. Not a familiar figure in the dream, no story remembered, no transitional period. I stirred, woke, then returned to a new confusion: a great army with flashing banners, gaunt penitential figures, castles in whose towers and cellars were immured melancholy ladies, waiting to be rescued, revived, knights prancing on gaily caparisoned steeds (or were the knights gaily caparisoned?), yawning graves, figures of death and decomposition, the beseeching face of Al Jolson, a joust, a tourney, a duel, hair shirts, pilgrims and penitents, dark conspiracies, courtly ceremonials, the Dance of Death, rose petals floating down from distant towers, and all the time a desperate sense of having to choose. It was an anxiety dream. The face of Al Jolson suddenly (in my sleep) provided a clue. *The Jazz Singer*. Huizinga, whose book, *The Waning of the Middle Ages*, I had been reading. These were images out of this work, naturally no familiar face (except Al Jolson's), everything faraway, and the anxiety of choice, to have to decide somehow among these distant images (what does it mean to decide among images?), this kaleidoscope out of the past, this medieval pageantry, pestilence, this romance, conspiracy, penitence.

41. *Who Won?*

There was a rush job the following day at my uncle's printing shop, and I stayed on into the night to help expedite the matter. Then there was a lull, I found myself with time on my hands, and a telephone at my side. It is my habit to use the phone for reasons of appointment, business, convenience, etc., and not for reasons of sociability, lengthy conversation. This disembodied talk at a distance is not altogether real, it has an element of irresponsibility—one likes to shake hands on a promise or to look into the other's eyes on hearing a given sentiment expressed or expressing that sentiment. Too much burden is put on the human voice. Nevertheless, in this lull, with a phone at my side, I decided to call Melanie.

Knighthood no longer flowers, but men will always try to impress women, whether it be a lad climbing a towering tree before an (apparently) indifferent girl, or a (grown) man testing his wit, knowledge, or intelligence before a woman toward whom he is preferably drawn. And he will attempt incredible deeds of athletics, valor, or dialectics, though she is not in distress, and the last thing in the world she wants is to be saved.

Of course I had to call Melanie and apologize for intruding the way I had. But I was also curious to know how I had fared in my joust with Arthur, in that hour-long tournament of minds. So I called during this lull at the printing shop, and on the third ring she answered the phone (I mention the number of rings as a naturalistic detail). After "How are you?" "Fine. And how are you?" "Fine," I said:

"I'm sorry that I interrupted that way yesterday."

"That's all right," she said, "Arthur dropped by without calling too."

It was as though my interruption had canceled out Arthur's, so that she was angry at neither one of us.

"It was a rather heated discussion," I said, trying to get an expression of opinion.

"He's not excessively open to reason," said Melanie.

This dispraise of my opponent implied that I had gotten the nod. I was mildly satisfied, but certainly did not feel as though I had won bay or laurel. Then I realized (as though I hadn't realized it before) that this was all nonsense on my part, acting like an adolescent trying to impress the girl of his choice.

"You know," I said, "when I was a kid I ran around the Central Park reservoir three times to beat another kid who had dropped out after two-and-a-half turns, and it was only to impress a girl who was there."

Melanie smiled over the telephone (such things happen). We chatted a while, easy and friendly-like, until my uncle called out that I was needed.

"Look," I said, "I have some work to do here, let's go to the *Living Newspaper* Friday night." I was talking from the vantage of Wednesday.

"Fine," she said, and so that appointment was finalized.

42. *A Bouquet for Melanie*

A youth will not only perform great deeds of daring for the one he loves or try to impress her with feats of gymnastic or mind play, he will also bring her gifts, and these gifts can be of varied sorts, from rock to jewel, or may not be material objects at all. The following day I met a chap named Wankowitz at the University. I naturally asked whether he was related to the woman of the same name in Melanie's apartment house. He said that she was a cousin, and fairly distant at that, deep in the thickets of consanguinity. Now, had I not knocked on this lady's door in error, I should never have known of her (unless idly recognizing her name from the names above the bells and below the letter boxes in the familiar apartment hall), and if I knew her name (learning it the way I did or otherwise) but was not in love with Melanie Craig I would surely not have enquired deeply (maybe cursorily, maybe not at all), but knowing her name and feeling as I did about Melanie, I enquired closely about Miss Wankowitz, not for her sake (whom I had seen only on stairway, through the chink of a door or swiftly, silently, closing that door) but for Melanie's sake, to bring her an offering, a gift of gossip, if not of truth or intuition, a humble offering, news of a neighbor. Adam Wankowitz—the cousin—answered my questions, feeling, no doubt, that the long arm of coincidence had shrunken the world, and, secure in this shrunken world, I made no pretense that I was his cousin's friend, or even that my friend was his cousin's friend, but must have intimated a connection less casual than the one that in fact existed. At any rate Adam (an eager undergraduate taking summer courses for extra credit) spoke freely about his distant cousin, freely in the sense that he gave me the external facts, her life's garment, so to say, for the fact is that he hardly knew her. Very likely I understood Miss Wankowitz better than he did!

But he knew the events of her life—her Polish birth, her thwarted love, her political flight, and loveless exile—and I gathered these facts together, lovingly, as a bouquet for Melanie.

43. *Reportage*

Then the interval passed, and Friday night arrived.

"I come to you," I said, "or you come to me, or we meet at a third place. That exhausts the category of Meeting."

"And now," she replied, for she was prepared to leave her apartment, "we go out together, rather than alone or in a group, and that exhausts the category of Going Out."

On this somewhat scholastic note we left for a production of the *Living Newspaper*, a unit in the W.P.A. Theatre Project. The production we saw dealt with the lives of the share-croppers. We saw the squalor and desolation, and behind these shacks, behind this desperation of families, were flashed figures of rent, income, etc., on a great movie screen. Generally speaking, these productions told the audience what it was that the audience knew, tending therefore to goad the social consciences of those whose consciences were already pretty well goaded. Occasionally, as by a rush of feeling, or sudden insight, the scene was illuminated for us in an unexpected perspective. Melanie was particularly interested in the *Living Newspaper* because of her interest in reportage. Dreiser, Sherwood Anderson, Waldo Frank and Dos Passos had come back from Harlan County in Kentucky and had written of the situation in the coal mines, in the coal towns, in the miners' homes, and of the feelings and attitudes of the miners and their families. It was reportage; the reporter takes a stand, he not only gives the facts but expresses his views as to the meaning of these facts and as to what ought to be done. You might call it a high objectivity, or a subjectivity in the cause of progress, an acknowledged bias—it is a style of reporting that hardly exists now.

"It is the raw material of the novel," said Melanie, as we walked away from the theatre discussing reportage, "before it is fused into the form of art. You do not have to move away from the material, you move into it, even become, for a while, part of it."

We were in the theatre section and went to Hector's Cafeteria on 43rd Street and Broadway; it had a balcony which commanded a view of the Broadway scene.

"When you come to write whatever it is," I said, "you *are* removed from the materials, you are at a desk and these people and actions must be reconstructed as though it had all taken place years ago."

But I could not deny the warmth and immediacy of the form. We drank our coffee, and I thought it time to give her my gift.

"I met a cousin of a neighbor of yours," I said.

She looked at me in surprise.

"Miss Wankowitz," I said, and proceeded to tell her what it was I knew about the music teacher. It was a kind of personal journalism, about a stranger, and Melanie was very much interested, the way we are about a neighbor, even though one we hardly know. The social context of her unhappiness was less apparent than that of the sharecroppers or miners; her troubles, so to speak, were more in the private sector of the soul's economy (though she was a refugee from the spreading Nazism). We discussed these distinctions, looking down at the near wonder of Broadway.

"People in a crowd," I said, "tend to be silhouettes, the way they were in the *Living Newspaper*."

And having said that, why, Melanie seemed all the closer, all the warmer, more palpable. I kissed her lightly on the cheek, and she smiled.

"What are you doing over the weekend?" I asked.

44. In Praise of Saturday Night

"I'm free tomorrow night," she said, and I immediately translated *tomorrow night* into Saturday night, for the next night *was* Saturday night, and I was very happy at the prospect of going out with her on Saturday night, for of all nights in the week that was my favorite night, the carnival night. *Everyone Loves Saturday Night*, and the thought of going out with Melanie on Saturday night revived for me all the Saturday nights on which I had gone out. Friday night was fine, with its no-school the next day and its Sabbath sadness sense (the burning of the lights brought back to me a secondhand image of the Old World, knowing it only through my parents), but let's not forget that one of the glories of Friday night is that it is close to Saturday night, that New Year's Eve of the week, night of joy, of social communion, night when our society throws a light, though fitfully, into the gloom of the unknown, that expressive night, forgetful night. And I was pleased that Melanie had chosen Saturday night as the night of our meeting, when she could have chosen Saturday afternoon (a far cry from Saturday night) or Sunday afternoon or Sunday night. Not that *any* afternoon or night was unpleasant with Melanie, but none could compare with Saturday night, the very sound of which enthralled me, conjuring up an infinity of Saturday nights, past and future, an infinity of joy (who remembers the miserable Saturday nights?). The free associations of Saturday night! its dreams and possibilities, opening out onto beauty emblazoned in the sky, in the lurch and sway of strangers, in the eyes of the girls you loved, or desired (and anyone with spirit is desirable on Saturday night), the star-crossed sadness of the night, for lovers can part on Saturday night, or not meet (there is a lonely Saturday night). Saturday night is the night of all nights in the week when the soul expands and dreams to the edge of possibility, and further, for how can the possibility expand unless the soul dreams further than it can achieve? And because Melanie had chosen Saturday night for us, I moved lightly down Broadway with her, past the whirl of the *New York Times* national and international scoreboard, traveling south and east toward her home, for it was another glorious night, star-bedazzled, holding out the glories of this night and the next, which would be Saturday night, eagerly awaited by all. Whoever does not await this night is most unfortunate, cursed by nature or circumstance into a neglect and denial of Saturday nights, into a flight from joy and social communion, attachés of gloom and perversity, for who in his right mind will not look forward to Saturday night, to the random expectations and to the lovely chaos of Saturday night, to the flowering and bloom of the night, to the blessing and beneficence of Saturday night?

45. *More Discussing*

"Great," I had replied (up there on the balcony), and now we were on our most pleasant walk, for the prospect of Saturday night enhanced the possibilities of the night in which we now walked and conversed, in which we walked, fell silent, walked, and conversed. "The other night," I said, and I had not thought of saying it, the way I usually think before saying something that is personal and important or may turn out to be so, "the other night I read *Craig's Wife*. Do you know the play at all?"

"I really don't," she replied, "Naturally it's been mentioned to me on a number of occasions, the way any oddity in a name will draw comment, but I haven't heard much mention of it since our divorce."

"It's about a woman," I said, "who is concerned, obsessively, with order in her house—she can't stand rose petals on the furniture and must have the very leaves of her trees dusted. Material possessions mean everything to her—she is prepared to sacrifice anyone, including her husband, especially her husband, for the sake of her house and belongings. Mr. Craig refuses to understand, but finally catches on, and takes off. You have absolutely nothing in common with Craig's wife."

"I am Mrs. Craig," she said, "not Craig's wife," and she said that rather sadly. Then she went on, more directly, "No sign of all that family disorder that bothered you so much when we first met."

"The disorder here," I said, "is radical, in the nature of her character and their marriage." It was my way of apologizing for my early reaction to the difficulties and accidents of her life.

We spoke about the tyranny of possessions, of how, ideally speaking, material objects should be used as means for a better life.

"But there's no point in talking about that now," she said, "when millions lack the most elementary needs. When the spread of goods is equitable, this problem will merit discussion." It was a way she had of criticizing me (and herself) for the superiority of our economic positions, though we were both in moderate enough circumstances. She (and I) were guilty about our economic advantages; radical politics was an answer to that guilt.

"All right," I said, "but the problem of justice, of the good society, would remain the same whether you and I were rich or poor. So we are back to the objective situation."

Then I pointed out that most of the revolutionary leaders came from the middle class, or better. We discussed politics for a while. Melanie had read some Trotsky as part of her effort to find political bearings.

"I was struck," she said, "by a certain scholasticism. Every strike has the potential of a social revolution, in the way that every disease has the potential of death."

"That's an odd criticism," I said, but then she went on:

"Of course, there's a tremendous dynamism, a kind of atheistic prophetic feeling."

"According to his doctrine," I said, "he's been defeated by historical causation, by the dialectic of history. Had the Revolution spread to Germany, France, . . . but it didn't."

Then we discussed the problems of bureaucracy and leadership, the role of the individual in social change, Tolstoy's epilogue to *War and Peace*, the meaning of political power, how it was (according to Sukhanov) lying in the streets before the Bolshevik seizure, waiting to be picked up. We discussed the relations between freedom and security, recalled how Lenin had sent Emma Goldman out of Russia, telling her, in so many words, that "this is not for you, you'll be happier elsewhere," analyzed the Thermidorian reaction, the role of the Second International, wondered where Marx would stand if he were alive today, discussed the emergent Freudo-Marxism, stopped at the Waldorf Cafeteria on 8th Street and 6th Avenue, the cafeteria from whose tables the sugar bowls were removed, and whose rest rooms were protected by guards, discussed (at the bare table) over more coffee, comparatively abstruse questions and questions of the day. We both loved cafeteria conversation—the bareness of the place (no sugar bowls or ketchup on the tables), the absence of waiters, the hum of the conversation at other tables (a steadier and deeper hum than restaurant hum), the joy of getting to know one another by exchange of views. It was a kind of paradise, if paradise is a life where time speeds easily, all pressures, fears, premonitions, and tensions are forgotten, where learning and pleasure go hand in hand.

"Here come Eric and Sandy," said Melanie, and looking up, I saw them, to my surprise, approaching our table.

46. . . . *through a heaven of vice a hell of virtue is reached*

—KAFKA

I was not surprised that they were coming toward our table but was surprised that they were together and coming toward our table, for I was unaware (and so, apparently, was Melanie, because she expressed surprise at seeing them together) that they had become friends in the brief period since Sandy's party, where they had first met. Then they were at our table, standing above us, and we naturally asked them to join us, and they naturally accepted and went for their coffees, which gave us the opportunity to express further wonderment at their being together, until we came to realize that it wasn't that surprising, that some people made friends quickly, and by the time they returned to our table our wonderment had pretty much subsided. They had gone to the movies, then wandered around, discussing, and had moved into the sphere of Utopia, of life and problems in the classless society, *after* the state withered away.

"Eric is concerned with the element of boredom," said Sandy.

"It's a question of a higher form of conflict," said Eric. "If the working day is reduced to a couple of hours, and the product is spread equitably, all material needs being provided for, I'm frankly puzzled about how the day will be spent."

"People will turn to whatever activities they enjoy," said Sandy, "study, travel."

"I just can't see everyone lying under the trees—look how bored people are on Sunday afternoons now. Is the whole week going to be a Sunday afternoon?" asked Eric.

"You forget," said Sandy, "that leisure time now follows basically unpleasant work."

"But the work will be the same" said Eric. "There will be less of it, very much less of it."

"That quantitative difference," said Sandy, "will amount to a change in quality."

"People used to the day-to-day struggle," said Eric, "won't know what to do with themselves, they will think up new forms of struggle."

"In that case," said Melanie, "we should make every effort to keep the class struggle forever alive."

"I don't say that," laughed Eric, "because we must move in the direction that justice and reason demand, but we're talking about Utopia."

"When the struggle for survival loses its sharpness, or even disappears," I said, "maybe the conflict between individuals will take on a sharper, but more meaningful aspect. There will be higher forms of love and friendship, of competition."

"I suppose," said Eric, dubiously.

"Look," said Sandy, "there's no question but that life is more interesting when the good and the bad, the deformed and the ideal, exist side by side, but can't you conceive of new forms of variety?"

"What I think of," replied Eric, "are people sitting around, drinking, getting on one another's nerves, a lot of woman-chasing, restlessness without results, much destruction."

"What about exploration?" asked Melanie, "and to the moon? What about research in the fields of disease? Don't you think that a terrific expenditure of energy will be required for all that?"

"That's true," said Eric, "but only a certain number of people will be involved in such activities."

"The whole level of human activity will be raised," said Melanie.

The conversation lagged, and we looked around at the scene, drab and yet curiously animated.

"Your argument," I said to Eric, "is similar to what you hear about how boring paradise must be. We find it hard to conceive of a situation that is qualitatively different from the situation we have, just the way, according to Lucretius, one can't conceive of himself dead, because he visualizes himself observing the dead figure. But it needn't be that different. Whatever greater good develops must develop from the good we have here and now. There's always a little paradise, else we couldn't have the notion of it."

"I wouldn't worry too much about the problems of Utopia," said Melanie, "while we have the problems of today to cope with."

"I understand that," said the active young Socialist, "but today's problems open into the future, and we must follow them."

Then we gossiped a bit, and Melanie and I left; Sandy and Eric said that they would stay on, and of course it was Sandy's delicacy in allowing me to escort Melanie home alone.

47. *Melanie Meets My Friends*

Then came Saturday, whose dawning I did not see (nor the dawning of hardly any day), and I awoke refreshed and happy. Why happy? I was young, healthy, had a reasonable chance to fulfill my ambitions (for they were possibly not beyond my powers), was going to see Melanie in the evening. Why not happy? I thought of a half-promise I had made (earlier in the week) to visit on Saturday night. Other friends would be there. It was a little group of which I was a part, and Melanie had never met any of my friends. Was it by design that Melanie had not met my friends (except by accident, in an intermission or at someone else's party)? Was I ashamed of Melanie? Was I ashamed of my friends? Did I think that she might not get along with them? I was no longer as happy as I had been on awaking—the day's problems were beginning to crowd in, but I threw myself into the day's work, at home and in the library; I thought it would be nice to get my thesis done by February. Why not by February? I worked steadily, covered ground, saw the lines of my work fan out, began to get the feel of the ending of the thesis. Tonight a date with Melanie, maybe a visit to my friends. Why not a visit to my friends? Back home from the library, I bathed, I dressed, and moved into the Saturday evening street. Wow, it was hot! No wind, hardly any air, sweat formed immediately. I moved swiftly through the streets on a route becoming increasingly familiar and reached Melanie's house early. Why not early? Why hide the fact that I wanted to be at Melanie's early? Should I have skulked around the neighborhood for fifteen minutes? She was pleased about meeting my friends.

"It's a kind of primal horde," I explained, "the way most of these groups are. Our hands are raised against the world, so far not against one another."

"I haven't seen a primal horde in years," she said, and so we took the subway to the 90s on the West Side.

Now there are various ways in which I can tell this episode of our visit to my friends, but the best way is to describe the action of a team engaged in a game in which Melanie was the spectator and in which I moved rather uneasily from the role of spectator to that of participant. I am trying to tell it from Melanie's point of view. The introductions were polite, friendly, but there was no small "hello" talk, no asking what the stranger "did" (that was a taboo question); it was as though we had walked in after the warmup, after the game had started. It seems that an old man had rung the bell about an hour back. He was apparently a Western Union messenger and had a telegram for the host. They had asked the old man to stay for a drink. The telegram was from a couple in Des Moines, saying that their visit was delayed. This was, for a reason not altogether clear, a cause for great merriment; what probably caused the merriment was that this couple from Des Moines would be unable to make the trip east. The telegram, which was passed to us, was analyzed exhaustively, in every conceivable manner, as though seven of our New Critics were orphaned of all literary texts except a telegram of fourteen words from Des Moines, Iowa. Historical allusions were offered, grammatical quirks were analyzed, much was made of a pause, its effect on the rhythm of the sentence; dozens of names, connected in one way or another with the sender, were whizzed around the room, and these names led to other names, twice and three times removed from the sender. There were sharp semantic bounce passes, swift overhand puns, long looping remembrances, hysterical scores of a personal nature. The talk shifted to the old messenger, who showed up one instant as a kind of chorus of old men, then as a kind of defective, then as the prime mover in the encounter we had missed, then as a bewildered old man, listening confusedly to the babel about this telegram which he had routinely delivered.

My friends were having a great time; I was enjoying myself and would have enjoyed myself more if I thought that Melanie was more comfortable, though she gave no indication of discomfort. My friends were, of course, being rude, in a sense that they continued a discussion in a manner that excluded the guest. They did not bring the game to a halt because a stranger, a guest, was present, but went on playing (stimulated, indeed, by the presence of an audience), made her perforce a spectator of a game whose rules she did not understand, though the content was as simple as I have described it. All reality possible had to be squeezed from this telegram, from the old messenger, from the couple in Des Moines, from the friends and acquaintances of this couple, who were themselves old friends (I knew of their existence) and had been away for a few years. It was a way of exploiting whatever happened to be happening. There was no whisky present, but after a while coffee and cake were served, and the conversation, which had dawdled (apparently a time-out), now speeded up again in a razzle-dazzle exhibition, the words caught up, zipped around in a free-associational orgy, a frenzy of wandering wit. The hour was late, though the game was not over. We rose to go, the men rose, the host and hostess moved with us toward the door, and then returned to the fray, for as we walked downstairs we heard the tumult rise to a new crescendo, as, no doubt, Melanie and I were incorporated into the saga of the Iowa telegram and the old man on the bicycle (it was a twenty-six-inch Columbia bike—the old man had apparently brought it upstairs with him, taken it into the living room of the apartment, where it was scrutinized, exhaustively analyzed, as though it were the last manufactured object in the world and this the last night to understand and make something of it).

48. *Together, Apart*

We walked toward the subway.

"It was kind of fascinating to watch them in action," she said.

She asked me about the individuals and I gave her somewhat swift sketches of their backgrounds, characters, and interests. We were a group, a band of (mostly) brothers, trying to make a world of our own—seeking fame and fortune in the great world, then returning to the security and excitement of the world we were making together. Melanie and I were now at 96th Street and Broadway, in front of the famed cafeteria near the kiosk. What more natural than we should buy the Sunday paper and go into this cafeteria? The place was crowded; it is one of our glorious mixed neigborhoods, with the pluralism which we considered a lesser evil to classlessness. We found a table in the midst of the animated crowd. We glanced at the newspaper headlines. Had we been married, we no doubt would have chosen our favorite sections and disappeared into them. But the way it was, we merely looked at the front page, whose format was menaced by the shadow of the Spanish Civil War.

"Hello Lila," said Melanie to a girl who came up to our table. She was shapely and serious. "Why don't you sit with us?" asked Melanie.

"Sure, let me get Jack," said Lila, and unable to attract his attention by waving and shouting (the place was noisy and Jack was busy looking for Lila and for a place to sit) she walked off toward him.

"She's on the Writers' Project," said Melanie, "and Jack is a union organizer. They're going to get married."

Then Lila and Jack appeared and sat down with us. Jack was vigorous, rather narrowly outspoken, with a charm that was honest, though perhaps too dynamic. Since Melanie hoped to be working for the Writers' Project in the autumn, the two girls talked shop, the kind of shop two people will talk when one is in the field and the other hopes to be. Lila said that they were in the planning stages of a project dealing with U.S. Route #1 that followed this famous road and described the countryside, the cities, the landmarks through which the road passed; also, the history of the road; you might say it was to be the biography of the road.

"You may get on that road project," said Lila. "It would probably involve some traveling."

Jack seemed restive, anxious to get going, and they didn't stay very long after drinking their coffee. I don't know how it affected Melanie, but the fact of their engagement threw me off a bit. It meant that some kind of line had been drawn in the area of confusion through which they moved, and it pointed up my own uncertainty—as regards Melanie, as regards my future (I had no idea, for example, how I would earn a living, for teaching didn't much appeal to me and what else can a historian do but teach?). I resented the engagement of these strangers in a way that I didn't resent the marriages (even of strangers) that were taking place, for you are always more envious of what is closer to the desirable, thinking that you know what the desirable is.

We didn't outstay the departed couple very long, but moved into the convenient kiosk. Our traveling plans were to take the Broadway train down to the Sheridan Square Station and walk east. The 14th Street exit would involve no longer a walk, but that famed thoroughfare was kind of glum in the early morning hours, the Village of course being much livelier. We had no trouble finding seats on the train; the paper was on my lap. Other couples, married (perhaps only engaged) divided the Sunday papers and wearily scanned the day's news, the weekly summaries, the rotogravures and comics. My wandering eyes caught sight of a familiar face on the opposite aisle, toward the end of the car. It was the woman who had once occupied my apartment, the one I had interviewed, who (as I had suggested to Melanie) might have been a member of the ancient profession, where the body is the weapon of livelihood. She was sitting with a gentleman, obviously her husband, who looked very much the well-to-do merchant. Why were they not in a cab? Musing momentarily on this question, I thought of a number of explanations. I quietly identified the strangers to Melanie. She looked at them with a more casual indifference than she usually showed for such unknowns. She said nothing. What was there to say? I felt that it was idiotic to have pointed out the strangers—what possible sense was there in identifying a woman who had, many years ago, occupied an apartment in which I was now living, she possibly an ex-prostitute, the man with her probably her husband, probably a businessman? What was I trying to prove? At the same time I resented Melanie's apparent lack of interest. The matter *was* related to my dissertation—shouldn't she show *some* interest in that? As the subway approached 72nd Street, the woman and her companion arose and walked toward the door closer to us, for the reason that this door brought them closer to the stairs leading to the street. Waiting for the train to stop, the stranger's eyes moved down the car, past me, and back again. Had she recognized me? It was hard to say. But why not? If I had recognized her, why shouldn't she have recognized me? It was only a lack of self-confidence, even of self-respect, which made me think that I recognized others who did not recognize me, a running down of my own appearance and importance. I asked Melanie whether she thought that the stranger had recognized me. She was angry at the question.

"I'm tired," she said, "of defining these nuances of behavior."

I thought she might launch into an attack on Henry James. But how often did I ask her to define nuances of behavior? I imagined that she was having a delayed reaction to our visit, a kind of moral post partem. Here, in the subway at two in the morning, she was weary, aware of others' weariness, their depression; behavior was gross, she saw individuals as part of the great social scene, citizens of the Great Depression, images for reportage, the individual described in the density of his economic and social surroundings. The psychological nuance was an escape from the overriding reality, from the bread line, from the relief rolls, from the unemployed, from Hitler, from the future of the Socialist revolution. And I, concerned with the problem as to whether that woman, the one I thought might have once been a prostitute (what difference? Wasn't I stigmatizing someone who may have come to the pass out of difficult, needy circumstances? Wasn't that why Melanie refused to make any comment when I pointed the woman out to her?), had recognized me in the instant when she stood at the subway door, the one closer to the street exit, for I had made that point to Melanie too? She was not interested in these attenuations, these distinctions, if not in the field of manners, then in that of individual psychology. Then Jack and Lila, the couple we had met—he active in a significant social area with a given purposiveness, they engaged. Had she been disturbed by the presence of this engaged couple, by the fact of engagement? Did that perhaps anger her, more than the question of the recognition of the woman who had once occupied my apartment, more than the subtleties of individual psychology as against the obvious social horrors? These were my thoughts as the subway proceeded south; we rode in silence, got off at Sheridan Square, and there we were again, in the midst of Saturday night drawing to its close. People were moving away from the sources of pleasure, carried under their arms the tell-tale newspapers, indicating that their Saturday night had ended. Silently we headed east. Not for us the pleasures of making love on this night. I wondered what the phrase "pleasure dome" meant. Should I ask Melanie if, why, she was angry? But I decided not to, being angry at her silence. I tried small talk, and she responded shortly, discouraging further small talk. This was the way our Saturday night was ending, in a silence growing grimmer by the minute. We continued to walk side by side as the distance between us widened. I should have liked to come closer, but did not know how. The stars shone pallidly in a far-off sky. We reached her corner, then the front of her house. She broke her silence, said good-night, and moved swiftly up the stoop stairs.

49. *In the Bosom of a Family*

Let me hasten on with the story. That night, that Saturday night, that Sunday morning, I fell into a deep sleep (the sleep was waiting for me in the bed and I fell into it), but it turned out to be (again!) a troubled sleep, where the narration, the story line, was blurred—shadowy figures moved across the screen, a veritable phantasmagoria. Nor could I recognize these figures, now gliding eerily across a room or a field, now milling around in a desultory fashion, as at a carnival about to break up (a carnival seems always about to break up). A dream of Obliteration of Identities, a return to some original chaos of personality. In this area of ambiguity (to coin a phrase) a firm line appeared, a dark insistent line, and this line had a sound, and the sound repeated itself, and the pauses between the sound were quite exact, and I stirred in my sleep, as the blur of the dream seemed threatened by the insistencies of a sound whose familiarity I was approaching. A telephone ring! a telephone was ringing in my dream, ringing so insistently, so clearly and meaningfully that I woke up from my dream (the shadows dissolved) to hear the ringing of my telephone. I seized it.

"Hello. This is Horace Dow. How are you?"

"Fine, Horace, and you?"

"Very well. This is sort of last minute, but we'd like you to come up for dinner tonight."

"Tonight? What time is it now?" and I was angry at myself for asking this question because I knew that he would now ask whether he had woken me.

"Say, were you asleep?"

"Oh, that's all right."

"I'm sorry, it's a little after twelve." Then he said something that sounded like "up here," but he couldn't have said that.

In the course of this interchange, I slowly remembered that I had planned to spend some time at the 42nd Street Library in the afternoon, but now I seized at the invitation, feeling let down somehow that Horace had not invited Melanie, or at least tactfully suggested that I might bring a friend, but he had only seen me once with the girl, so why should he make assumptions?

"Thanks, I'd like very much to come. What time?"

"Oh, 'round six."

Great, I thought, as I showered and dressed, I'll do some work at home, and then walk over to Washington Square and take the Number 5 bus uptown. I saw myself on top of a double-decker bus going up 5th Avenue to 57th Street, turning west to Broadway, north to 72nd Street, then west again to the Drive, and so up to the Columbia area where the Dows lived. It was a dream easily actualized—at a quarter after five, with some work behind me, I was seated on top of a double-decker Number 5 bus, which followed exactly the route I had earlier followed in my thoughts. I rang the Dow bell and was admitted into a house overflowing with domesticity. Horace was sitting in the living room in a comfortable chair, reading one of the sections of the newspaper which you tend to put aside at first (with no intention of looking at it again) and then come back to in the restlessness of the late afternoon. Playing on the floor, in the middle of the room, among the scattered sections of the Sunday *Times*, was the Dow's 5 year-old daughter, Claudia. Her eyes lit up as she saw me, not so much for the real me as for me in the role of tea-consumer. For she had in front of her a toy tea-set, complete with a tiny kettle and genuine tea bags.

"Would you like a cup of tea?" asked Claudia.

"I would be delighted," I replied, in the elaborate tone I reserve for the 5-year-old daughters of friends with whom I am having dinner.

"Wouldn't you like something a little stronger?" cried out Mathilda, appearing from the kitchen, tidily aproned, though her face was not smudged with flour.

I waved to her, shook hands with Horace, who had risen from his chair to greet me, and told Claudia that I would certainly have the tea before I drank anything else, for she was upset at the prospect of my first consuming a drink that one of her parents would bring. I was in the bosom of a family, seated on a comfortable sofa; in front of me was a coffee table, on whose surface was soon placed a bourbon highball and a cup of Lipton's tea. I sipped the tea thoughtfully.

"Just perfect," I said to Claudia, "even better than what the Emperor drinks, in the Court of Peking, or fabled Cathay."

The child was pleased, and asked if I'd have another cup; I cheerfully agreed, and while this was being prepared, made a considerable incursion on the Kentucky product. The conversation moved narrowly between family matters, school matters, and news of the day. By the time we sat down to dinner, I had had four cups of tea and two drinks.

"Which do you like better?" asked Claudia.

"Your tea," I replied, "is unquestionably the superior beverage from the point of view of taste, appearance, and long-range therapeutic value. Not only that, but it's much better."

Claudia beamed and offered me another cup of tea; after a complex interchange of views among the four of us, it was decided that the next cup of tea would be served at the end of the meal. It was very pleasant sitting in the bosom of this family. I was involved in the security of an ongoing process. For me, there was no responsibility, no choice; I would later rise from this table and walk out of this apartment with no business unfinished, in the warm sociable glow which suffused us all. We finished the main dish, and Claudia served the tea next to the coffee, next to the tall drink. Then we rejoined the living room, and after a number of false starts and alarms it was Claudia's bedtime. She kissed her mother and father, then kissed me. My impression was that the kiss she gave me was the most passionate of the three.

"Goodnight," I said, "may pleasant dreams attend thee, in the arms of —" I hesitated.

"Morpheus" said Mathilda, thereby proving her supremacy in the field of classical scholarship.

Horace and I then kicked it around until Mathilda returned; then the three of us discussed, over and around drinks which had no competition from Claudia's tea. When the rigors of night set in for all of us, I took my leave. It was 10:33, and there is absolutely no significance to the exactitude of this time.

50. *I Praise Her to Myself*

I walked to Broadway, and then into the well-known Bar & Grill near the University. This was not done as a matter of course—I am one of those who can take or leave alcohol, and generally I leave it. I am not even a social drinker, in the sense that I will not necessarily drink because others are drinking, and do not scorn the lonely drink. I had had three drinks with the Dows, the effects of which had worn off in a manner that created a desire for beer. I thirsted for beer. As is true of many people who are infrequent drinkers, the activity tends to be something of an "experience," to which I am drawn, from which I am repelled. I am repelled because I dislike the idea of using external stimuli to create a more interesting inner world. It is a Puritan reaction, though my people are not of old New England stock. In fact, they are not of New England stock at all. Then I think of Coleridge and his opium, Keats and his claret, Leonardo and his youths, Dante . . . . It becomes a fine question as to what constitutes an external aid. You fall in love; is that love, that person, an external aid to the inner life? This way leads to the hermitage, and since I am not meant to be an anchorite and realize that I cannot push my position to its absolute I fall in love, take a drink, make a friend, and so resist the urgency of conscience which demands that I do on my own what it is that I think I have to do. This is a somewhat summary explanation of my move into the bar. I ordered a beer and looked around approvingly. Why, this place was a model of order: the whisky bottles, stacked by kind and brand, each man at his bar place (the women at theirs), the space behind me evenly broken into booths. It was a clean, shining bar, the drinkers on the contemplative side, no signs of rowdiness, but in the style of Sunday night drinking. Standing alone (for no one was making an effort to talk to me, nor was I making any effort to talk to another), I gave myself up to thoughts of Melanie ("giving oneself up" describes the act of a man guilty or of a cornered criminal). There is an aspect of Melanie's character that I have hardly mentioned. I mean a lack of envy, an absence of the endless criticism of others which one hears on all sides, a criticism that rarely shows an interest in the other but is a kind of self-gratification, a way of inflating the self, as though it were a tire lost its air. But Melanie was truly absorbed in the object, and so the criticism was never self-inflating. This may not sound like much, but I find it a thing of great wonder that she could be selflessly absorbed, patiently seeking the truth without the maddening self-congratulatory attitudes of so many others (*Look, I am seeking the truth*)—that was surely part of her beauty, and I stood in a certain awe of her, the way one feels awe in the presence of beauty. But was I thinking that *in order* to move away? How confused the situation was between us. Why did we not approach one another in a marriageable way? There was a hindrance, a silence, an intervention of powers not easily identified. Surely I did not know what I wanted. I was surely confused, seeking perhaps to avoid the long commitment. And perhaps she the same. The beer had lost its savor, so I walked out and down Broadway to 96th Street. The morning papers were out! The weekend was over! I bought the *Times* and the *News*, went into the cafeteria and immersed myself in the horror and confusion of others.

51. *Her Sad Departure*

An hour later (such is the maddening certitude of time) I was fast asleep, in my bed of singular blessedness, and once more dreams began to prowl in the cavern of my mind—dark beasts of prey, a shining tiger, and the clatter of the Mergenthaler machines, running off, as fast as the eye could follow, copies of my thesis, to be hawked in the streets. They were being hawked in the streets by Algerian urchins (I mean Horatio Alger)—rugged, canny, basically sound, each shouting the slogan he thought most conducive for the sale. Then, back to the forest glen, the slouching beasts, primordial, unnamed, and the snake but lately bruised, moving and slithering the way a line might waver on some electronic screen, or the insistent sound wave betokening once more the ring of the telephone. Drenched in sleep, I awkwardly reached for the ringing instrument, brought the mouthpiece to my mouth, the receiver to my ear, thought for a long instant what it is that one says on picking up this humble wonder of the communications world, knowing that there was a certain word absolutely necessary under the circumstances, couldn't for the life of me recall that word. And then it came to me, aided, no doubt, by the presence of my mouth at the mouthpiece, my ear at the receiver.

"Hello," I said, and I heard Melanie's voice, explaining that her mother was ill and that she was flying out West. It was Monday morning. The summer session was ended, my arrangements with my uncle were flexible, so I told Melanie that I'd see her to the airport (the plane was to leave at 12 noon, it was now 9:30).

And so it turned out, in time's curious passage through eternity, we were at the airport, all particulars avoided. Melanie's mother had come down with pneumonia, and Melanie thought that if all were well she'd be back in the

city on the Friday afternoon train. We waited siliently until it
was time for the plane to take off. Then I kissed her on the
cheek, pressed her hand, and watched as she walked up the
stairs leading to the plane. She turned, waved, and disappeared. I waited for the plane to take off, watched its
awkward performance on the ground, then followed it up into
the sky. It is different from a train, where it is possible to
wave good-bye to one you see, and different from a ship,
where you can catch the familiar face in the waving, shouting
crowd. Ways of saying good-bye, according to the means of
transportation used. Some come to airport, harbor, or terminal,
see their friends or loved ones aboard, then make a point of
leaving before departure. Enemies of sentimentality, and the
guilt in the hearts of those who wait for the departure, hiding
the relief. And the death buried in every departure, the tears
as the ship moves down the harbor, the chance that every
leaving is a final leaving, because of the hazards of travel and
because any journey adumbrates the final journey. I watched
the disappearance of the plane, then moved back into the bus,
into the sobriety and security of the bus rolling through Jersey
toward the heart of Manhattan. I was sad at Melanie's departure, sad at her sadness, and that sadness carried through the
afternoon's work at my uncle's printing shop.

52. *Waiting, Missing*

Waiting is a habit of the soul, the way getting from one
place to another is a necessity of the body. These are areas of
transition, the time and space preceding an act or event (that
act, event, being the transition to another act, event). There
are some of us whose lives seem a perpetual waiting, all
behavior swallowed in that endless expectancy. At the other
extreme are those of us who by endless movement, an incredible unceasing restlessness, swallow all waiting, all ex-

pectancy, create the illusion of something happening all the time (the movement from place to place is what is happening, the way, at the other end, the waiting is the experience). In-between we all move and wait, the way I was now waiting for Melanie to return and missing her while I waited. "Missing" people is a form of mourning for the departed. Some leave in order to be missed. Absence makes the heart grow fonder—the mourning is premature, the beloved returns. See, she returns from death and distance, our mourning premature. We are ever so glad to see her returned, whose departure we greeted with the anxiety of loss forever, whose return we greet with the anxiety for one forever found. And miss the one we have not been getting on with, in whose absence all difficulties are composed, all confusion harmonized, so she returns to a reconstructed life, something built in her absence, an ideality destroyed by her return. I waited for Melanie, missed her, mourned her prematurely, harmonized our differences, plainly missed her, she being gone and not at my side—the primordial ache of separation, one proof of together.

53. *Seeking the Mechanical*

Work of a routine or mechanical nature (if it is not the way you must make a living, if one sees an end or a near end of it) can have, if not a liberating effect, then certainly a soporific one, this side of euphoria; the imagination, forever seeking the unknown goal, probing the glories of futurity from the dim hints the present sometimes allows, is grounded in the recurrent exigencies of the day's task. So we sometimes seek drudgery in order to escape the hazards of chance and contingency, the way I plunged into the work at my uncle's printing plant (a plant! ungreen, seedless) during those days of Melanie's absence. I rearranged the fonts of type, brought customers' lists up-to-date and in alphabetical order, cleaned

up the corners, straightened out the stock—all work beyond
the call of commercial duty. Yes, yes, I was creating little
pockets of order to exclude the contingencies of experience,
holding off, if not time itself, then the glories of time. The
possibilities out there, dimly felt, presaged, life's never ending
opportunities, the lovely pluralisms, all the marvelous things
coming to be. And it was I who had listened in a somewhat
superior manner to Melanie's description of order in her
mother's house! I who had commented philosophically on its
meaning, as though from a distance!

"Hey, what's with you?" asked Gino, a linotype operator
with whom I had become quite friendly.

"Just getting things in order," I replied, from the depths
of my self-chosen prison, deep in the dungeons of self.

I moved from pocket to pocket, plunging, if not joyfully,
into these vacuums from which the uncertainties of the external
world had been sucked. So I was tired, first by the mechanical
nature of the work itself and then by the movement from
one area to another. That is how (without the emphases and
refinements) I spent the four days at my uncle's shop while
Melanie was away.

54. *Sky, be blue, and more than blue*
—KENNETH FEARING

Looking out of my open window on Thursday morning
(probably because the sky was blue, a perfect blue, as blue
as blue can be but not more than blue) I thought of the lines
of the poet who brought to life the snarling moralities, the
justice hunger of the metropolitan radicalism of the time, and
clearly delineated the mood, sometimes the nature, of the
surrounding horror, in long artful lines (the length of 13th
Street) compounded of cynicism, sense of personal outrage,
tendentious, or selective, objectivity, and special prayer. By the

prevailing literary canons the lines could have been interpreted as a retreat from the struggle or, symbolically, as a demand for a more than perfect society, as if to say: "Nothing is too good for suffering humanity"; to demand more than the reality can be expected to deliver. I thought of all the arguments about the perfectability of human nature, of human society—*you can't change human nature; you can't change the institutions unless you change human nature first; change the institutions, then human nature will change of itself; it's a question of the dialectical interplay between human nature and society.* Was too much being asked of us (Freud and the destructive impulse), was it possible to ask too much of us, for deeds of courage, examples of stoical acceptance of unnecessary suffering, were not unknown? But the poet was making two requests—and the first was that the sky be blue, asking from a sky only what can be expected from a sky (it was certainly not irrational to ask the sky to be blue, and particularly when the sky was most often not blue, but gray). Once blue, however, then why not more than blue? If you ask only that the sky be blue, you are making a rational request, and it is possible that the goods will be delivered. If you are asking that the sky be more than blue, the demand is beyond the call of nature. It is perhaps the difference, I thought, looking at my patch of blue sky, between Scientific Socialism and Utopian Socialism. And that went back to the polemics of Kautsky and the Austro-Marxists.

55. *It is very much easier to shatter prison bars than to open undiscovered doors to life*

—D. H. LAWRENCE

Friday was gray. For the first time in a week, the sun had not made a powerful appearance; it shone wanly through a bank of clouds. Dark days are conducive to thought—one tries to understand on these days what it is he has experienced on the glorious clear days. But that's all nonsense—we experience and reflect at the same time (maybe not during the stormiest experience, or in the *very* low-pressure ones). Some even maintain that reflection is a kind of experience. Well, why not? Let's say that the overall meteorological situation conditions the nature, certainly the tone of the thought—that way of putting it ought to satisfy most everyone. People get angry (I thought, on this dark morning) for reasons of which they are not necessarily aware. I was thinking of Melanie, but parenthetically, so to say, recalled a friend who used to get angry at one person or another, disassociate himself for days, weeks on end, but no one knew why, he'd never explain, even after he came back, for he always came back. He had apparently suffered some insult, fancied or real, someone had unwittingly said something that had a peripheral connection to something that ought not to have been said, or someone omitted to say something, perhaps a word of thanks or approval, a sign of recognition, hard to say what, for the devil knows what it was upset him, so you couldn't be careful, choose your subjects, your words, the way you might do knowing the nature of the sensitivity (if one is sensitive, for example, to a given facial feature of his own, a reference to any kind of facial oddity, on any stranger's face, might create an atmosphere of insult, indignity, followed by anger and withdrawal). But we couldn't, as I say, puzzle out what it was disturbed our friend—it might have had nothing to do with us at all, some old memory, some ancient wrong that threw him off balance, out of sociability—and we used to discuss the matter with a kind of hysterical seriousness. I was trying to understand why Melanie was angry, withdrawn, was trying to get a long view of the matter, for it did not require years of historical research for me to understand the difference between an underlying and an exciting cause. In the last week I had been considering that Melanie's withdrawal was based on a critical view of my character. She felt the absence of risk in my life, that I made things easy for myself, didn't move into the world of contingency and danger, where one's ideas are tested, where one's courage is tested, where life itself may be in the balance. My confusion was real, my ideas in relation to action were not clear, but wasn't it possible that it was an insufficiency in character that made me tolerate that confusion, made me indeed seek and welcome that confusion? The fact that the decisiveness of many others was mindless did not absolve me. That mindlessness involves another kind of criticism. Often, in those soliloquies of conscience with which we are all familiar, I lashed at myself for not making life critical, for not making a life in which the whole man was involved—his ideals, his courage, his mind and imagination. *Every day as though the last day*, I'd say to myself, and meanwhile I was working on my thesis (a bit of municipal antiquarianism, or nostalgia), or making a little money at my uncle's shop, or seeing a girl, or talking with friends. Surely something was missing; I felt the incompletion, the absence of commitment, countered with the thought of a commitment to truth, but that sounded hollow, my involvement in scholarship was not that deep. To make life critical! Every day as though the last day! Yet I somehow mistrusted these formulations as overdramatizations, fell back on Epictetus, on an ideal of modesty. Perhaps I was asking too much from myself, asking for a kind of heroism, maybe martyrdom, of which I was not capable. Was love the answer? But here was love, here was further difficulty, for love makes extreme demands, points up the insufficiencies of character, makes clearer, more shining, the ideals that you seem incapable of achieving, or even of coming to grips with in a proper way. Yes, she no doubt saw a weakness in me, a kind of shallowness, I made things easy for myself, accommodated myself to the views and attitudes of others, creating a factitious absence of hostility and conflict. Shying away from the difficult, the trying! Afraid to test myself! Looking away from the horrors and the suffering everywhere, or somehow containing them, to create a phony neatness, a soulless order. And if I was perhaps more critical of myself than she was of me, what difference did that make? Her criticism was more important than my own—I tolerated my insufficiencies, made of them a way of life, but she suffered because of them, she wanted more from me than I wanted from myself, for what I wanted of myself I did not reach, and the life that fell short of what I wanted was the one that I tolerated, contained, half-heartedly accepted. And that angered her, that I should make a way of life of my insufficiencies, of my lashings of conscience, my confusion, my refusal to use myself, my caginess in holding back, building reservoirs of emotion and idealism, burying ever deeper my unused powers. Wouldn't that explain her anger more than the episode on the subway, or wouldn't it put that episode in a wider, more understandable context? And it was with these thoughts that I approached the terminal and awaited the arrival of the train.

56. *Melanie Returns*

I waited outside the gate of the track on which Melanie's early afternoon train was due. A railroad official (dressed like a conductor) opened the gate, and strangers began to appear from the recently arrived train. Some looked tired, some relieved, some bewildered (perhaps their first visit to the city), all travel-worn, finally free to move on their own. I saw Melanie moving up the ramp, looking very reposed, very beautiful, and moved swiftly towards her, noticing a stranger in her company, apparently helping her with the baggage, perhaps a friendly chap seated near her on the train. I reached and embraced her, she responded warmly, for time and circumstance alter relationship. She introduced me to Dan Craig. That was a familiar name. I must have understood who he was before I recognized the name, because I looked at him in astonishment, and that look must have turned into one of horror when I understood that this was her ex-husband I was facing, and now I was shaking his hand. My reaction was extreme. I mumbled an apology, turned, and sped up the ramp, through the unattended gate, became part of the swift-moving, anxious crowd.

57. *In skating over thin ice, our safety is in our speed.*

—EMERSON

As I lost myself in the anonymity of the Grand Central crowd, I recalled what happened a little before the end of "White Nights," I am thinking of the moment when the heroine (a child of seventeen, what we would call today a slip of a girl, rushed off from the man in love with her (that confused daydreamer) into the arms of the one she had been so anxiously awaiting—he finally arrived—thereby affirming the love she had so vehemently, so tremblingly tried to deny. Then she turned and expressed her sorrow to the other man (that fumbling fantasist). I (now contrasting, certainly not identifying myself with the girl in the story) had rushed off from the arms of the girl I loved (it is only a paragraph away since we embraced) into the anonymity of a crowd, and that is much less interesting than rushing off into the arms of the one you love. I was confused, angry, ashamed, bitter, and bewildered, very upset by so unexpected a confrontation. And after all that self-criticism (for my imagining what Melanie thought of me I construed as self-criticism), all that purging, to prepare myself—though hardly anointed in oil—for this meeting, to begin again so difficult a round, to try once more to help create a closeness in which the both of us might be enveloped, call it a web of happiness, a productive ongoing process. The first thought to cross my mind was that she had lied about her mother, all a ruse to meet Dan Craig, who, as the careful reader will recall, was stalled in the Midwest with a spark-plug cleaner and tester that wasn't selling like the Bible. But that was obviously a ridiculous thought—she might tell that to me, she might tell it to the super and his wife, but not to her own brother, unless indeed she had told him both the truth and the deception, coached him in the deception, and that was the act he had put on for me when I met him the night before in the Café Royale, in the company of Jill, and my mind raced over the interpersonal relationships among the four of us. But Melanie had never lied to me, all my suspicions (from the night we had met, when she gave me her address without a name) had proved unfounded. Every one, without fail! She did have an older brother who had died! (For so Frank had confirmed, when I spoke to him at the party and turned the conversation to his family life.) And thinking of this series of unfounded suspicions, I was angry with myself, angry for making accusations that I knew were false and yet could not help making (due to my suspicions) and so could not help being ashamed. Why did the sight of Melanie and her ex-husband together upset me so? There were areas which I had only faintly explored, matters I was reluctant to approach. Yes, yes, reluctant to approach, for the reason that my feelings did not jibe with my views, call them principles if you will, and one does not like to think that his principles are at the mercy of his feelings, that these principles are merely a superstructure to be leveled by the first gust of wind. I was walking the streets, moving swiftly, determined to achieve some understanding, for an unexamined life is not worth living, and what if one fears the examination, fears to learn the truth about himself? It was so difficult and unpleasant a task, so easy a task to avoid. Who was forcing me to do it? Who cared? My suspicions, my shame—which Blake called "Pride's cloke"—my anger (inner directed)—what a monstrous psychic amalgam, that was the exact phrase I used, the word *amalgam* having a definite connotation of disjunctions arbitrarily yoked together to create a factitious political position, that was how I explained it to myself, though the position itself varied from self-criticism to suspicious anger (there is no suspicion without anger, but there is anger without suspicion) and a certain amount of self-pity, creating thereby a further amalgam, one of a congeries of amalgams, a phrase that I actually used in the course of these deliberations, toward what I hoped would be some kind of self-understanding, that to be followed by a proper move. Then I took up each emotion in turn, for I wanted to be clear and orderly about the matter, in that typical reflex from disorder and confusion. First, suspicion. What is suspicion, I asked myself, what do we mean by the word *suspicion*? It is an absence of trust, thinking that the other is hiding something from you, either in the way of thought or act, and that something which is being hidden is a blow against your honor, your wife, your principles, your pocketbook, whatever it is you hold important, for one is not suspicious of the good but only of the bad (though the word is sometimes used loosely, or jocularly, in regard to the good). What was it that I thought Melanie was hiding from me? Simply (!) that she had taken up with her ex-husband again. This would involve the fraudulence of her trip west, but my suspicion had not clouded my reason sufficiently for me to accept this proposition. However, couldn't she have taken up with Dan Craig again without so elaborate a design, without this fraudulent frame? My suspicions now tolerated this possibility, I saw in my mind's eye the story of what had happened. Melanie at her mother's bedside—the room is wide and tidy, the light streams in—Craig somehow (how?) hears of his ex-mother-in-law's illness and appears on the scene, at the bedside, next to Melanie, so that the mother would not have to turn her head, and also to be next to Melanie. Maybe Mrs. Bogen was very fond of her son-in-law; I had even heard of cases where the mother-in-law was named as the corespondent in a divorce action between daughter and son-in-law and of marriages between a man and his ex-mother-in-law. At any rate, Dan is all sweetness, there at the bedside, full of attentions and flowers, creating all manners of ease and comfort, and Melanie is pleased, the mother improves, she is out of danger (so the doctor proudly declares), and she encompasses her daughter and her former son-in-law with one of those sickbed glances which is said to bring people closer together, causing them to depreciate their problems in the face of the mortal enemy, now routed. They are brought closer together, all that had been good in their married life comes to the fore, the bad is buried in the drama of the illness, in the serenity of the sick room, where the danger is fled. The mother continues to improve, there are no reversals, her daughter is happy, and with her ex-husband, maybe she thinks (who knows?) that Craig's presence has aided her mother's recovery. Melanie and Craig walk together in the evening, they tiptoe out of the room, making sure that the mother is asleep, and stroll along the river. There is a sensual charge, they wonder if all is as dead between them as they had imagined, they walk, hand in hand, along the river shore, they are together again, and back on the train together. And I, as I run down the ramp, thinking he was a stranger, a friendly stranger helping with the baggage, a fellow across the aisle naturally attracted by a pretty girl, the way it is done in trains for an attractive, or an old woman. Imagine it! And her coolness when I ran to embrace her! Had she embraced me in return, or had she passively accepted my ardor, my homage? I wasn't sure, hadn't thought of it at the moment, and now it was difficult to decide. How does one draw the line between a return pressure that is polite and one that is loving? And the introduction to Craig—again so cool, so measured, and I gazing at him as though he was a friendly stranger, embarrassed, maybe wary, trying to figure out my relation to this attractive young woman. But wouldn't it have been *more* suspicious if she had acted unsurely, introduced us hesitantly, wouldn't that have been more indicative of a new situation, something awkward and unexpected, a blow to my honor? Yes, yes, knowing Melanie, that unsureness (I reasoned) would have been more indicative than the coolness which, nevertheless, I found most infuriating. So obvious an absence of warmth—not only to me, but to Craig as well. Perhaps my impression of a friendly man carrying her bags (even if that man happened to be her ex-husband) was not so far-off after all—he could have met her on the train by accident! That was not inconceivable, he had been out West, his business affairs were not prospering, he would have to return to the main office, to the city, his car had broken down, and she had never given any indication of anger against Craig, disappointment yes, but not anger, and so (meeting him accidentally on the train) she acted in a friendly manner towards him, and he the same towards her. Was she supposed not to speak to him? Divorced couples are sometimes friendly. True, it is a special kind of friendliness, a kind of relieved friendliness, the war being over, the armistice signed, but yet friendliness, enough to make a chance meeting not unbearable (is that friendliness?). I saw them riding together on the train, making small talk, both a bit uncomfortable, Dan Craig the more eager one, for it was my impression that Melanie had decided on the marriage break, but both now relieved that the agony was over, and holding onto the positive, or whatever was left of the positive, but without the charging of the sensual currents (except maybe on Craig's side); they looked somewhat sadly at the passing landscape, as at a life finished. But I was angry at Craig, and now, moving at a good clip through the streets, I considered the meaning of this anger. Having concluded (for my reason was not clouded over by suspicion) that Melanie had not taken up with Craig and that they had traveled back together in innocence, or call it relief after agony, my anger must therefore have another basis. I knew perfectly well what that basis was, I had always known what it was, but I approached it only in a glancing way so as not really to come to grips with it. It was the fact of their marriage that angered me, the fact that Melanie had come to me, so to say, at second hand. Now this feeling, which I hardly dared to admit to myself, ran absolutely counter to the views I held, or thought I held, on the sexual question, on the fetish of virginity, woman's freedom and emancipation, etc. But deep in my soul was buried the feeling that a woman who had belonged to another man could never belong to me. The word "belong" in this context is open to all sorts of meanings, but as thoughtful as I was trying to be, I did not move in on this area. The formulation of the feeling was a blow to my ego, showing that I did not truly believe what it was I made out to believe, and that's a rough enough definition of a hypocrite. But there was no dodging the feeling, no other way of explaining my anger with Craig—was it really with Craig, wasn't it with Melanie as well, or with the fates which had created this situation? Think of it! I, a liberal, maybe even a libertarian, a professed enemy of dogma, a young man seeking freedom, justice for strangers, feeling angry because the woman I loved had not come to me "pure," that I could never forgive her for having belonged to someone else. And opposed as I was to the Puritan tradition, to its bitter, life-denying aspects, to its joyless dogmatism, its stranglehold on the future! Is it any wonder that I was ashamed of myself? I was now at the point of analyzing my shame, and thought of the poem which Sandy Warren had given me a few nights back—we had met on the street as I was walking home from work one evening, and he had given me a copy of a poem which he said he had just written. He said that I could keep the copy. I thought that was rather odd on his part, for his early animosity toward me had never fully died away, and handing a person a poem is surely a friendly act. But I was even more puzzled when I later read the poem. It was entitled

A POEM TO NOBODY IN PARTICULAR

Thou be a liar, a betrayer of trusts, an executor of indigence,
Thou createst evil issue, deformations of the clandestine real,
Cook the essence of being in the stolen skillet of surcease.
My friend! My admirer! you mongrel transcendentalist
Deafening day by day the brave whispers of time,
Strangling the violet (its death buried in your palms),
Sealing the home Nature made for Jack-in-the-Pulpit,
Did you no harm, must suck the dying air
In the coffin you casually created (Evidence! Scotch tape!),
Forger of promissory notes on the First National Bank of Duty,
Drowned desire in the swamp disguised as a lake,
And now you sleep the sleep of the self-forgiven,
Fatuously bow to the fangs of circumstance.
Thou listless torturer of nameless children, wake!
Wake! your niche is being hollowed in Eternity's closet
Foul fumes assail you, who deflowered our pure air,
Sprayed lies over a hungry field of bluebells,
Keeper of Double Books! Hypnotist of the Innocent!
Wake. But your gas mask no longer fits,
Your soul, distended, bulges from the body you won
From dearest parents, transfigured into an eternal astonishment—
Thou swindler of hard-won visions, thief of poems
Won by bloody joy in love's forts and caverns.

What the devil did he mean by it all—these surrealist
effects were never to my taste anyway—and why had he
handed the thing to me? Again suspicion. But we had met
absolutely by accident—had we not met at this time I surely
would never have seen the poem—and he said that it was a
poem he had recently written, which would explain why he
had it with him. He was the kind of person who handed his
poems around (that I knew), though not indiscriminately, and
therefore why not to me? But why Keeper of Double Books!?
One can take as meaningful what is not personally directed,
but now the tone of the lines followed the sense of my feelings
about myself, the shame in regard to my suspicion and my

anger, in violation of the views I was trying, however shakily, to turn into principles. Shame (besides being "Pride's cloke") is self-criticism based on the violation of norms of behavior you have set up for yourself. I was ashamed. And shame is often pervasive, it moves in on you, on long-forgotten deeds (suddenly recalled), and fills the soul with self-loathing. Then the rational element intervenes, asking: what is this extreme preoccupation with self, why are you denying the great world outside, even if it be, in Whittier's words, *"the clouding grey of circumstance"*? And I was ashamed of my shame, ashamed of my self-loathing, and walking more vigorously, at a terrific speed, through the streets of my native city, I observed with interest the life of the street, and particularly the play of children, that nostalgia made palpable, to escape for a moment the self and its problems and as a preparation for the ordeals and acts of the self. And all the time the sickening sense of an end.

58. *To affect the quality of the day, that is the highest of arts.*
—THOREAU

I looked carefully around me. It was four o'clock on a Friday afternoon, toward the end of summer. The city lived around me; I breathed its grime, smelled its odors compounded of monoxide, industrial fumes, and whatever nature had to contribute, tasted my tongue, touched here and there a wall, a railing, a window protecting merchandise against marauders, and saw the lovely mobility of our people, thinking of my friend who had gone south and felt that he was moving so *fast* down there. The faithful uses of objectivity, the strong sense of the reporter absorbing (*Queen of the Senses, renew me*) the life around. What was it that St. Augustine said about the world? That it was a place where the dying succeed the dead; why not where the living succeed the lifeless? But this was a shallow optimism, what we call, in the political sphere, a *vulgar* optimism. Look there! a strange sight. Two boys are teaching a blind boy how to catch a ball. He has the awkward stance of the blind—his feet are spread, his arms outstretched, anxiously, hopefully awaiting the arrival of the ball. One lad throws the ball, the other stands close to the blind boy. The ball is in the air. "Now!" The blind boy closes his hands, feels the ball, holds the ball close against his body. He smiles the agonized smile of the blind. "Great! Great!" and the youth takes the ball from the blind boy and tosses it to his companion, who prepares again for the throw; again the blind boy adopts his curious, awkward stance, awaits the ball with all that pathetic eagerness. Poor blind child, dear suffering boy, dumbly doomed. If you had to choose between blindness, deafness, and dumbness (for who is without sense of taste or smell?), which would you choose? Then I had rounded a corner, and the scene became a memory, something that had once happened. Here were now five youths—none of them could have been more than twelve—hurling kitchen matches against a wall. A somewhat odd activity, nor is every throw successful. They are keeping count, it is a game, twenty-one fires win, and one lad is throwing with unusual accuracy. He has apparently figured out some kind of spin in the movement, and his match flares up again and again. This game would be more dramatic, I thought, if played at the twilight hour, or maybe in the night-time itself, but this was certainly an irrelevant addition to the basic elements of competition and chance, I thought, and then stopped in front of the Empire State Building, where I could not help overhearing a conversation among another group of twelve-year-olds. They were challenging one another—it's a fact—to race up to the top of the Empire State Building and down again. Some of the boys were eager for the try, some drew back, some were hesitant, in a ratio probably quite typical for a venture of this sort.

"Come on," said one, "what's the big deal of it?" "Nah," said a second, and a third was silent, between the anxiety and the shame. Now the Empire State Building, as is well known, has 102 stories and is 1472 feet high. That, I figured swiftly, is about 491 yards. Now the 440-yard record, on a flat, circular run, was about one minute fifty seconds, and the extra 51 yards could certainly be run in eight seconds or so, let's make the time for the distance two minutes even. How fast could a fairly swift twelve-year-old boy (for there was no reason to think that there were champions here) run this distance? Say four minutes. Now how much longer would it take to run this distance up as against straightaway? That was hard to figure—I estimated ten times as long, which would bring the time to the top to about forty minutes. And the down time maybe fifteen minutes. Could one of these lads run up the Empire State and down in less than an hour? If a world champion runner could run the marathon distance of more than twenty-six miles in about two-and-a-half hours, could a twelve-year-old boy (presumably not a champion) run this vertical distance of a little less than one thousand yards, up and down, in about an hour? It is a theme for idle speculation. "Ga," said one of the kids, "we'd all keel over," and another said that they could rest at the landings. Then the kids, who were discussing this matter in front of the entrance, were shooed off by a civilian, undoubtedly part of the maintenance staff, and that is why I did not see the beginning of the race up the Empire State Building, or even find out if the race came off, for I was beginning to weary of the life in the streets, someone else's life. It was then that I thought of Thoreau's statement, and saw the great difficulty there, for it is so much easier to be carried off by one's own difficulties, or to become absorbed in the lives of strangers. But "to affect the quality of the day"—that requires a dangerous struggle with the reality to change the course of events, to satisfy the hungry self in the ideal cause, holding transformation above acquiescence.

59. *A Difficult Encounter*

Ten o'clock that night, after all the childish wandering, a great way for a twenty-three year old to behave, I decided to call Melanie, seeing the difficulty as one that had to be aired, if not solved, now or never at all. I first thought of writing her, even started a letter, but that seemed cowardly, and so I called her. She was at home, and I asked if it would be all right to come over, not acting casually, but just not wanting to talk on the phone.

"Sure," she replied.

Whereupon I moved into the streets, walking anxiously toward a difficult confrontation. I knocked on her door in a manner between the aggressive covering fear and the timid masquerading sadism. It was a middle-of-the-road knock, and she came to the door, opened it without asking who it was, in the way you do when you expect one. She flung out her arms in a gesture that was unusually theatrical for her.

"Nobody here but you—and me," she said, in a tone that compounded anger and forgiveness. It was, as ever, an accurate representation of her feelings, for her speech was never hypocritical.

"I want to apologize," I said, "for the way I behaved this afternoon."

She smiled, in acceptance of my apology. "I imagine you were pretty surprised," she said, "when you saw Dan."

"I was surprised when I saw him," I answered, "but I was flabbergasted, shocked, when I met him."

"You had neither a reason nor a right to be," she said. "We met by accident on the train."

She said this as a matter of fact—the statement had the content but not the ring of an explanation. For some reason I thought of the slogan: "National in form, International in content."

"I ran into your brother Frank last night," I said (but he was the only brother she had, so why name him? or having named him, why describe his relationship?). "He told me that your mother was much better."

"She is," said Melanie. "Frank told me that he had seen you."

The preliminaries over, I moved stubbornly on. "Look," I said, "I'm not very outgoing in personal matters (I was going to say *frank*, but didn't, because it was her brother's name), I find it difficult to express my feelings, particularly when what I have to say is discreditable to me, shows up— how do you call them?—character deficiencies."

"Don't we all tend to hide our weaknesses?" she smiled. "Isn't it the human thing to do?"

I thought immediately of the popular song: "Was That the Human Thing to Do?" to the effect that *you left without leaving a note behind* (or maybe *without EVEN leaving a note behind*), *was that the human thing to do?*

"But it is exactly the one who hides his weakness," I replied, "who finds it absolutely essential to flaunt his weakness, in a certain sense he glories in his weakness, he is a parasite on it. At any rate, I find personal discussions very difficult, even have a habit of waiting for the passage of time to do away with the need for personal discussions."

"Time buries the problem alive," said Melanie, "in a shallow grave, but if this is so difficult for you, why not just skip it. This is not a moment of crisis."

"That's exactly in line with one of the things I was thinking about!" I exclaimed precisely, "how difficult it is to make things critical, to bring them to a point of decision. *Make things critical!* I say to myself, *every day as though the last day!* Then I see all sorts of possibilities, see what is wrong here or there, draw back, become indecisive, confused, and then the problem is covered (alive, in a shallow grave) only to pop up another day."

"*Every day as though the last day*," repeated Melanie, "one cannot live at that melodramatic pitch; when you're that demanding on yourself, you are only protecting yourself against what has to be done."

"True," I said, "you put it very well. One makes impossible demands in order to avoid the necessary behavior. I have a friend who is in a bad way; I don't mean that he is unhappy, merely unhappy. He doesn't function productively; I mean, he can barely hold down a job, talks interminably of painting—only gigantic murals, canvases depicting the crucial moments of world history. But he does nothing, says that he is priming his psyche—that's the way he talks— preparing himself by study, etc. I once mentioned psychoanalysis to him, and his attitude was not so much that psychoanalysis could help *him*, but that he had something very special to offer psychoanalysis, his difficulties and problems being so special, that they would illuminate this discipline, create a whole new set of problems, but you must know such people yourself. The conclusion is that only Freud can properly understand him, he sees himself as a significant addition to the characters in the case histories—another little Hans, another Dora—and feels that Freud would be very fortunate to be able to learn from him the true nature of the creative process, the circumstances being so profound, and only the profound can illumine the ordinary, and so on. But Freud is not available, so my friend goes on with these perfectionist delusions. The fact is that he's afraid to travel in a subway (a fear of burial alive), that he can't go to bed at night without first performing all sorts of ceremonial acts, he's afraid to sleep for fear of dying in his sleep, he has a wife and child to support, can barely, as I say, hold down a job, but if it is not the very, very best, then it is not for him."

"He's certainly in a bad way," said Melanie.

"Bad," I said, "he's practically around the bend, he keeps going precisely on the basis of this perfectionist dream."

"Back to Utopia," said Melanie, "back to two pieces of bread—people reaching for the sky, who can't find their way around the corner."

I was enough of a Utopian (how can the good be approached without a notion of the good, even an image of the good?) to be annoyed by anti-Utopian remarks, though I had brought the matter up, certainly spoken very critically of a friend involved in a kind of super-Utopianism, Cloud 9 style. I was now twice removed from what it was I had started to say. I had started to explain my feelings about her marriage, then gotten into the question of my own difficulty in talking about my weaknesses, in talking about personal problems (not only mine, but anyone's), and then onto the insensate demands made on reality by a friend. So I moved one step backwards and said:

"I know how angry my political attitudes make you; I understand your anger perfectly well, too, for I am often angry at myself for the same reasons. I find that one party or grouping is too dogmatic or fanatical, that another doesn't have its roots in American life, that still another is too sectarian, etc. It is another kind of perfectionism, asking of an organization what it cannot provide, for any organization must reflect the disharmonies of the society in which it lives. It is a way of refusing to make a choice, and then I justify this refusal by holding up as a goal an independent, critical attitude, gadfly, but am I in fact acting that way, as a critical solvent, the voice of independent reason, etc.?"

"There's no reason for you to live an organizational life," she said. "It's just that effective social change is accomplished through political organization; you don't join for the sake of joining."

"You're right," I said, "today I'll join the AAA as a start."

But she didn't think that was very funny, or if she did, her reaction was hidden.

"No doubt," I said, "this difficulty of choice relates to childhood experiences, forgotten ones at that."

"Look," she said, impatiently, "we've all had childhoods, we've all had to choose, between one parent and another, among all sorts of simple and complex matters, but at a certain time you have to put these things aside. If you're trying to tell me that your political behavior is based on infantile neurosis, well, that's too easy a way out, that's a way of avoiding the problem. Explanation doesn't justify."

That's how we got into a discussion of causation—many economic determinists refuse to accept psychological causation, later a more elaborate Freudo-Marxism came into existence. I was angered by this approach (she was arguing a position which she was in the process of giving up).

"Forget the childhood part," I said, "but it's not so difficult to join an organization, especially if your friends are doing it, it's a way of being in the swim, as well as avoiding the displeasure, even the contempt, of friends, and then there's an aura of righteousness about it, you are on the side of history, of the progressive forces, you are doing your share in destroying a society that is dying and does not deserve to live. By so joining you have recreated the security of a childhood world (back we go again), extended the family, so to speak. Or it plainly gives you someplace to go a few nights in the week or creates a banding of the brothers against the far-off father. You don't think that everyone joins a party for the best of political reasons, or for a political reason at all?"

"I don't question that," she replied, somewhat wearily, for she had been through all that herself, "but there must be a way of dealing with the objective reality on its own terms. People find their way by trial and error, you have to test your beliefs one way or another, you have to be sure that the beliefs are meaningful for you, that they are not a cover for some unexpressed or unacknowledged needs. You don't judge organizations by those who join them for the wrong reasons."

Here spoke the veteran who had seen people join for all sorts of reasons, often without the faintest relation to politics or to the state of society. Now I was back to the place I had earlier started from, the place from which I had wandered off, finding it difficult to discuss these matters with her, but the avoidance was no longer possible, in the sense that I would be making a fool of myself if I failed to return to the high road.

"What I started to say," I said, "was that my anger at the terminal was really based on my anger that you had been married at all. Seeing you together dramatized that fact, it awoke the slumbering feelings, feelings that I have hardly dared to express to myself, because of the principled objections I bear towards them. Yes, I wanted to have had you first, not at secondhand."

"In that case," she said smiling, "I suggest that you find yourself a ten-year-old girl, keep her under constant surveillance (there are agencies of private detection), and marry her the day the law allows you to marry her. But even in such a case, there will remain a certain amount of doubt—you know the joke in Freud's joke book, 'Doubt, doubt, always doubt.'"

"But there is another point," I said, "the fact of your previous marriage was one of the things that drew me toward you, not the most important thing, for when we met down there on the East River Drive I didn't know that you had been married. But once known, it was a factor."

"Naturally," said Melanie. "It is well known in the literature of psychoanalysis that a woman previously married has a certain fascination for a given kind of man, the deeply buried incestuous feelings make themselves felt. Doesn't that sound reasonable? And how lucky you are that I had no children with Dan, for in that case you might have been drawn to me all the more, and recoiled with more horror. So you see that the trauma could have been worse, there is a saving grace in everything."

She spoke with an unfamiliar tone of irony, but did not

seem angry. In fact, she suggested that we go out for a walk, and when we reached the ground floor we ran into Sandy and a friend, whose name was Bellin (Sandy introduced him that way, using my last name, too, but introduced Melanie by her full name). I recognized his name as that of one of the young proletarian poets, having seen his work in *Partisan Review*, or maybe *Dynamo*. He and Sandy were outward-bound for coffee; mutual invitations were tendered and we decided on Rapoports, another of the famed East Side dairy restaurants (uptown it is Steinberg's). I was relieved, in a way, that we had company, for I had pretty much said what I wanted to say, had felt pretty stupid saying it, and welcomed the change of situation, maybe an interlude.

60. *Poetry and Life*

Bellin, surprisingly young, hardly more than twenty-one (I make the point because of his reputation—a modest one— but then we know how early some poets flower), was talking in the vein of Self-Criticism. This was not unusual, was almost called for, was an indication of a given flexibility, a sign that one was not unaware of the changes in the material situation and of the effect these changes must have on doctrine, on ideology. We are standing here before the interaction, the famed dialectic, the process in which the real and the ideal mingle to create new forms and contents, forever subsumed, in a never ending spiral. Some found this Self-Criticism more rewarding than criticism from others, from the outside. Now, Self-Criticism here does not mean criticism of the self, but of one's position, and Bellin was delivering strictures on the current condition of proletarian poetry.

"For one thing," he said, "we see signs of an undue simplicity, part of the tendency toward the direct, agitational style, as though the poem must be understood by the most-exploited, most-ignorant worker. But the fact is that the working class is permeated by middle-class values, so this attempt at an extreme simplicity, the spare, agitational style, runs counter to the workers' cultural attitudes and expectancies. Of course, these bourgeois values are in the process of being destroyed by the economic crisis (and the moral crisis in its wake), the class distinctions are being sharpened. But we cannot underestimate the strength of the bourgeois ideology, the bourgeois cultural apparatus, and the difficulties thereby created in reaching the masses with our revolutionary, Marxist message. There is a tendency in this connection towards a certain idealization of the worker; he is somehow removed from the nexus of everyday life, torn, so to say, from his actual social relationships, even from his personal relationships, and becomes a creature unknown on land or sea, nothing more than an ideological target. In that respect, Empson is correct in comparing our treatment of the modern proletarian to the idealization of the shepherd in the pastoral poetry of earlier times. In the depiction of these shepherds, we see how far removed they are from the exploited peasants of the period. It is very difficult for us to make the necessary contact with the industrial workers. Let me give you an example, in some quoted lines of Funaroff:

> Look!
> There is Karl Marx.
> There is your Spring.
> There is such a woman.

These lines have a certain strength but at the same time an awkwardness; we are approaching a form, but have not yet found it. I should say 'created' it, not 'found' it, and that opens up the problem of tradition, what is called the 'usable' past. I think there is a tradition in American (and world) poetry from which we can learn much—Whitman, without his curious passivity, acceptance, without that extraordinary *kind* of wonder in which he embalmed himself; Sandburg, with his real immersion in popular life, though he lacks the dialectical touch, is perhaps too descriptive. And a writer like Villon is more important to us, than, say, Pound and Eliot, whose personal tones and social attitudes are quite antithetical to what it is we are trying to do. I am not denying their skills, even their ability to achieve what it is they want to achieve, but we are seeking other ends, and we must find other means. Our task is to reach the masses with our revolutionary message. For us, Marxism is an arsenal, art one of its weapons, and we do our part in destroying the society that is destroying us and help into being the classless society, the next necessary stage in human history."

"I myself," said Sandy, "always approved of Keats's comment about 'schools' of poetry: he felt that fish, and not poets, should swim in schools."

"I'm not so sure about that," I said. "In my field there are 'schools'—universal historians, metaphysical historians, etc.—those with the same interests tend to come together. Don't we talk of the Elizabethan dramatists and see a certain resemblance there, or the Romantics?"

"The Elizabethans," said Sandy, "wrote as individuals. It is we of later times who have put them together, as though they constituted a school, a kind of collectivity. And so with the Romantics. In every period there is a certain spirit abroad, and given people, in the arts, etc., reach for it as well as help make it. Then history decides that such or such a style represents that period. But these people did not necessarily know one another or work together in any way, and there are always diverse, even contrary, tendencies."

"You know," said Melanie, addressing the proletarian poet, "you are trying to do something which is quite unusual. Intellectuals have often gone to the people with messages they considered of the greatest importance—consider the Christian apostles, or, to come closer, the Populists of the nineteenth century in Russia. These Populists, mostly from the big cities, fanned out into the provinces, bringing their message of enlightenment and freedom. No doubt many of the townspeople and peasants were astounded, baffled, by this word from the far-off cities delivered by strangers. But this intelligentsia spoke, or tried to speak, the language of the people, tried to explain clearly what it was they thought and felt, what they thought the people ought to understand and act on. They were speaking, that is to say, in an expository prose, though often in a heightened emotional tone and with a kind of fervor that contributed to the bafflement. But you proletarian poets are going to the masses with a philosophy that is alien to most of your readers and are expressing it in a poetic form, an ancient art with all sorts of structural complexities. You burden yourselves with a range of difficulties . . . ."

"But that's it," interrupted Bellin, "it is precisely as poets that we want to express ourselves, we do not want to divorce our poetry from our politics, our morality. Should we write about matters that do not interest us because of the inherent difficulties in expressing what it is we want to say? It is precisely our art and our political morality that we want to bring together."

"I've seen poets," said Sandy, "who go into organizational and journalistic work, find it so much easier to make contact that way, and either give up their poetry, or write it in a more traditional way. Usually they give up the poetry."

"There are all kinds of people," said Bellin. "You are talking about personal needs; I would be unhappy to give up poetry for organizational work."

"It's possible," said Sandy, "that the kind of poetry you would have to write would require a simplicity, an abandonment of historical forms and complexities, of the kind of sophisticated rhythms and tones which poetry demands. I have heard it argued that the ballad, the catch, is perhaps an answer to your problem. There is a tendency toward the impoverishment of poetry for the sake of the socialism. You will perhaps find yourself cutting down on the range of your poetic power and sensibility in order to achieve a certain clarity, to make a given point. You will be suffering as a poet. The masses should be reached in the simplest, most effective way, by slogans and explanations, by graphic descriptions, by everyday moralities, etc."

"I think that's so," said Melanie. "I am interested in writing reportage, in describing how people are living, how they are suffering and struggling under exceptional circumstances. This is a type of journalism. People read newspapers— the news article, the news story, is an absolutely familiar form. The ordinary reader does not have to puzzle over this form. Our problem is to give that form a more meaningful content."

I listened with interest to Melanie. I looked at her with interest. How tiresome and stupid my earlier feelings now seemed! How self-indulgent and unimportant! And so much of excitement in the outside world, so much injustice, so much to be done, to use one's self, one's best self, in these meaningful struggles, in this continual examination and re-examination of reality.

"As far back as 1901," said Sandy, "Yeats asked the question: *What Is 'Popular' Poetry?* He was trying to reach the people with his verse, thinking of what it was that the people would read, or recite, or sing to words, with pleasure, for the sake of the poem's beauty and meaning, the poem being the experience, and not seen as an incitement to political action. The popular poets, like Burns, wrote of experiences that the readers shared. They were not making demands outside the poem."

"As far as that goes," said Bellin, "there is an old tradition of didactic poetry. It tends to be scorned, but who is to say what poems should be held to, what feelings they should arouse. New kinds of poets are always arising."

"There is Mayakovsky," said Sandy, "but was he really

a popular poet, is he a popular poet? He is a rather difficult writer, his images are often strange, his rhythms most unusual, pitched so high, outside the ordinary range of intensity."

"We write in another language," said Bellin, "we have different problems."

61. *More*

The conversation paused, then spurted ahead again, grew even more hectic, as we moved into the early hours of the morning. These are the hours, the company congenial, when the mind sharpens, the imagination grows more vivid, conversation comes into its own. But I was more involved with Melanie, looked at her across the table—she and Sandy were on one side of the table, Bellin and I on the other. I thought of my early "police description," saw that the better you know and understand one, the more difficult to describe, or the more meaningless the description. I admired her for the way she had toned down my confessional—it was part of her way of making one's problems not quite as sensational as one thinks, of putting those problems in proper perspective, not only showing that everyone has such problems, but that they are part of growth, of change, of living, and must not be allowed to get out of hand. What was going to happen now, how would it work out between us? I saw the situation as an open one, inconclusive, with no sure sense as to how it would work out. But I was sure that however it came out, whether it was an end (I had been sure of that for a while, but now I wasn't so sure), or a new beginning, or, for that matter, a continuation, it was somehow all for the good. She gave one a sense that there was so much to be done—so much to be done for one's own sake, for the greater good, because the injustice, the disharmony was present, and had to be dealt with, and if one didn't deal with it, that was an indication of weakness, of moral deficiency. She had a way of making life more meaningful, she was a creator of values, the kind of person you would never forget, no matter what the outcome. Isn't it a fact that some people make a permanent impression, one has them forever, but others fade, because they are not involved with the reality, or fear it, shy away? The conversation moved from the field of literature into the realm of politics, social morality, preconditions for choice, the meaning of freedom, the means of achieving justice—all the problems that agitated us, our problems. Life opened up as an arena for accomplishment. There was so much to do, and we had so much strength to do it. Melanie was radiant. How could one not be carried along with her? I thought that when we would leave later on, when Sandy had excused himself, with his decent tact, hiding the hurt, going off with Bellin (so I imagined it), we would walk down to the East River Drive, down to the bench where we had met—over the river, and the slow-moving gravel boat, the policeman who hesitated, then moved on (I heard his footsteps, that dying clatter); all the particulars of that first evening came back to me. But now I decided against that move, saw it as a phony move, a gesture in the Hollywood manner, a kind of regression, a false new beginning. But one of the things I had learned from her was to avoid the extremes of the heroic posture and of self-pity, to move along the main road, between the disappointment which comes from asking too much (what is too much?) and the glory which cannot be won swiftly but is the end of a process. And I felt confident that we'd continue on that main road, felt, for a moment, the extraordinary confidence of those youthful Sherwood Anderson characters whose mawkish disappointment (*Gee Whiz, I'm a Fool.*) is followed by a sense of the wonders of what may yet come, the mysterious openness of life, and I joined again in the discussion of all those difficult and troubling matters.

You're *It*

It was a little after five, the sun was beginning to lose its power for the day, and the three couples were sitting on the screened porch, in the early summer time, mostly with drinks in hand. They were all on vacation, had begun to soak up sun and surf, and, now, in the established ritualistic manner, were spending the time between exposure and dinner in this social communion.

"You're *It!*" cried Teddy Horton, the eight-year-old child of the host and hostess, and he tagged Danny Levy, son of one of the visiting couples.

From their vantage point, the six adults became, in an instant, the audience of a most ancient game. The five children —three from neighboring houses (for the Thurlows, the final couple, were childless)—who had been playing in a haphazard manner, with occasional struggles of a short-lived though sometimes dramatic character, were suddenly transfigured, being chosen for parts in a drama of unusual intensity.

The four fled from Danny as though he were the carrier of a plague, one whose touch meant danger, desecration, humiliation; they fled from Danny to avoid the touch that transmitted the nameless horror.

Teddy, Barry, and Jackie scattered in various directions, but Gus, who was the youngest, made for the scrub oak. This tree was a sanctuary; holding it, one could be tagged with impunity, for then nothing baleful could pass between the *It* and the tree-toucher.

Seeing Gus safe at the sanctuary, and scorning, moreover, the thought of going after the youngest (although he would have carelessly brushed him if he were in the open), Danny lit out after the others. As soon as Danny disappeared, Gus, who had been holding onto the tree quite firmly, now became rather bold. He walked away from the tree, sat down on the grass, followed with fascination the flight of a bird— but all the while he was on the lookout for Danny's reappearance. Tempting the fates this way, he nevertheless strolled back to the tree occasionally, made contact with it, sat down at a point midway between temptation and absolute safety.

When Gus moved away from the sanctuary, he was taking the chance that Danny might suddenly reappear from an unexpected quarter (conceivably behind him), touch him, and transmit the awful thing. But the temptation made the game: by running for the tree and holding on for dear life, the four could put an end to the game—for what self-respecting *It*, under the circumstances, would not have walked off in disgust?

Suddenly Barry appeared from around the corner of the house, Danny Levy in close pursuit. Roused, Gus ran to the tree and reached it a step before Barry, who, breathing heavily, encircled the oak and gazed triumphantly at his unsuccessful pursuer.

"Safe," he cried at Danny, who paused, keeping a lookout for Jackie and Teddy while resting within the shadow of the sanctuary. Then he went back in pursuit.

"That's not quite how we used to play the game," said Mr. Levy, who was a trifle upset that his son had been so ignominiously made *It*, and continued to be *It*. "We had no tree; if you were *It*, you just ran till you tagged someone, and then that person was *It*."

He wished that his son would tag someone, for he felt *It* himself, some of the untouchableness had passed into him. Quite by accident, he brushed Mr. Horton's sleeve as he reached for his drink. Mrs. Levy thought it unfair that the young host should have tagged *her* child when there were three strange children playing, but she said nothing.

"There are different ways of playing the game," said Mr. Horton. "We used to play just this way, except that we'd use a lamp post for *safe*."

He tried to think of other variants of the game, for he saw himself at the moment as the analyst and historian of the game of Tag, but nothing more came to mind.

"It's a fascinating game," said Mrs. Thurlow, "so simple and kind of . . . awful."

Just then Teddy Horton broke into view, in a mad rush for the now deserted base (for Gus had gone into the field), but Danny was close behind, made the tag, cried "*It*," turned round, and was off. The chase must have been a long one, for Teddy was winded; he sat down next to the tree which he had vainly tried to reach.

"You see," said Mr. Thurlow, "how the sanctuary receives the unclean as well as the clean."

"I beg your pardon," said Mrs. Horton.

"I mean," went on Mr. Thurlow, "that the notion of a sanctuary interests me. I remember reading in St. Augustine that, in the sack of Rome, the barbarians recognized the churches as sanctuaries, made no move against the Christians or the pagans who took refuge there. It is one of the more noble features of human society that there should be a place so recognized, even 'mid the horrors of war, when all restraints are thrown aside, in which man, relieved of conscience, destroys in a fury of anonymity, all sanctions gone. Why, even in the last war there was a *tendency* to avoid the destruction of certain buildings, call them, if you will, hallmarks of civilization."

The three couples on the porch were not well known to each other; Mrs. Horton, who was a friendly type and believed in bringing the world closer together, had met the Levys at the house of a mutual friend and the Thurlows at a museum opening in town. She never hesitated to invite to her house people whose acquaintance she had recently made, a habit whose social consequences were unpredictable. Until now the conversation had been scattered, for the group did not share enough close friends for serious gossip, and had somehow not been able to hit on any subject that brought them together.

Mr. Thurlow's remarks, however, did have the effect of starting up a fairly spirited discussion, touching on the importance of a room of one's own as a sanctuary from domestic confusion, on bird sanctuaries, on the modern pressures—as shown in Hitler's extermination of the Jews and other examples of genocide—to destroy the concept of sanctuary, a pressure finalized by the appearance of nuclear weapons, whose total destructive power made a mockery of the ancient notion of sanctuary. Then the conversation moved on to nuclear testing and the possibility of its abolition, sane nuclear policy, the French nuclear blast in the Sahara and the awesome possibility of *small* countries becoming members of the Nuclear Club, the problems of detection in underground testing, the hazards of fall-out, with particular emphasis on Strontium 90, the feasibility, architecture, and cost of shelters, concluding—after a slowly diminishing masochistic thrill at the prospect of being involved in so inconceivable an orgy of mutual destruction—on a note of futility.

Nullified by contradictory elements and their sense of "What can I do about it?" the conversation died, and they all looked with interest as little Gus suddenly appeared from nowhere (out of the brush) and sank down beside the tree, happy that he had been out there on the battlefield, and happy, too, that he had been able to return in safety. And all were happy for the child—for his courage in testing himself against the older ones, some of them strangers, and his good fortune in avoiding the awful touch.

"Safe at home," sighed Mrs. Thurlow, and then Teddy appeared, trying to pass the thing on to Barry, who dodged and turned, made a dash for the tree, but was overtaken just before he reached it.

"He's *It!*" cried Mrs. Horton, triumphantly.

"It's rather curious," said Mrs. Levy, "that the neuter 'it' is used, as though the person tagged has become a thing. Why not: you're *He* or you're *She?*"

But the question answered itself; they all laughed at the prospect raised.

"It's one of those disguises," said Mr. Horton. "The neutrality of the name (I just can't get myself to use the word 'neuterness') was an attempt to cover the horror of the content, but then the word itself took on the unknown horror, and so was despoiled of its neutrality."

"I can remember when *It* meant sex appeal," said Mrs. Thurlow, but the other women said nothing, either because they did not remember when *It* meant sex appeal or did not want to acknowledge that they remembered when *It* meant sex appeal.

"I am reminded," said Mr. Horton, "of, shall we say, the social difficulties of the lepers in the Middle Ages, who moved from town to town and were denied admittance, out of the darkest fear of contagion."

"And the medical fact is," said Mr. Levy, "that the disease is not at all as contagious as was thought. Modern miracle drugs are said to be very effective."

"We know," said Mr. Thurlow, "that such fears tend to be irrational. I need only point to the prevalence of syphilophobia only twenty or thirty years ago. You remember the phrase: 'The Syphilis of the Innocent'? But when it became known that salvarsan was able to cure this disease, the fear of syphilis declined; it is hardly of any significance today."

Whether the fear of syphilis was irrational *before* the introduction of salvarsan was not discussed.

"Well, then," said Mr. Horton (the women were discussing, for the moment, another matter), "this game carries on in the tradition of the ancient uncleanness—the tagged person is become a leper, his touch brings contagion, what is there to do but flee?"

"But did the leper pursue the nonleper?" asked Mr. Levy.

"The healthy ones," said Mr. Thurlow, "always feel that they are being threatened by the diseased ones, and in this game of Tag or *It*, we have a dramatic confirmation of that feeling."

"The fear of the diseased one, by the way," said Mr. Horton, "relates to all sick people, not only to those with contagious or infectious diseases."

"I think that you're going too far there," said Mr. Levy. "I think the fear is confined mostly to infectious and contagious diseases."

"I agree with that," said Mr. Thurlow. "You'd be surprised how many people there are who, after shaking hands (even with a close friend), will not eat till they wash their hands. That also refers to doorknobs, old books, and other objects."

"That's getting into the area of mental disease," said Mr. Levy, who gave the impression that he did not prefer to get into the area of mental disease.

"Well," said Mr. Thurlow, "you are dealing here (and he waved towards the game, where Barry had just come up noiselessly behind Jackie and put the hex on him) with the realm of the unconscious and irrational; the kids don't know *why* they're afraid of being *It*. This is a game that they pick up from the older generation, and the fear seems to come along with the game."

"It would be fun," said Mrs. Thurlow (for the women had rejoined the conversation), "if we could play this game sometimes."

The thought of the six of them rushing off in all directions to avoid one another's contact made them laugh, and Mr. Horton said, with a bit more sageness than was absolutely required, "In a certain sense we are playing that game all the time."

"Haven't you ever been touched," asked Mrs. Horton, "in a way that makes you feel absolutely filthy for days—you can't wash it away?"

She hurried off to get some more ginger ale, the conversation subsided, and the adults looked out more closely at the game.

Jackie, who was *It*, was not pleased with the distinction (but some were, loved and sought to be *It*, enjoyed the significance, if not the desecration—and that was another way of destroying the game). He was very anxious to be rid of *It* and moved as swiftly as he could to transmit the unpleasantness. As is often the case, he was betrayed by his anxiety; the others dodged and escaped him in a way they never would have been able to had Jackie been playing in the style of the games where he was not betrayed by his anxiety. Jackie slipped, he ran past his prey, he lunged and broke his stride, when in another few steps he would have caught up.

"He certainly is worried and anxious," said Mrs. Levy, in the absence of (not instead of) Jackie's mother.

"He seems actually frightened," said Mr. Horton. "Something seems to have gotten *into* him."

"True," said Mr. Levy. "He's behaving as though something awful will happen to him if he doesn't rid himself of this . . . this incubus."

"The Devil," said Mr. Thurlow. "Casting out of the Devil."

(Mrs. Thurlow giggled, for the three men had given the effect of a kind of academic vaudeville team, each delivering his set piece. She thought it would have been more appropriate if they had risen, advanced a few steps, and then said their pieces.)

Mr. Thurlow's mention of the Devil opened up a new conversational vein, the game was viewed as a self-exorcizing chain, requiring no Black Mass, no Witch's Sabbath or incantation (unless the "You're *It!*" was the incantation). All that really was needed to rid oneself of the Evil One was simple contact—touching one who was involved, but touching a stranger was useless. This led to a discussion of the history of Satanism, a glancing reference to *Paradise Lost*, a comment on the remnants in popular speech of devil worship ("You Devil, you," said half in admiration, or "You lucky devil!"), mention of the Evil Eye (which Mrs. Horton said had been cast on her by a stranger in a passing car the day before), a rave remembrance of Dreyer's remarkable film *Day of Wrath*, and so into witch-burning, Salem, Miller's play, the rise and fall of McCarthyism, conformity (especially of the young), the unusual tensions that might account for that conformity, the desire for hedonistic and material satisfactions in view of possible universal holocaust, and so back to the hydrogen bomb and a sane nuclear policy.

"Oh," gasped Mrs. Thurlow, "the little boy is *It!*"

Swiftly side-stepping the anxious Jackie, Gus had headed for the oak, tripped over a branch, and been fallen on by Jackie, who had either tripped over the same branch, or had just plainly fallen on the small boy to make the tag as complete and indisputable as possible.

"He couldn't be more *It*," said Mr. Thurlow, as the child rose from the ground, angry at his bad luck, missing very much the security of the oak, for, tired of the constant dodging and shifting made necessary by his short legs and his inability to cover ground as quickly as the others, he had planned a long stay. But he pluckily set out to divest himself of the unwanted thing.

"I hope he's not *It* long," said Mrs. Thurlow, who had adopted the child as her own. Indeed, they all felt a certain sympathy for this six-year-old among the eights and nines.

"What puzzles me," said Mrs. Levy, after a pause long enough to create the need for a new beginning, "is how the game started, suddenly, without warning."

She had not yet recovered from the shock of that unexpected tag that had started the game and catapulted her son into the unwanted commanding position.

"Why," said Mr. Horton, thoughtlessly, "I guess the kid who made the first tag had that *It* feeling and wanted to pass it on."

"Nonsense," said Mrs. Horton, who had not forgotten that it was their son Teddy who had started the game. "Kids get tired of one game and they decide to start another, the way we get tired of one conversational area and move on to another."

"That's true," said Mr. Levy, trying to bury deeper Mr. Horton's unfortunate remark. "I don't think we ought to make a mystery of everything. Take this game, for example, about which we've talked so much. Haven't you ever felt like wanting to get rid of something, and in a hurry? An old suit that you're sick and tired of looking at, although it has plenty of wear left; a piece of furniture that has suddenly become a burden, you can't look at it any more; some old thought or scheme that you want to get rid of, forget once and for all? Maybe this game dramatizes that desire to get rid of unwanted things, a kind of efficiency kick."

"You throw out a piece of furniture," said Mrs. Horton, "or you give it to a charity and do not know its final disposition, but here the excitement is in passing the thing on to a specific individual."

"One child passes on his own particular fear," said Mrs. Thurlow, "and the child who is tagged replaces that fear with his own."

She was wondering what fear little Gus was struggling with, and was saddened as she watched the boy outdistanced by his four tormentors, who came up close to him, and, as he made his move, scattered and opened up a space with their unfair long-leggedness.

"Of course," said Mr. Thurlow, "he doesn't *have* to play with kids two and three years older."

"How brave he is!" cried his wife. "He seeks the difficult task."

The absolute contradiction between these two points of view created a silence, and the adults watched the flashing figures, listened to the medley of cries—playful, fierce, and honeyed.

"Of course you've got to give him credit," said Mr. Thurlow, realizing that his wife's position was the nobler one, "but there's such a thing as taking on too much, more than a body can bear."

There was general agreement on this, too.

Someone asked where Gus lived, and Mrs. Horton replied that she wasn't quite sure, but thought that he came from a house down the street. At least, that was the direction from which she had seen him coming one afternoon. She didn't know his second name, and thought that he might live out here all year. All this uncertainty added to the pathos generated by his diminutive size, his current *It*ness, and his difficulty in passing along the stigma; all this created, most certainly for Mrs. Thurlow, the image of an orphan, a waif, but there was no real reason to think that he didn't come from an absolutely secure home—a point someone would undoubtedly have made if Mrs. Thurlow had voiced her gloomy sentiments.

But Mrs. Thurlow's gloom was suddenly dissipated when little Gus, hidden behind a bush, lured his colleagues into the open (they came stealthily, but into the open) and sprang on Danny, who was closest, and so transferred at last the accursed thing. Then he sprinted to the sanctuary, and hugged that tree as though it were a spar in a tumultuous ocean. (He had learned the great danger of being retagged, so in making the touch he was moving away at the same time.)

This dramatic change in the circumstances of the game led to a new conversational spurt, this time on the question of the underdog. There was talk about those who made it against the most severe hazards, of long shots in horse races, odds against poorly rated contenders, of David and Goliath, the haves and the have-nots, of big and little nations—and this led, imperceptibly, to the possibility that these little nations might get possession of hydrogen bombs, or at least obsolete atom bombs, and that led right to the shelters and a sane nuclear policy.

Mrs. Levy was not as disturbed this second time as she had been the first time that Danny was *Jt*, but she was disturbed, partly because he *was Jt* and partly because he was *Jt* for the second time, being therefore the first one *Jt* for the second time. But, like all the others, she was somewhat impressed, even a bit mellowed, by the fact that the game had now come full circle, underlining the elegant statement of Copernicus:

for the circle alone can bring back the past

They sat waiting for the game to end, for that would give a formal character to the departure envisaged by the two visiting couples, one end leading to another, although it would be more proper for the Levys to make the ceremonial move than for the Thurlows, whose sentimental adoption of Gus did not quite qualify them as parents.

While waiting for the game to end, Mr. Thurlow could not forbear a final probe into the nature of the game they had been watching.

"When kids that age (I mean Oedipus-wise) harbor a guilt, a shameful thing that they want to share—for passing the guilt from one to the other is a kind of sharing—can we exclude the Freudian interpretation?" Nobody took a strong stand excluding the Freudian interpretation, and he went on: "Parricide and Incest, that is the stuff of their guilty imaginings, and the band of brothers transferring and sharing this guilt."

"That was concise," said Mr. Levy, admiringly.

Out on the field the game was over, the kids were milling around, making comparatively meaningless contact, and Mrs. Levy said, in the prescribed ceremonial manner, "I think the kids are sort of tired. We ought to get started."

Which they did, and, in the cool dusk, they heard Mrs. Thurlow say softly, *"The world's slow contagion."*

A Note on Chivalry

1. *Introduction, with Jokes*

Jokes. Ha! Ha! I am among those willing to become a captive audience (or whatever the singular of the word "audience" is), if only the joke is funny (not unfunny) and is told well, either in the elegant *or* the embroidered style. A joke is a bit of folk art. Why scorn it? And the joke cycles—fascinating, are they not? Traffic jokes, psychoanalysis jokes. . . . Have you heard the mother-in-law joke?

> A mother-in-law gives her daughter's husband (son-in-law) two ties for Father's Day. Daughter, son-in-law, and children come to visit Grandma on this occasion, all properly dressed. Dad is wearing one of mother-in-law's ties. She opens the door and says to him straight off: *"What's the matter, you didn't like the other tie?"*

Curiously enough (why curiously enough?) I have recently heard a number of other jokes in what I call the mother-mother-in-law-grandma complex. It is a recurrent trend. I have a sociological friend, he is in fact a sociologist, and I plan to ask him to explain this trend to me, in its urban-rural sociometrics and all the rest of it. If I remember to, I will tell him the following joke:

> A woman is running along the ocean beach, and she cries: *"Help, help, my son the doctor is drowning."*

trusting that he (the sociologist) will be cognizant of the Jewish middle-class prestige propulsions involved here and not be unaware of the tragic status-destiny dichotomy which provides the atmosphere for this fine current joke.

Then there was that party a while back at a friend's house, and an elegant girl came in. I don't mean that she was elegantly dressed, but there was something fine and real about her, one of those absolute strangers you feel you have known forever and will continue to know forever. What a lovely, warm, and reasuring smile! And she brought into the room romance, I mean, the coming into existence of so many possibilities, beauty to be sought and never reached, all those forgotten streaks of glory. It was something that the room needed very much.

You know how even the prettiest girl gets lost in a room full of noise and drinking, and then suddenly you are standing together, in all that noise, all that (suddenly) lovely confusion, and she tells you, what? A joke:

> A grandma is wheeling her grandson; an acquaintance looks into the carriage and says:
> "My, what a pretty baby."
> Says Grandma: *"You should see his picture."*

We discussed the formal problems raised by the last line of this elegant joke. There are possible variants: *"You should see the picture,"* or *"But you should see his picture,"* and we discussed these variants, seriously weighed them. Her smile was warm, reassuring, I felt very much at home, not so much in the house of this friend, this stranger, but at home in the world, once more at home in the world, this cold and bitter world, this monster of a world. I was home in a world suddenly made warm and reassuring, a glorious world, full of infinite promise, round and golden, a world in which it was no longer possible to fall off.

2. *The Middle Ground*

Let us by no means forget the great middle ground of experience—the American Midwest, the Victorian novelists, Wednesday at three o'clock in the afternoon, the land lying between woman's breasts, all the forgotten working hours—and through the confusion of friends and strangers talking, for we were among friends and strangers, it seemed that she had a position with, worked for, earned her livelihood—was it with the B & O?—sounded pretty much like the B & O, an established transit corporation, no doubt one of the few corporate organizations that had in its title the name of a city *and* a state. It struck me as pretty odd that she should be *with* (that's a nice way of saying that you work for somebody), that she should be with an organization half-city and half-state, a kind of industrial mermaid. She was with them in a capacity, and you can spend an awful (in the sense of long) amount of time with a company if you are with them in a capacity, but it really wasn't so long, it just seemed long because it's an everyday thing, you've got to be there or give an excuse, like a marriage that way. It's a way of paying for your leisure. But she spoke pleasantly of the task (not an ordeal at all), she was not among those who suffered in order to enjoy later, she gave the impression of enjoying the working day (but who knows?), caught it all up in that warm reassuring smile, the one mentioned in Section 1.

3. *A Connection*

At a certain point, between old friends and between friends newly met there comes a pause. We are all acquainted with that pause: nothing is said—some are embarrassed, some are relaxed, some absolutely relish this pause (enjoy the embarrassment and upset by the relaxation). If the friends are old, and the pauses numerous and lengthy, well, then, the situation requires grave analysis. With old friends newly made, it is always possible to ask, as I now asked: "Do you happen to know Mr. Indleberg, who is connected with your firm?"

"Certainly I know Mr. Indleberg, we are in different departments."

"So you *know* Mr. Indleberg. He happens to be my brother-in-law's cousin."

"Would that be your wife's brother or your sister's husband?"

"My sister's husband, of course."

"Do you know him very well?"

"I've met him exactly twice, on family occasions."

"I don't really *know* him, not only are we in different departments, but the departments have no connection with each other."

"I'd say that he's about 5'8"."

"That's right, he's rather stout, somewhat stooped."

"Obviously the same fellow."

This is a way of making a connection to destroy a pause. Ah, Indleberg, wherever you were at the time (and it would have been nice if you were at a party, enjoying yourself), you surely never understood that you were being used, as a pawn, as a pause-destroyer, between old friends newly met, to establish, for a brief moment (as compared to a lengthy moment) a connection.

4. Surrounded by Sociologists

I yield to no man in my admiration for Thorstein Veblen, that genuine (as opposed to phony) eccentric, that hard-bitten Northwoods stylist, and I can read with pleasure many a page of Sumner, but I must say that my blood boils, my gorge rises (not necessarily in that order), when I see a pretty girl surrounded by sociologists. Seeing it now, it struck me as a kind of allegory of the English language (why is a pretty girl like the English language?) in its purity, menaced by the killers of that language. By "purity" I mean the ability of the language to reach what is true and beautiful in experience, and to clothe that truth and beauty in appropriate images and ideas. By "killers" I mean those who smother the new-born truth and beauty (for truth and beauty are always new-born) by an apparatus, an effluvium, gobbledegook, words that have lost all relation to the object, to language itself. How to save her from the sociologists? I assumed that she wanted to be saved from the sociologists (though she was chatting with them in a friendly enough way) because who would not want to be saved from the sociologists? Looking around the room (for support or for weapons) I noticed a set of the English Classic Poets. I picked one of the volumes from the bookshelf—the book was solidly constructed, weighed perhaps two pounds, and had sharp edges. I determined to hurl at the heads of the sociologists these Classic volumes. What would be more fitting weapons, in this new *Battle of the Books*, with which to save this maiden, or in distress? I gripped the volume, got the feel of it, so to speak, and then noticed that she had fled from the foul circle, and was wandering alone, in an aimless freedom. I regretfully put the volume back in its place.

5. *Responsibility*

It suddenly occurred to me that I was an engaged man! My fiancée was wearing an engagement ring, *my* engagement ring, there had been an announcement in the metropolitan papers, if not her picture, and only the date had to be set. My fiancée was visiting her grandparents in Kansas City. She is very devoted to her family and has an extensive family, mostly in the Midwest and the Far West. I realized (also suddenly) the *outlandish* and *irresponsible* nature of my behavior. True, my connection with the girl I had just met at the party (I didn't know her name, the introductions were slurred) had not even reached the flirtatious stage. We merely spoke to one another with a more considerable interest than you might statistically expect (equating interest with percentage of meetings over a given length of time), we merely looked at one another (the romantic mixing of the glances) in a manner that bespoke the possibility, circumstances allowing, that we might get into an involvement more personal than the next, though not necessarily very personal. Why, it was very possible that on this very evening, at this very party, a number of people, meeting for the first time, were interested in one another in just the same way. And it was possible that my fiancée, off in Kansas City, if she were at a party, could easily become just so interested in a stranger whose name she had not quite heard. Nevertheless, it being a fundamental law of life that one thing leads to another, I thought that I ought to act more *responsibly*, for it is, if not a law of life, then a fact of it, that we can be *carried away*, and that would take me far from my fiancée, far from my engagement and prospective marriage (though no date had been set) down some turbulent river, into some unknown sea. In order to avoid this fascinating possibility (and responsible behavior, if it does not *have* to destroy fascination, can very easily chill or contract it) I determined to avoid this young woman, whose warm reassuring smile had carried me so quickly down turbulent rapids to unknown seas. I've only known her twenty minutes, I thought, and here I am engaged to my childhood sweetheart (I meant by that thought that I knew my childhood sweetheart ever so much longer). I was pleased with this truly responsible thought.

6. *Indleberg . . . the Old Razzle-Dazzle . . .*
Contact-Continuation

"He's married to a girl his own size."

"Indleberg's child once came to the office. He's a boy."

"When I last saw him," I said, "we discussed Red China, the four-minute mile, and the soul's immortality."

"He used to be in my office," she said, "that is, before I was there. Then he was moved into another office, then into another section, then into another division, and now I hear his name mentioned occasionally."

"He told me," I said, "that Red China would spill over into Soviet Russia *before* the twenty-first century, that the four-minute mile was in its infancy, and that he was working up evidence for the soul's immortality."

"He told me," she said, "that he loved his work, but wanted to retire."

"He drinks bourbon on the rocks."

"He used to write with a ball-point pen."

"Did you know that he was married previously?"

"That's incredible," she said, "I mean, he doesn't give that impression."

"His previous wife," I said, "is now married to a man in the diplomatic corps."

"He eats tuna fish for lunch," she said, "with a strawberry float."

"He's sort of nice," I said, "he lets you say so many things about him."

"I didn't know we knew him so well," she said.

"We know him very well," I said, "and why shouldn't we? He's our oldest friend."

"Who?"

7. *Kinds of Doing*

To do for the sake of your living parents is filial gratitude.

To do for the sake of dead parents is ancestor worship; otherwise (if they be not parents), it is to honor the mighty dead.

To do for the sake of the work is dedication.

To do for the sake of dear ones is gratitude, for the sake of friends is love, for the sake of strangers is sacrifice.

To do for the sake of the future is alienation, and distrust of one's powers.

To do for the doing's sake is animal joy.

To do for truth's sake is nobility.

To do for God's sake is presumption.

To do for fame's sake is neurosis.

To do for money's sake is tragic.

To do out of fear is degenerative.

To do out of duty is necessary.

To do for beauty's sake is romance.

8. *Romance*

I lifted a volume of the Classic Poets. If I hurled it at the head of an offending sociologist, and thereby saved a maiden not exactly in distress, would that get me into the arena of Romance? This style of Romance is quite out of fashion, particularly in the metropolitan society which I frequent. Of course, there are girls in trouble, there will always be girls in trouble, but the help they need does not seem to require courage. It might require understanding, it might require the scientific knowledge of a psychoanalyst (plus understanding), or it might require just simple friendship (as compared to complex friendship). The growth of protective institutions—police departments, fire departments, etc.—makes the old kind of courage irrelevant. The emancipation of women has helped to destroy the old Romance. The point is to save someone weaker than you. But men are in trouble, and are saved by women psychoanalysts. Nevertheless I gripped the volume, I felt as though I had the feel of it now, thinking that the old Romance is not dead, that Beauty will yet be saved. Man needs woman, so woman is in trouble. Beauty is menaced in all sorts of ways, by the ogre of uniformity, by the resentment of the ugly in spirit, by the cold Hell of mediocrity. I heaved the volume of Blake at the head of a sociologist (for she was once more in that circle).

9. *The Fight*

Angered by the unprovoked assault (for the man was unknown to me, so he mistakenly thought that it could not be personal) the sociologist retaliated, the struggle took the form of a fist fight. Neither one of us was particularly skilled in this form of struggle, but we fought fiercely, I for the reasons already disclosed, and he (not knowing the provocation) because of what he considered an unprovoked attack. It was the first fist fight I'd had in about ten years, but boxing is a skill that you do not easily lose. I began, as though this were an everyday occurrence, to use the old feints and combinations. Now the point about a fist fight is that in all probability no one is going to be killed or seriously injured, it is not a duel, not a struggle to the death. We both observed the Queensberry rules, did not hit under the belt, did not deliver the murderous rabbit punches, it was a clean bitter fight which we were both bound to survive. The overwhelming possibility of mutual survival naturally weakened the romantic conception. Nor was the spirit of Romance strengthened by the fact that the girl (whose name I had not caught) was unaware that she represented Beauty encircled as well as the purity of the majestic English language, likewise encircled and endangered.

She may have thought that I was jealous, or more likely thought that I was drunk and irrationally combative, but I did succeed in breaking up the circle of sociologists. After some ten minutes of fighting, our host hurled himself in between us, cried that our behavior was absurd and that any differences we had ought to be settled in a civilized way.

"What's it all about?" he asked.

"He threw a book at me," said the sociologist, "and for no reason."

I refused to discuss the matter, but the fight having stopped (by the intervention of our host), neither one of us was anxious to continue, the sociologist because he felt that he had retaliated sufficiently (my eye was cut), and I because I did not want to continue in a struggle that was bound to be inconclusive (for nobody would be killed, though his nose was bleeding). But the girl was once more freed from the circle of sociologists, and, catching her glance, I recognized my error in thinking that she was unaware of my motive, for she smiled at me most graciously.

"This is plain stupid," said our host, and added, inconsequently, "You don't even *know* one another."

10. *Our Host*

Our host was upset for two reasons. The first reason for his upset was that he felt concentrically trapped: by his difficult marriage (that is, by his marriage), by the constrictions of his social and professional life, by the apparently irreversible loss of contact with his old friends, by time's tyranny, the slow erosion, body and soul. The second reason for his upset was the feeling that he had been too late to save the girl in distress. Feeling young in heart (the way dissatisfied people often do, having missed the great early experiences) he dreamed often (for Romance dies hard) of a woman who needed to be saved, dreamed of himself, strong, wise, wily, fighting his way to the heart of the maze, and taking her off to some place where life was forever real. That dream had died hard, but it had died, not altogether died, for he was young in heart, but for everyday purposes it had died. And he was upset (a third reason) because I had come to the aid of the girl in the grip of the sociologists. He was the only one in the room (with the possible exception of the girl herself) who understood that my act was neither erratic nor drunken, he understood that my hurling the book and the struggle not to the death which followed was an effort to save the girl, and he was resentful that another had come to her aid, he bitter and unable to make the swift move (for it is the young hero who comes to the aid of beauty and the future).

11. *Outside*

Standing at a window in the moment before the coming to the end of the party, and then the end of the party, I looked out the window. The apartment overlooked the river, though up to this moment I hadn't at all felt that I was in an apartment overlooking the river. The river flowed silent and powerful towards the sea. Across the river the Palisades endured, in their ancient struggle with time and erosion. And in the obscure depths of the sky shone the steadfast stars. I indulged in the traditional melancholy reflection that we and all our chatter would soon disappear but that this river and sea, these cliffs and stars, would go on and on. This is an absolutely inconsequential thought, I said to myself, because nothing follows from it. Thus I had apparently come to the conclusion that in order for a thought to be consequential something should follow from it. These rather pointless reflections were interrupted by a remark addressed to me.

12. *The End*

"That's a glorious view," she said, and she smiled reassuringly. "Except for the fact that we're on the fifteenth floor," she went on, "it's the same view that the Indians saw five hundred years ago."

"The rocks and river endure," I said, but refrained from adding that *we* would disappear. The chatter in the room had died down. Most of the guests had gone. The host was wearily serving coffee to the hard core. The volume of Blake had been kicked into a corner. We heard someone tell the joke about the grandma who, walking with her three grandchildren, tells an admiring acquaintance:

> This is Albert, nine years old, the doctor. This is Stanley, six years old, the lawyer. This is Gordon, two years old, the accountant.

and: *"He is beautiful, but you should see the picture!"*

"Thanks," she said, looking at the book on the floor, in the corner. So she surely had understood my quixotic blow! for had I really meant business, I would have hurled the Wordsworth, a much heavier volume. "Your eye is cut," she said, and passed her hand softly over the bruised area.

"It's only a superficial wound," I said idiotically, for I had never expected that she would touch me. Had her touch not been so soft, I would have been angry at her for touching me, but since her touch was so soft, I was not angry. I have known many people for ten years and longer, and we have never touched one another. There was a pause before the departure. "Remember me to Indleberg," I said. Her smile, following so closely to her touch, reassured me. The age of the Palisade cliffs was somehow not so impressive. "It will all be part of the Great Memory," I said, thankful that she did not shake my hand, for she was leaving with a group (three men, two women) and the other four were impatiently waiting. "It is a phrase of Yeat s," I said.

"I know," she said, "*The last of the Romantics.*"

"That was a bit presumptuous of him," I said, "there will always be a last romantic."

She smiled reassuringly.

"Would you like some coffee?" asked our host.

"I certainly would," I replied, thinking of Kansas City, of doing for beauty's sake, of the youthful Palisades. I picked up the volume of Blake and gravely replaced the book in its proper place.

The Dream Issue

Frank was assigned to the Friday issue on Wednesday, and it looked pretty good from the beginning. Friday issues generally looked good because Friday looked good and because Thursday was the extracurricular day, all sorts of personages spoke before the various student clubs early in the afternoon. Also, the big basketball game of the year was scheduled for Thursday night, and that generally rated a streamer, particularly if the College won.

So Frank was kind of pleased as he assigned the club meetings and the odds and ends late Wednesday, and then the fellow who wrote the literary column came in and left his copy, written out in an excellent, clear longhand on those long ruled yellow sheets, very unnewspaper-like. It was a brilliant piece on the metaphysical poets. His analysis of the "flashes of wit," of the relation between wit and metaphor, of wit as a superstructure, added up to one of the best literary columns of the year.

"This will pull the English majors," said Frank to Karl, an upper freshman who was his assistant Issue Editor.

Karl shrugged; it wasn't his type of criticism.

On Thursday Frank came up to the office after his eleven

o'clock class, his last of the day. He had spent a good part of that hour in sketching out the first page of the issue. But it was mostly to pass the time, because things didn't begin to shape up till later in the afternoon.

He looked through the copy that had been turned in. Among the releases and stories he saw a piece that set him back. It was a slashing review by a student of a book written by an instructor, pointing out certain elementary historical errors as well as a number of grammatical ones. The critic thought that the author had misunderstood the nature of the crucial problem and left some doubt as to his ability to grapple with the problem even if he had understood it. Some aspects of the work were praised.

Frank handed this review over to the Managing Editor without comment. The latter looked at it carefully and penciled an O.K. on it.

"That's all right," he said. "It's a straight review, nothing personal."

The Sports Editor, a rather glum character who was lost between what were once described by Stanley Walker as the "Gee Whiz" and "Aw Nuts" schools of sportswriting, was busy typing his column in a corner of the office, which was beginning to get crowded. He suddenly pulled the sheet off the roller.

"Here," he said to Frank, "read copy on this yourself. I wouldn't trust another soul.

"Do *you* know what a dangling exclamation point is?" he asked a freshman on the staff, and walked out.

He left behind a masterly column on gate-crashing, in the form of a tribute to One-Eyed Connolly, who was then in his prime, and with a number of examples from the local scene—the fellow who walked in backwards and collected a return ticket, the one who got into uniform and *dribbled* past the astonished gatekeeper, the disguised Western Union messenger, and many another famed stratagem. And, he pointed out,

> We must not omit the classic method of avoiding the bite—just plainly getting past the ticket collector by capitalizing on withdrawal or momentary abstraction or by sheer, unadulterated, old-fashioned speed.

"What a column!" said Frank, as he and Karl went out to lunch with Van, who was beginning to take over the main feature assignments.

"He's a good boy," said Van, "but he's a little weak in knowledge, real background of sports history. I mean, take Joe Vila."

This was a curious comment on Van's part, for he himself was noted for a stubborn mythological streak. Between the interesting and the true he sometimes wavered. His copy was excellent, but troublesome, dean-bait.

"How's the issue shaping up?" asked Van, at the lunch table.

"Good," said Frank, "everything but spot news. What happened to your interview?"

Van tapped significantly over his inside coat pocket. "It's cooking inside," he said, "just a few little changes. You should have it by three o'clock."

He had interviewed a prominent business figure who had gone on record as saying that the city ought to cut off funds to the College, close it down because of its radical record.

"He was kind of wild," said Van, "walked around his office screaming that he was paying taxes to educate people to take his money away."

"What did you say?" asked Karl.

"Oh, I offered to loan him a dollar," said Van, laughing. "Then he said it was for our own good to close down the school, because we'd never get any jobs anyway. When an employer finds out what college we come from, why, that's it. Wait till you start looking for a job, he said, just wait. So I said there were some economists who thought it was more difficult to get a job during a depression, mightn't that be a factor? So he blew his top again and said that if it wasn't for the radicals there'd be no depression.

"He was a good scout, though. Told me to come and see him after I graduated, might have something for me."

"Does he think this interview is for the Harvard *Crimson*?" asked Frank.

"Just dialectics," said Van. "A man's views don't necessarily jibe with his character."

Police sirens blew. We hurriedly paid our checks and left.

"It's the Norman Thomas meeting," said Karl, and he was right.

The veteran Socialist had spoken before a student group, and in the question-and-answer period at the close tempers had grown short, words flew, there was some pushing, and there were a few punches thrown between Socialists and Communists, with a few Trotskyites and Lovestoneites in the middle. With the aid of Norman Thomas and a number of listeners, this scuffle was soon broken up. But someone (described by police as an "unknown informant") had called headquarters and said there was a riot in progress. Metropolitan reporters appeared in the wake of the police cars. There was no battlefield, there were no injuries, but the story made front page in a couple of the afternoon papers:

Radicals Riot

"This story," said Frank, "is a search story. Who turned in the alarm? The rest is routine."

It was the busiest part of the day. Copy was flowing in —club meetings, faculty notes, previews of weekend events, fraternity news, movie reviews (for the paper had to justify the free tickets), and all the oddities that go to make up the news.

"Here Karl," said Frank, "you'd better take this copy

down to the printer. They're hollerin', and I don't want to run too much on the overtime. I'll be down in a couple of hours."

After Karl left, someone said: "Do you think he'll pull a Kessler?"

Kessler, in the lore of the paper, was an unfortunate youth who, some years back, had lost the copy on his way to the printer. He claimed the package was stolen from him by a thief who mistook him for a bank-runner. The Issue Editor called as many staff members as he could reach, and they labored long into the night reconstructing the morning paper.

"The Business Manager must have had babies when he saw *that* overtime bill."

"Don't worry about Karl," said Frank, "he'll make it."

Just then Sawyer walked in and, with exaggerated carefulness, deposited an envelope on the table. It was *Gargoyle*, a kind of catch-as-can column, specializing in paragraphs, poems, witticisms, and comments.

"Treat her tenderly," said Sawyer, "she may have a sister, she may have a brother. Is that Tom Hood or Tom O'Bedlam?"

"Listen," said Frank, who had rudely torn open the envelope and was looking at the copy, "what language is this, and what does it say?"

"Greek," said Sawyer, "the best Attic numbers. A quotation about nobody you know."

That was about all Frank could get out of him. The columnist left.

This poem (in English) was contributed to the column:

HOMAGE

1

A bank wreathed in flowers
A clock without a face
Gone the glittering hours
Without a trace

Buried in fathomless vaults
In the darkness of the ground
With the rose and the peonie
Dying without a sound.

2

Hours are wreathed in gladness
Far from the naked clock
Banks are plunged in sadness
Though built on rock
Only the buried can flower
Only the losers have won
Homage to Samuel Greenberg
And to Emily Dickinson.

"The poem is O.K.," said Frank, "but I don't know about this ancient Greek stuff. Is there a classics student in the house?"

"I'll take it down to one of the professors," someone said.

"No you won't," said Frank.

After a while Winkler came in. He was a student in Greek and Latin who occasionally contributed a gossip column to the paper.

He whistled that short-long whistle with the dying fall as he looked at the passage in question.

"Boy," he said, "this will get someone into hot water, or, if you'll pardon the confusion, into the cooler."

"It figured," said Frank. "What does it say?"

"Well, it's kind of garbled, but it refers to a man with three testicles. People come to see this wonder from far and wide, even *Thracian rubbernecks*, which is how I'd translate it."

"Just as I thought," said Frank, and with a swift move of the crayon, he obliterated the offending phrase.

At about six o'clock, the Editor came in with his editorial, and after going over the dummy for the issue with him Frank gathered up his copy and left. It was dark, the first stars shone faintly, the Gothic halls, the stone campus, were faintly bathed by an early moon. Day students were leaving, night students were coming in, knowledge hungry, from factory, from office. Frank thought of some of the famed alumni who had fought their way to the top, redeemed the pledge, and he felt proud of his college, maligned as it was, proud of its students, hungry, bitter, noisy, but keeping alive the ancient flame of learning, the search for truth.

On his way to the subway Frank stopped for a sandwich and looked professionally at the front page of his evening newspaper. He was interested in makeup, the shape of the news. Lively news did not necessarily mean a lively looking paper—he had seen too many issues crowded with news and features but spoiled by thoughtless arrangement, inept choice of type, unimaginative use of pictures. It is just like content in painting, he thought, the richer the concept, the more expert the execution must be. And there is no greater spoilation than the botching of a worthwhile concept. What difference does it make *what* you do to a worthless concept? You could dress up a newsless issue, but there was something hollow about this success.

The paper in front of him carried a meaningless picture of police and students at the College aimlessly milling about, in a confusion desultory and bare. There was a picture of President Hoover addressing a farm group. An unemployed demonstration. First news of spring training in the South. A feature writer was reporting on three nights he had spent in a Bowery flophouse.

Frank thought that he had a good issue in the fire. He sketched out, again, the front page. Nothing hidden, no unexpected prominences. And the danger, when you had so much live news, of a jumpy, a nervous effect, where everything and nothing stood out, with no place for the eye to rest. The result of the basketball game might throw things off balance. A victory would clinch the metropolitan title. What decides importance? What *you* think, or what you think the majority think? The balance between private judgment and the popular interest. No pandering, no inflaming. To appeal to the common reason. Voltaire, Condorcet. And the common emotion. Tough figuring.

When he reached the printers, he found things in good shape. Most everything had been set up, and John and Whitey, the two linotypists, started right in on the copy that Frank brought with him. Proof had been read, and Karl was a demon proofreader. Frank sent the other two staff members home and went to work on the front-page dummy with his assistant.

In a little while Whitey came over with a wet proof. "Here's your editorial, boys," he said.

Frank looked carefully at the sheet in front of him. Copy always looked better in proof, a new air of reality. This was one of the editorials, breathing the spirit of the great doctrinaires of free speech, which never failed to bring criticism from all areas of the undergraduate political spectrum. It was between the period of the "fighting liberals" of muckraking days and the "confused liberals" of the late thirties. The next issue would probably run two letters, one from the right which would criticize this playing into the hands of the left, opening the hole in the dyke and so opening the floodgates of Bolshevism, and the other from the Communist left, pointing out that this editorial was "confusing the superstructure with the base, making a fetish," etc.

"Damn good editorial," said Frank to his assistant. "Read this sentence."

Karl read:

There is no conceivable form of society where we will not have to fight for freedom of expression.

"There's something to that," said Karl.

"That'll burn 'em up," said Frank.

"Some more copy for you demons," said Whitey, "I'm going to start making up your front page, if you're ready."

Whitey was a fabulous figure in the history of the newspaper. He was one of those "naturals," there was nothing in a printing plant he could not do. Frank remembered, from his freshman days, the time that an important story had broken at the last minute. The Managing Editor rushed downtown and dictated the story to the imperturbable Whitey, who worked away at his Mergenthaler with the ease of a typist at one of the new electric machines. Frank copyread that story— it was flawlessly set up, without an error.

"Good," said Frank, handing him the dummy, "I'll be with you in a little while."

He divided the proofs with Karl. There was an odd letter being printed, dealing with problems of curriculum. It had a very old-fashioned air, slow and full paragraphed, amid the choppy rhythms, the active verbs. The Editor had told Frank to be sure to make room for it, though it ran almost a column.

"Most of the students *do* spend most of their time in the classrooms," he said.

The letter was excellently written though a little on the pedantic side, defending certain compulsory subjects, etc. Frank shrugged. At the moment he was more interested in the newspaper than he was in his studies.

While they were so occupied, Van walked in. "I was in the neighborhood," he said, "and thought I'd see how you slaves were coming on. Let's go out for coffee."

Frank said he'd go down with Van. "Can I bring you fellows anything?" he asked.

Whitey and Karl went for the coffee. John passed it up, saying he was going to knock off soon.

Once they got downstairs, Van said he felt more like a drink than anything else, so they went into the first bar, where Frank ordered a beer and Van had a couple of drinks, fast. A cheerful man, bobbing along with the music, was at the piano, and a girl who looked like a sociology major by day was singing, with an abstract interest, "The Moon is Low."

"I'd like to get moving," said Van, "I'm getting tired of college."

"What do you have in mind?" asked Frank.

"I like to go where the trouble is," answered the young feature writer. "You get a build-up of pressures, and then there's bound to be an explosion. The way you had in Manchuria, the way you'll have in Germany soon. I like to be where the naked struggle for power takes place."

He had a habit of using in speech the extreme terminology then current in political writing.

"What about you?" asked Van.

"Well, I've got another year and a half of school. I guess I'll start worrying toward the end of next year."

He was anxious to get back upstairs, to the makeup, to the excitement of the end of the issue.

"I'm going to beat it," he said. "The basketball score should be coming through soon."

"What the hell?" asked Van aggressively, "are you a makeup man or a reporter?"

"Craft snobbism," said Frank, as he put down his dime.

"I think I'll hang around for a while," said Van, and he gazed morosely at the sociology major, who was giving "Sweet and Lovely" a going-over.

Frank found everything in order upstairs. John had left, Whitey was working at the form, and Karl was down toward the end of his proof work.

"Here's your coffee," said Frank, putting down the containers he had bought in the diner on the corner. He had bought one for himself, too.

"Where's Van?" asked Whitey, "on his way to the Cape of Good Hope?"

Karl said that Kress, who was covering the basketball game, had called between halves and said we were two points behind, and that it was anyone's game.

"We'll win," said Whitey, who had adopted the College. "We always win the tough ones."

They worked silently for a while, and then the collegians finished their proofs and worked along with Whitey.

"That looks in good shape," said Whitey. "I'll finish my coffee, and then I'll make these new corrections."

The three of them sat around the desk, waiting for the final score. Frank enjoyed these lulls—the expectancy, the easy camaraderie. He and Whitey talked about some of the recent graduates.

"What happened to Isaacs?" asked Whitey. "That boy was a crackerjack. Never had to change a word of his."

He never praised any contemporary staff member this way.

"He's school correspondent for a couple of papers," said Frank.

Whitey nodded. This news confirmed his expectancies. He remembered one of the riot stories that Isaacs had written so coolly as to make it sound like a meeting of the Chess Club.

Karl listened with interest to the tales of these giants of the very recent past.

After a little more of this gabbing, Whitey said, "Here, give me those proofs, and I'll set up the corrected slugs."

While he was working on these corrections, the phone rang; it was Kress on the phone, exultant.

"We did it," he said to Frank, "69–67, pulled it out in the last two minutes. I'll be down in about half an hour."

"I told you," said Whitey. "I knew we'd catch them."

By the time Kress came down, Whitey was finished with all the resetting, and had set up the streamer headline. All they needed was the lead story, and, of course, the banks for that story. Everything else was ready for the press.

"You can take off," said Frank to Karl.

"Nah," said the kid, "I'll stick around."

"I thought you would."

Kress burst in on schedule, waving his copy and half-dragging a girl with him.

"I wrote most of it on the subway," he said. "Meet Marcia. Whitey, Frank. What is it again? Karl?"

"Look," said Kress to the girl, "examine the fonts of type or something. I'll knock this story off fast."

Marcia was kind of pretty, and pleased the way girls are when they've crashed an all-man's place. But then she got bored as the others went to work. Karl didn't really have anything to do, but he made himself busy. He was kind of shy with fairly pretty girls.

Frank read copy; it was a good story, maybe a little on the flamboyant side, but it *was* the big game and deserved the spread. As he finished a page, he passed it along to Whitey at the machine. Frank was trying to keep the overtime down, but he was very careful, he wanted no boners on the outside column.

Marcia saw that Karl wasn't doing anything important.

"What's this?" she asked him, holding up a cut.

"That's a line cut," he said, "it's a way of reproducing pictures."

"Well, here it is," said Kress. "Just wait till Ring Lardner, W. O. McGeehan, George Trevor, and Grantland Rice see this!"

"Are they friends of yours?" asked Marcia.

The laughter was low and respectful.

The sportswriter and his girl left, and it wasn't long before the story was set, banks and all, corrected, and placed.

"O.K.," said Whitey, "how about a page proof?"

Looking at the wet proof, Frank was pleased. Karl grinned. Even Whitey, giving it a quick professional glance, nodded in approval. You could tell that Whitey would be talking about Frank in the years to come.

Frank caught one or two minor errors, which Whitey quickly reset. Then Whitey locked up the forms, and the two students watched as he set up the press. In a little while the first copy rolled off. Whitey stopped the machine and looked at the paper.

"Smudgy, uneven," he said, and crumpled the paper, threw it away. He adjusted the machine, ran off a few more copies, then gave one to each of the young journalists.

"Your baby is born," he said, smiling. "All yours now."

"Good-bye Whitey."

"Good-bye boys."

They walked uptown slowly till they hit a cafeteria. It was lively and crowded, people were sitting with the early editions of the morning papers, reading with the anticipatory interest that the paper bought on the morning itself never has.

Frank and Karl pulled out their copies of the college paper and looked at them as though for the first time, the way you do when a thing is made and there is no chance to change it anymore.

"It's a dream issue," said Karl, and the kid meant it.

Frank was very happy with the issue, it wasn't one of those that sparkle on the front page and then die inside. It was strong all over. The story of the "riot" was well handled:

> A scholastic hassle on the "nature of world imperialism," a few unfriendly shoves and blows, and the zeal of an "unknown informant" brought the police to the campus yesterday on a wild-goose chase.

The interview with the agitated business man

CLOSE COLLEGE FOR OWN GOOD, DECLARES IRATE MERCHANT

SAYS RADICAL AURA SPOILS EMPLOYMENT POSSIBILITIES; OFFERS REPORTER JOB

was handled a little too facetiously, but it was pretty funny.

Kress's lead story made good reading, though he was occasionally carried away by his own hyperbole:

Houdini-like cross-court razzle-dazzle

and it was always nice to start off with a victory, it gave the paper a head start.

The editorial looked and read as strong as ever, and the columns, including the new one which reprinted editorials from leading undergraduate papers throughout the country, had a very readable air. Even the fillers seemed well chosen.

They pushed the papers away and talked for a while. Karl was a Socialist; he was lively, somewhat of a jokester on occasion, but when it came to Socialism he was very serious. He'd talk about Austro-Marxism, the revisionism of Bernstein, the theories of Kautsky, the activities of the Second International in the Orient. He was left-centrist in his thinking, a devoted follower of Norman Thomas, admirer of Debs this side of hero worship. He had tangled with the Communists on many occasions, and was able to give a good account of himself. He was going on seventeen years of age. His father was a garment worker.

"You Socialists," said Frank, speaking from the outside, not exactly sure *where* on the outside, "are going to be squeezed between the Fascists and the Communists."

"I don't think so," said the youth, who was kind of puzzled by Frank's range of interests, hesitating to label him dilletante. "Our ranks will thin out only if capitalism expands, grows stronger."

"Is that bad?" asked Frank. "People will go back to work."

"It'll take a war," said the lad, "and then another decline. But the Socialists are the least neurotic of the parties in opposition, they'll take advantage of job openings, etc. Short range it's to our credit, but long range the fanatic wins out.

He doesn't want happiness, he wants power. *Very* long range, I don't know."

The college paper looked kind of thin under the weight of this conversation.

Frank felt foolish, as you do when younger people pick up the serious aspect, and he was kind of tired too, so he let the conversation lapse. So did Karl, who wasn't the monologist type.

It was close to two in the morning; the brisk air of early March revived Frank as they walked toward the subway.

"Do you read poetry?" he asked. "Who do you like?"

"Sure," said Karl, "Shelley, Emma Lazarus."

Frank grinned. He envisioned Shelley and tried to imagine what Emma looked like. Then he recited:

> *Wherefore feed, and clothe, and save,*
> *From the cradle to the grave,*
> *Those ungrateful drones who would*
> *Drain your sweat—nay, drink your blood!*

"A violent image," said Karl, "but basically correct."

"Wow," said Frank, "farewell to Fabianism, you're moving left, boy. Whither Karl?"

"Home," he said, "home to Brooklyn."

The early March moon followed them crazily down the street, shedding a dim light on the structures and superstructures.

> *The cold chaste Moon, the Queen of Heaven's bright isles,*
> *Who makes all beautiful on which she smiles;*
> *That wandering shrine . . .*

recited Karl.

When they reached the subway they picked up the morning papers.

"Goodnight," said Karl. He pulled the college paper out of his pocket.

"Real good issue," he said.

"So long," said Frank, as he boarded the uptown train.

The Business of Poetry

Goaded by economic necessity and inspired by the famous recommendation to the disgruntled recruit that he buy a cannon and go into business for himself, Ned Norris, a youth, decided that he would mix art and commerce in the most unashamed way.

This was how he reasoned: "If I send my poems to an editor or to a publisher, with a polite note, etc., it is only another way of selling my merchandise, except it is called acceptance and rejection instead of buying and selling.

"Why do I need these middlemen? I will go to the consumer direct."

This was how he went retail, and joined the ever growing ranks of those who bring their wares directly to the attention of the ultimate buyer.

He differed from most of the peddlers in other lines in that he manufactured his own product. True, there were some gadgeteers who manufactured their own products and then took to the road as salesmen. Ned differed from these individuals in that each one of *his* objects was unique.

This was a point of great honor with Ned—he would

not sell the same poem to more than one individual, and resisted the temptation of the carbon and the mimeograph.

In fact, there was a time when he refused even to *offer* the same poem to more than one individual, but his sound business sense triumphed over this rather insane purism.

Later on, his sound business sense triumphed also over his disinclination to sell the same poem more than once. He found himself in a position where he could put the carbon, if not (alas!) the mimeograph, to good use. This was the occasion of the triumph of his poem:

THE SKY-BLUE WEEK

So contrived his life that experiences were consumed in a weekly poem
Depository of the frightening moment of apartness
And the well-planned reconciliation
Of the week without drama
    The unadorned trembling week
    And (speak it low) deliverance.

In that week love retreated further
Appointments were broken
Boundaries altered
Mothers immobilized

Everyone feels his reaction is wrong.

That was the sky-blue week
Praise the temperate zone!

This poem caught on. It sold in the fives, his first modest success.

Unlike the egg men, the brush people, and the repairers of household appliances, Ned had a wide open field. The only competitive area in the city was Greenwich Village, from which he at first stayed away, realizing that his youth and inexperience would place him under severe handicap against the downtown veterans. So he determined to season himself before trying his hand in the big time.

In resisting the lure of the market which provided ready-made customers (many a night Ned would go down to one of the Village bars and observe the veterans in action) he displayed a canniness hardly to be expected from a practitioner of this unworldly art. But in determining that he would make his way in the world by means of this unworldly art, Ned displayed a commercial enterprise and ingenuity topped only by the great modern French painters.

Nor did this business activity (at first) in any way interfere with the quality of his verse-making; he displayed a controlled schizophrenic talent which put him far in the van of his competitors who approached their selling activity with an aggressive pride and effrontery which failed to cover the deepest shame.

"After all," sometimes reasoned the poet, who dreamed of a time when goods and all created objects would be freely exchanged on a no-cost basis, "is there radical harm done to an object as a result of its being sold? Does the bread lose its savor at the precise moment of the purchase?"

He often felt that there was radical harm done to the objects in the process of sale, but he was able to dismiss this vague feeling in the interest of self-preservation.

"After all," he reasoned, "who am I to stand outside the frame of a society created by people more or less like me (all of whom I wish to reach) and declare that I will not enter into their methods of moneymaking and their elaborate techniques for the distribution of goods?"

But at the same time he recognized without hesitation that no business sale he ever made (and he was fated to be involved in some extraordinary transactions) gave him the satisfaction of a gift freely and lovingly given or freely and lovingly received (whether the object was bought or made, but especially when it was made).

Ned's methods were very simple—he generally did his own work in the morning and then would take to the road in the afternoon. He'd first decide on the neighborhood and then choose his wares accordingly—forasmuch as the neighborhoods were dying, the differences remained—between the Battery and Times Square, between Williamsburg and Hunts' Point.

He did not particularly write for the neighborhoods, but some poems were more fitting than others. Of course, he was not in the mass-distribution game, the individual he sought could be anywhere, but still he had to play the angles. He had to take advantage of what remained of the neighborhood differences. Wherever he went, he had to seek out with extraordinary care the potential buyer. In this way he differed from other kinds of salesmen, who knocked on every door.

Too, for Ned, everyone was a potential buyer, but he realized (sadly) that he was in one way at least outside the economic situation. How often would he hear: "I wouldn't take this stuff for nothing."

In many cases they would not take it for nothing. Such was the poem beginning,

Life being hope plus disappointment,

which he simply could not give away:

> Life being hope plus disappointment minus pleasure plus pain
> Times the painstaking regret times the momentary prospect minus
> the forlorn hope
> Plus desire despair disillusion
> Minus the inhibition of abstract thought and the sudden unifying
> experience
> Divided by multiplication
> The square root of surprise
> And those numberless swooping gulls, fading in pairs, groups, and
> solitaries.

One approaches people who are in a fair state of repose, in a public place, with a little time on their hands. This rules out passers-by and subway or bus riders (there are exceptions to every rule, such as a subway in the early morning hours, between the end of pleasure and the beginning of work). Bars, cafeterias, parks and squares, playgrounds, bus and railroad terminals are excellent trading areas, but caution must be observed at all times. One ought not approach an individual who is nervously awaiting a train.

But the basic approach is on an individualistic basis—I have halted passers-by, rushing, in no state of repose, and effected a quick sale. It is a meeting of the minds, that uncanny premonition which brings together the buyer and the seller in a consummation rewarding for both.

One has to become acutely aware not only of the stranger's character but also of his mood at the moment. Appeal to the mood as it relates to the character, and you have a sure sale.

There is no one, correctly approached, who will not buy your poem. A record of failure (percentage-wise, sales against efforts are very low) only means that you have not come to the necessary awareness.

It is precisely when this awareness is weak that one has need of the grosser categories of salesmanship. It is not reasonable to expect anyone (especially a poet, whose moments of inspiration, by a confused tradition, are reserved for his work) to be at the top of his game at every moment. That is why we have the rules of grammar and manuals of salesmanship.

I wish to boast of some of my successes (for I am the Ned of whom I have been talking).

A youth was idling on a corner, obviously waiting for a girl who was late. I whipped out these

TWO WAITING POEMS

1. Waiting for the distant sound
   His eyes are closed
   His ears to the ground.

(Four years is his master dead
Safe in his vault
He asked to be burnt instead.)

There is a murmur along the ground
The beast is aflame
It is the sound of his master's voice
(Alas, in a foreign tongue).

2. Waiting. Between trains
Between infancy and childhood
(To learn to walk, to learn to read)
Waiting for love to walk in,
Or for the point of saturation,
Waiting for disaster, for death to walk in
(You're dead a long time)
Waiting for Spring which is already gone
For the case to end (the jury is hung).

which I presented to him. I made a quick sale. He saw a chance of using up the intolerable time.

This is an important social function of the poem, to use up the waiting, the intolerable time. The poem, read in a comparatively short interval, creates the illusion of a completed experience and so compensates for the time one feels he is wasting as he waits, and especially when he waits with pleasure. Such an individual is an excellent prospect.

The rules are not hard and fast. Sometimes, one makes an offer of a poem that runs *counter* to the mood and behavior of the prospect, as in the case of the following poem which I sold to a noisy individual in Bryant Park:

A SONG OF SILENCES

A song of silences
Of the sea, of the night,
of Jonathan Swift in the year 1742
(year of remorse, madness, and silence)
Silence where no words are spoken

And where no words are unspoken
(A dead silence)
Silence after the shriek of agony
All are immobilized, silent witnesses,
And of the streets before dawn:
The stars disappear without a sound,
Fade like the memories of eternal loves.

The tendency, however, is to present a poem that is in tune with the prospect's mood (the homeopathic dose). On this basis, I made a very profitable sale to an elderly woman, who was sitting with a friend in Goldberg's Park on 72nd Street and was involved in one of those deep silences which must be distinguished from mere quiet. Reading my poem, she silently reached into the depths of her pocketbook and, without a word, handed me a five dollar bill, which I silently slipped into my pocket, before slinking off.

AGAIN SILENCE

Again: silence,
The chattering of the apes
The even breathing of Norton,
Normal man with the requited desires
Who makes money without guilt
And love without force or gentleness.

Again: silence,
The tapping of the blind
Ringing down the alley,
Measuring out the blocks
(Twenty to a mile
In the New York style).

The silence between the heartbeats
Measuring out a life
Life doubling back on itself.
Chattering, breathing.
Swinging 'round in the empty alley
Hearing only the intervals
In the beat of the blind heart.

After a while I became so adept at sizing up the mood, the overall Gestaltic situation of a prospect, developed such a refined sense of empathy, that I was able to write a poem on the spot. Such was the poem I wrote for the man sitting in the Automat below Columbus Circle, gazing moodily out at the falling snow:

SITTING IN THIS PLACE

Sitting in this place, rather than another,
Watching this snow, instead of another,
Waiting for what will never happen
(It is all in your head)
Forgetting the joy found and the joy already won
(Not altogether in your head)
Recognizing that what does not come to the hand
　　That is not yours
And what does not leap from the imagination
　　That is not yours:
These belongings are elsewhere, otherwise possessed,
Or not belonging.

What is yours comes to you, seeks you,
These the glad cries of my children
Welcome in eyes and bodies
And this snow, swirling and blowing
Twisting around you—
This is yours, this seeks and envelops you.

In this case, the man would not buy my poem—he read it carefully, said that it was very interesting but that he did not care to own it.

(As it happened, I sold this poem years later to a wealthy roué staring out of Rumpelmayer's window.)

This power I developed of writing on-the-spot poems cut down considerably the inventory I carried with me. Naturally, I never went out without a small stock, but, with my new skill, I was not so dependent on this stock.

I could not help comparing myself favorably to my downtown competitors, who carried their poems around like so many potatoes and offered them to their customers one after the other, in an effort (often growing hysterical as the bottom of the bag was reached) to make the sale.

What a distortion of the concept of the uniqueness of the individual! What a travesty on poetic justice!

I realize I am overstepping the ethical bounds in talking so of my competitors (many of them worthy men and women in other respects), but I must appeal here to a higher standard than the one dictated by narrow professional demands.

Now I reach the question of price, about which, as a beginner, I used to be very sensitive, being unable to reconcile my product with the cash nexus which binds, where it does not strangle, the buyer and seller. I have learned to transcend, if not to harmonize, this conflict. I have never failed to accept an offer (except where it was made in bad faith) feeling so confident of my productive powers that I found it unnecessary to hold back for material reasons. My main problem was to make it clear that I *was* in the market, that these objects *were* for sale.

Here is a rough breakdown of the would-be customer reaction:

Most refused the paper—gently, fearfully, angrily, as the case was.

Some accepted, glanced, and returned—gently, fearfully, angrily, etc.

Some read and returned without comment, and with evident lack of interest.

None of these I pressed further.

There were, however, those who read with interest and were prepared to discuss. At first, as I say, I was ashamed to have to explain to them that it was necessary for me to sell these objects, and in my embarrassment lost many a sale, for this is the effect of an apparent lack of confidence in your product.

I overcame this difficulty by evolving a presentation announcement:

"Would you care to read and buy this poem?"

which I varied according to circumstances and, on certain occasions, did not feel the need to use at all.

I accepted any price offered, but I made it a habit with strangers never to give the poem for nothing, even where I was forced, in some cases, to maintain the fiction of a sale by making a small loan to the indigent purchaser to put him in a buying position.

I have made some interesting sales on the basis of these offers freely made and freely accepted.

In this game one never knows what he is appealing to, and must be prepared for the most unusual reactions, financial and otherwise. I have had to revive fainting women, console weeping men, and make a hurried getaway from some irate individual whose aggressive instincts I had succeeded in awakening by some line or other.

Often, of course, the reaction was of a very rewarding sort, as in the case of the gentleman, slightly drunk, but not enough to cloud his reasoning faculties, who offered me $100 for the lines:

In the moment before the moon faded
Love was born
And died with the fading of the moon.

I freely accepted this offer, for I could understand how these lines could be highly valued.

Difficulties arose when the customer asked for the price. "How much do you want for it?"

It was difficult to put a quick valuation on the object, there were so many things to consider: the reputation of the poem (among friends), the amount of time put in, the quality of the effort, the number of lines, my needs at the moment, the economic status of the customer. The only thing I did not have to consider was the market, which in this commodity is blind. You never know when you're asking too little or too much.

I am always prepared to bargain for the reason that I do not know myself the value of the commodity that I am offering, and will therefore accept, on the spot, any offer that does not sound too ridiculous, or too cheap in the sense that the offer is patronizing or otherwise not qualitatively acceptable.

My terms are cash, but I reserve the right to turn down any offer for any reason, for the reason that I am sometimes unable to formulate a reason.

I have, on rare occasions (for mine is a fanatical flexibility), extended merchandise on credit, where I thought the risk was reasonable. I must say, that with one exception, I have never gone wrong in my analysis of the moral character of the customer.

The exception was a middle-aged man whom I found in the Central Park cafeteria. He said that he was a little short of funds, but that he would be at the same table the following week. Sure enough, he was there, but much to my astonishment, he blandly denied ever having seen me. Persistent efforts failed to shake this lying structure: the case will soon come up for settlement in the Small Claims Court. I have no witnesses and naturally no receipt, but think I may perhaps shake the defendant's equilibrium by reciting, as much as I remember (for he has my last copy) the lines of this poem:

THE JOB

Before the occupational psychosis is shaken off, the
    grooving and the divisiveness,
Before the sense of insignificance is lost, the absence of
    grandeur,

Before signification reasserts, binds itself with building
    and passer-by,
Before the depths and the heights come to a clearer
    connection, and the casual meeting is heightened.
Before the present horror is made clear, bomb and
    scream,
We are back to the post from which it is necessary to
    shake off, lose, reassert, heighten, and make clear.

I have adopted a flexible attitude toward the problem of barter. I happen to dislike using objects that have been used by others. My feeling toward these offered objects, which tended to be household furnishings, personal belongings, apparel, was one of revulsion, like moving in on somebody else's fifth. I made some exceptions in the case of books and other art objects, on the principle that they are merely imitations of things that can never be used up. I have made exceptions, *too*, in the case of personal belongings, where the pleas of the other or the attractiveness of the object in question proved sufficiently compelling. I am in possession of a remarkable red scarf which I took in trade for an old narrative poem. I have gotten a night's lodging out of a poem and many a fine supper (excellent trades), and I am always ready to trade poem for poem, even though this results in the reduction of my own inventory, for I will never sell another man's poem, and, having traded mine for his, feel that I have lost right to mine.

I mean that I will never sell another man's poem as long as my business is constituted the way it is. I have thought of going into the business of selling other people's poems—it opens up a profitable field. I may perhaps hire a young man to handle this phase of the business, or go into it myself when my own stock begins to dwindle. The duration of my productive powers is, after all, uncertain. Today, my imagination is in good shape, but poets go first in the "shaping power" and

I sometimes see signs of weakening there. But I am talking (I hope) of the distant future.

Meanwhile, business was pretty good. I was, thank God, making a good living in a way that pleased me. It's a healthy life, on the outside most of the time, a lot of walking, and an occasional game of handball in one of the public playgrounds.

Emboldened by my success on the outskirts (this was the period before the disappearance of the centers) and feeling that I had scouted my rivals long enough to gain a sufficient awareness of their weak points and strong points, I decided to move in on the big money and to test my mettle against these experienced merchants, some of whom were in business before I had learned to read or write.

I made a careful stock choice, a selection wide enough to cover any eventuality (I was not going to depend on the inspiration of the moment), and then picked my clothes out of the extensive wardrobe of clothes turned into costumes, which I considered to be an important element in my modest success.

You can imagine my feelings as I boarded the subway en route to this climactic encounter, to find out once and for all whether the long struggle had been in vain! Prepared to throw all caution to the winds, I held an iron grip on myself. I reviewed all possible eventualities, made plans for any conceivable contingency. In a word, I was ready.

I walked briskly into the well-known Village bar, with an air of self-confidence which made me feel very confident. I sized up the situation in a moment. Two of my experienced competitors were in the market, circling around their prey. I must present the picture this way for the reason that she was unaware of being stalked, and this rather unsavory situation gave me the idea of having a business card printed, just my name and, in small italics in the corner, *J sell poems*.

This elderly woman who was the center of our attraction

was clearly benign, philanthropic, and interested in the perpetuation of the arts. She wore a charming Victorian brooch and looked as though she had spent the afternoon in John Wanamaker's. I do not mean to run her down, for she did not try to be anything except what she actually was, and she cut no sorry figure in the midst of the phonies, the would-be's, and the incompetent eccentrics with which the place abounded. I am not proud of myself for having singled her out and joined the buzzards, but this was the exigency of the moment, I could not avoid it. I bided my time.

Both my competitors (I do not know whether they were working as a team or not) approached her at the same time, and she graciously invited them to join her.

(From the next booth, I could not fail to be an eavesdropper.)

Neither of my competitors mentioned their business— they brought up various other matters, then warily (so they thought) brought the subject around to the arts and to the difficulty of the artist in a world of Babbitry, of narrow and self-seeking materialism. . . .

I moved to their table, angrily, and put my poem down (I would have thrown it down if it were possible to do that) at about the same time that my competitors presented their works, one of which (as best as I can recall it) follows:

Uncovered an odd lot of stinking souls,
Ex-humans struggling for immortality.
How they squirmed in the noonday sun,
Yearning for the underground.
The wind whistled through the ephemeral frames,
Shivering spirits who once strode vigorously
Through the corridors of the halls of justice,
Who freely gave their bodies to unlovely strangers,
Lovingly gave their unlovely bodies,
Who dreamed, waited, and hoped,
Cunningly destroyed, sickened, and lived.

These are the citizens of the dreamless world,
(Who unlovingly gave their lovely bodies
And died and died and died).

"Madam," I said, "would you care to buy and read this poem of mine?"

"Young man," she answered, "you are very rude."

She let the three poems lie on the table. Mine was the only handwritten one. The other two were typed, one was a *carbon* copy.

The older of the two competitors picked up my poem (which I had written while sitting in the next booth) and read it aloud:

A dream, an entry into the secrets of the past,
Heavily disguised, like the villain,
Who hoping to appear as someone else
Appears only the more himself—
False mustache, false gleam,
False gait in the falsest dream!

There is a bird of prey, the cormorant,
And the delicate child, bemused
In the fearful forest.
The bird circles, the child is lost,
It is a narrative, an agony of waiting,
Deliberate, the way a stream is crossed
Or the way a master sets the stage
For a drama of retribution:
    The lost bird, the circling child,
      The random beasts in the forest wild!

The bird swoops, the child is seeking
The yellow flower,
And bemused, walks out of the dream.
The bird is baffled,
Talons spread, betrayed
By the extra dimension.

"What'll you take for it, kid?" he asked.

So this was the way one broke into the big time!

This was an eventuality I had not figured on, so I shrugged my shoulders.

He named a reasonable sum.

I accepted his offer and immediately presented the lady with another poem (thereby violating one of my firmest business principles) :

> Drunk and disorderly, a-dream in the alleys,
> I saw the brightest star
> Agleam, aglow.
> Neither distance, nor loss, nor the brooded hopes
> Affect this clear image.
>
> Look! look! a man arises,
> Alley-wise, alert, kneels and prays
> Under the rising moon,
> Reaches beyond himself,
> Asks protection, asks joy.
>
> Lucky star! shine bright
> Upon these helpless ones,
> Cover with thy bright mantle
> Years, years, years.

My competitors grinned at the speed with which I produced this poem, but the customer proved very recalcitrant, explaining that she only bought objects that were durable in the material.

"Because we work on paper instead of on stone," I began, indignantly. But one of my associates waved me down.

"Every lady," he said, "has her right to a choice of materials."

I could see the justice of this remark, and we all chatted pleasantly until the elderly woman arose and excused herself.

"I hear you've been doing pretty good uptown," said one of my competitors.

So they had heard of me!

Then they proceeded to talk of their business problems. They were both *Printed Poets* and were incredulous at my disinclination to be printed.

"You think *these* people are so much better than editors and publishers?" they asked.

I asked them why they never ventured out of their neighborhood.

"What?" they asked, "talk to strangers?"

That was how it went, parry and thrust.

I began to see their point of view: to work at close quarters, in familiar surroundings, rubbing against familiar bodies, seeing the same customers, drinking the same whisky over bars and tables worn down and scratched up by themselves and their own.

And there I was, freezing up in the country, courting rebuffs by strangers.

We shook hands cordially, though what I considered novelty and adventure they considered idiocy and though what they considered intimacy I considered a narrow and sectarian return to the womb.

After this experience, Ned Norris (for he is the I of whom we have been telling you) returned to his accustomed activity, the better for this additional area which he now included as part of his route. He became increasingly preoccupied with his economic status in the society. His youthful idealism refused to wither, he clung to his individual, his unique self, with the fury of a Protestant reformer. He was of the opinion (which he sometimes felt as a principle) that all possible ways of earning a livelihood were corrupt and self-destroying, for either you had to sell yourself or you had to make unconscionable use of others.

Of all possible ways he felt his method to be the least self-destroying. He made an object and sold it. But was he buying cheap and selling dear? In the creation of his objects he had reduced his contact with the market to an irreducible minimum; he swapped poems for pencil and paper with a friendly wholesale stationer, and these were his only materials.

The fairness of the price continued to plague him. His mark-up was absolute. Was he not buying cheap and selling dear with a vengeance, infinitely more so than the manufacturer or the merchant, who paid a price and then sold for a higher price? It cost him (Ned Norris) nothing, and he sold for something. But did it cost him nothing?

Why, the truth of it was that he created these objects with much absorption and pleasure, certainly without the boredom and unpleasantness of other work he had tried. Then, too, he *learned* from this work, which cost him nothing and gave him pleasure. The mark-up was absolute, he was the greatest extortioner of all!

Against this he measured the absence of exploitation, the willingness to meet the buyer on the latter's terms, and the pleasure his objects gave.

From this pondering he returned to his thought that it was better to give with love than to sell any way at all.

Then he realized that when one is no longer a child he must give up childish things. Children give (and take) and men sell—they sell goods, service, and/or themselves. Men sell in order to buy. He (Ned) also sold in order to buy protection from hunger and cold.

There was the possibility that you could allow other people to *give* you, then you would not have to buy. But there was nobody who gave without buying you, for only a child can be given and not bought.

All the time that he was living the mystery of the Fair Price and the morality of the Market, he was engaging in business with an excitement created precisely by the doubt. He made a good sale on his poem,

GOODBYE AND HELLO

Goodbye to that, analysis of the known
And the probe of those encaged
In prisons all their own.
Prisoners of conscience
Drawn toward bars
They are holding at arms' length!
Men whose chiefest offense
The promise broken to the self.

There remains music and dance
Solemnity close to trance
The wonders of Paris France.
Consider acrobats and kings
The line of Klee
And the horrors of yesterday.
(Lord, the bureaus of the soul
The self-sealing self
The sovereign spirit on dole).

and dreamt of striking it rich.

He dreamt of striking it rich partly because he was in love and realized that the time might come when he would have to sell *more* and *regularly;* this brought to light problems of such a puzzling and contradictory nature that the youth, baffled by the necessity of expansion, dreamt of striking it rich.

This is one of our difficulties, that new problems never solve old ones but make us yearn for the old problems we could never solve.

Solomon's Wisdom

When I came into the office, after an absence of four hours, the phone was ringing.

"For you," said Miss Roth, my assistant.

It was a business call which I handled with my usual despatch, for I work on the principle that people want to consummate their business as quickly as possible, even though nothing else particularly interests them.

"Any messages?" I asked Miss Roth a few minutes later, and she said there was nothing.

A few days later, I was again called out on an errand which kept me out of the office until quite late in the afternoon. No sooner had I hung up my hat and coat, than the phone began to ring.

"For you," said Miss Roth.

It was a business call which I again handled with my usual despatch, even though the party at the other end of the wire was more interested in conversation than he was in business, he being an elderly gentleman who clung to the fiction that he was in the heyday of his commercial career, though actually no merchandise could be delivered without the written consent of his nephew, a young man of very few words.

"Anybody call?" I asked Miss Roth.

"No," she said.

I was a little shaken by her answer. I received the usual number of calls in the afternoon, but not too many, it is true, for most of my business is transacted by mail, and business has not been too good anyway . . . How was it possible that there should have been no calls during my *absence* from the office?

As I became caught up in my work, the sense of uncertainty was absorbed until closing time, when Miss Roth rose and said her usual good-night to me. Then I looked more closely at my assistant, who had been with me for about three months and had come highly recommended by an old business associate.

I had no complaints about her work—she was conscientious and intelligent about the files and books, wrote a reasonable letter, had a pleasing telephone voice, a comely figure, and a personable manner.

The next few weeks found me in the office most of the time. A few deals came up all at once, and they required my close and detailed attention. I generally went out for a quick lunch, though I sometimes asked Miss Roth to bring me a sandwich and a container of coffee. Things were going very smoothly; if the deals went through as I hoped, my end-of-year statement might prove unusually congenial.

Then, a few weeks ago, on one of those clear autumn mornings which we New Yorkers so quickly forget (for we consider the spring and autumn inbetween seasons), I received a call from a very dear friend of mine, who was in town for the day and who had to see me on a matter which he said was of the utmost urgency.

I explained to Miss Roth that I would return sometime

after lunch, and, putting my desk in order (as though I would never come back) I left, with a sense of misgiving which I could not explain to myself, nor did I particularly try.

My friend, naturally, detained me beyond my expectations, though not past my hopes, for there is nothing I like (and dread) so much as a really broken-up day; this pleases my sense of disorder, which I generally keep in close rein. There was really very little that I could do for him—he was ostensibly asking my advice about a contemplated marriage (his third), but, since I did not know the woman in question, I did not see what possible value my advice could have. He was not interested in discussing the general question of marriage; he, like myself, was altogther for it, though we naturally differed in details. He really wanted to talk about himself a bit, to glory in his troubles, which are always interesting when discussed with a third party, to gain some sympathy for his long-forgotten frustrated ambitions, which speedily revived under my apparently sympathetic attention (I could not politely show my lack of interest), and to boast a bit about the money he had made. So we dawdled over lunch, smoked cigars, and when it became clear that neither one of us was going to make a disclosure of any real interest, shook hands firmly and wished one another the best of fortune, all in a glow that just failed to be real.

When I returned to my office, it was almost four in the afternoon. I had called earlier and been told there were no messages for me. Miss Roth was her usually composed self.

"Anything for me?" I asked, at the door, and as she was answering "no" the phone rang; it was a call from one of my best customers. I could not fail to be struck by this coincidence—Miss Roth merely lifted her eyebrows, to express disdain, I suppose, at the possibility that I might be accusing her, ever so inwardly, of any negligence whatsoever. And then the phone rang again for me.

From that moment, things were never the same between us.

The next day, while out on a completely fabricated errand, I called my office and in a heavily disguised voice asked for myself, giving the name of Mr. Andrews, and saying that I would call again. I was gratified at Miss Roth's telephone manner—so businesslike, so intelligent, giving so much the impression that she acted as the ears for a highly complex, smoothly functioning business mechanism. Exactly the girl for the job, I thought, and when she asked me my business, I said in a voice surprisingly similar to my own, that I was calling on a private matter.

"Any messages?" I asked on my return, with all the casualness I could muster.

"Yes," said Miss Roth, "a Mr. Andrews called, he said that he would call again. A private matter."

"Mr. Andrews?" I asked, allowing a puzzled frown. Then, after some phony deliberation ending on a definite note, I said:

"Oh yes. I wonder what *he* can want from me."

Then I threw off the mystery and went back to my work.

A few minutes later I rose abruptly and said:

"Miss Roth, I am leaving immediately and will be at the Hellespont Barber Shop for the next forty minutes. The number is Innisfallen 8080. Please call me there if necessary."

Then I wrote out this number in the large scrawl that I use under these circumstances and put the slip under her telephone. My exactitude was evidence of my anger. I was working on a theory of partial amnesia, induced by my absence from the office (contradicted by her faithful recording of the Andrews call), which absence had the effect of erasing me from her mind so that any calls for me were calls for a nonexistent person. I thought that this telephone number, so prominently displayed, would act as a constant reminder of my existence.

When I returned, forty minutes later, I stood outside my office door for a few mintues, thinking:

"By rights I should be in the office now, and hear the ringing which so often accompanies my entrance. I will wait for that ring and enter a moment afterwards. *Then* I will ask her."

I waited a few minutes, and then another few minutes, till people began to look at me suspiciously, for I was lurking. So I entered, crossing the threshold just as the phone began to ring. There was no way back—I moved to my desk and took the call, the only one, as I immediately ascertained, since my departure.

My office is situated in between a large manufacturing loft and another office at least three times the size of mine. I am on excellent terms with the manufacturer, he certainly would not object to my standing for as long a period as I pleased against the wall that separates our establishments. However, that wall is thick enough to deaden the ring of my phone, which has been pitched to its highest potential. The wall between the two offices is a thinner one; here the sound would penetrate. But, unfortunately, I am on the worst possible terms with Mr. Ritter, whose business, like his space, is about three times the size of mine. Our businesses are not exactly similar: I do not consider him a competitor, though he apparently thinks of me as one. This dates back to the episode where an out-of-town customer came into my office and bought a sizeable amount of merchandise which, though not exactly in my line, I offered to pick up for him. This was before he discovered I was not Mr. Ritter. By this time we were rather on friendly terms; we laughed at the confusion, and let the matter stand. In buying the merchandise from Mr. Ritter, I was forced to work at a slimmer margin of profit than usual, but where business and friendship are mixed, one does what one can. I was never able to understand how this matter came to the attention of Mr. Ritter, but a noticeable cooling in our relations followed. Above my office was a cement roof.

It was the habit of Miss Roth to go downstairs every afternoon at about four o'clock for some type of refreshment. This privilege was one which I had not exactly granted her, but into which she had drifted, nor did I gainsay. On this particular afternoon we are considering, she left at the usual time. I walked to her desk and glanced at the report she was preparing for the home office. The arrangement of the type seemed unnatural. I am near-sighted, looked closer and read:

> let it not be said of me:
>   (it is a fantasy
>   nothing is being said)
>
> i had a child
>   she is wed
> i had a dog
>   he is dead
>
> the neighbors are therefore whispering:
>   she is bereaved
>   nothing cleaves to her—
>   neither money nor love
>   nor memories of the adolescent king.
>
> but the wind is talking low
>   and the courtiers bow
>   and the deaf bees buzz
>   remembering the First Cause.
>
> on the ceiling of my familiar room
> there is a shadow broom dance
>   my mother is weeping
>   my sister is in a trance
>
> (weep not, mother
>   though ye be alone;
> good cheer, sister dear
>   ye are not alone
>   for mother is here)

As I was leaning over her desk, rereading these lines, Miss Roth returned.

"What do you mean by this snooping?" she asked. "How dare you?"

"Snooping," I repeated sarcastically, "this is a fine report to the home office."

And I seized her by the shoulders and shook her. Her response was to move against me with a tenderness and a yearning of a sort that I had long forgotten. My anger died down, I looked with amazement into the face of this girl who was giving herself to me with such sweetness and ease. She became more beautiful for me by the instant—the quiet breathing, the gracious movement of the soft breasts, the clear and forgiving eyes. Transported, I caressed her with a crudity which embarassed and infuriated me.

Then our lips met in a kiss soft and deep, a long melting of souls which I would fain continue indefinitely, so truly did it carry me from the workaday world whose bleakness and emptiness I experienced now to the full, for it was only in this transport that I dared to experience such bleakness and emptiness, only with such protection that I dared to experience such bleakness.

And the facade of the organized sentence fell away, revealing the amorphous image, starting point of the organized sentence.

As a young man I had read indiscriminately in the Bible, a book that, though it fascinated me (I am a sucker for anthologies), had little effect on my words or my deeds.

But now, to my amazement, I began to quote from the *Song of Songs:*

Behold, thou art fair, my love; behold, thou art fair,
thou hast doves' eyes.
Behold, thou art fair, my beloved, yea pleasant; also
our bed is green.
The beams of our house are cedar, and our rafters of fir.

Miss Roth stirred in my arms, opened her eyes.

> *Thy teeth are like a flock of sheep that are even shorn, which come up from the washing; whereof everyone bears twins, and none is barren among them.*

We laughed at this conceit.

> *Thy lips are like a thread of scarlet, and thy speech is comely.*

The telephone rang five times and then stopped abruptly.

> *Thy two breasts are like two young roes that are twins, which feed among the lilies.*
> *Milk and honey are under thy tongue . . .*
> *A garden enclosed is my sister, my spouse; a spring shut up, a fountain sealed.*
> *How beautiful are thy feet with shoes, O prince's daughter!*
> *The joints of thy thighs are like jewels, the work of the hands of a cunning workman.*
> *Thy navel is like a round goblet, which wanteth not liquor; thy belly is like an heap of wheat set about with lilies.*
> *. . . thine eyes like the fishpools in Heshbon, by the gates of Bath-Rabbin.*
> *How fair and pleasant are thou, O love, for delights.*

The telephone rang. I disengaged one hand and picked up the instrument. I engaged in a spirited business conversation. I chaffed with my opponent, laughed at his humorous efforts, and contributed not a few witty remarks of my own. The result was that I succeeded in closing (subject of course to the usual confirmation) a very profitable deal.

Hanging up the receiver, I returned to Miss Roth. There was an edge of annoyance to my behavior, close to distrust. She disengaged herself and returned to her desk.

"I am terribly suspicious of you," I said. "Why do you never give me the telephone messages? Are you trying to destroy my business?"

"You ask foolish questions," she said. "You are very imaginative."

"Delusional you mean," I replied. "Delusion is a self-aggrandizement, based on jealousy of those who can express their greatness, or make their way to it."

For love is strong as death; jealousy is cruel as the grave.

Tears came to the eyes of Miss Roth as she turned to her work and I to mine. There were no tears in my eyes, nor in the eyes of any man whose heart is drained by delusions and afraid of love.

Homage to
Benny Leonard

"What's wrong with him?" asked Mr. Flaxman, as Davey got up from the table, where he had sat morosely through the meal, and walked off.

Mrs. Flaxman shrugged, as though to say that she could not choose among the numerous possibilities.

When, a moment later, Davey walked back into the dining room to pull out the ball which was securely lodged between the floor and the bottom of the bureau, his father asked him, "What is it, David?"

It was David's turn to shrug his shoulders. "Nothing, Pop."

"A fine nothing," said his father. "One could die looking at you."

"I'm telling you, Pop, it's nothing," and he walked slowly out of the house.

When the door closed quietly behind him, did not slam, Mr. Flaxman said to his wife, "What is it, they don't tell you anything?"

There was an implied criticism here, the burden for the child's nonconfiding was suddenly put on the mother.

"You were probably no different at that stage, that's how the children are."

Mr. Flaxman was momentarily bemused, as he thought of his far-off childhood, the childhood that is twice as far off for the immigrant as for the native-born.

"To tell you the truth," he said, "who remembers?"

Since the problem had not come into full light, he shook it off, the more so when his wife said, "I wonder what's bothering him. You think he's not feeling well? Maybe I'll take his temperature."

Mr. Flaxman shook the thing further away from him, shook it almost into nonbeing.

The sports pages of that morning's newspaper told the story of Davey's grief. It was the defeat of Benny Leonard, one of the three defeats this remarkable champion was ever to suffer in the ring.

Benny was the boy's hero. On the short side himself, putting his reliance on skill, speed, dexterity, what the kids called "form," it was only natural that Davey should identify this way with the peerless lightweight.

Stories he had heard at home of the Old World pogroms and persecutions had created an uncertainty, a fear, which required a defender. This defender was required against no present foe but against some unknown future enemy, even against the monstrous foes of the past—Haman, Antiochus Epiphanes, the thundering Black Hundreds.

It was no accident that at this time (later his heroes were the mighty figures Ruth and Dempsey) he needed the prince-hero, the 135-pounder who could weave, parry, outguess his opponent, jab, feint, dance off, and yet throw the sudden knockout punch, and then come dancing into the middle of the ring, his dark hair unruffled, saying into the microphone: "Hi Mom, he never even touched me."

At this moment Daniel Mendoza would not do, but Benny Leonard would.

He remembered his mother's story. She was taking care of the store in their Russian village. Suddenly the cry "Cossacks!" She quickly locked up the store, ran desperately. How Davey wished he could have been there to defend her. . . .

"Hi Davey."

It was Chick, also out in the street for that glorious hour between supper and sleep.

"What's eatin' you, Davey?"

When Davey mentioned the fight, Chick was surprised. He couldn't understand that much of a reaction.

"So what," said Chick, "you can't win them all."

Chick was one of those kids who had more easily thrown off his ghetto past. He did not seem to carry within him the ancient walled cities, the night-time assaults and terrors; he did not dream of the bearded Jew shot to death in the tunnels under the New York Central Railway up on Park Avenue. He took for granted the prevailing freedom, was not drawn to the ancient midnight, nor was he disturbed by vague and monstrous presentiments, menacing shadows. He was well-adjusted historically.

This rather flippant attitude on Chick's part both angered and relieved Davey, the anger because his friend did not share his woe, the relief because his friend kept him from sinking deeper and deeper into this woefulness.

It was not yet dark, just light enough to see a ball, so they had a catch, throwing the ball back and forth in a leisurely manner—slow balls, curves, floaters, and an occasional fireball down the groove. Allie and Richie joined them, and they got into a quick game of boxball, playing under the lamp post. Then it was too late to play, and they sauntered down the block, toward the candy store.

"Last one down is a rotten egg," said Chick, and the four of them were off in a flash. Allie, a P.S.A.L. runner, won easily, by four or five boxes. Richie, who was kind of heavy, pulled up a game last.

"You're the rotten egg," said Chick, but the satisfaction was not abiding.

Inside the candy store they picked and chose among the sponges, the caramels, the licorices, the creams, in the secure and exciting candy world.

Coming out, at their ease, chewing, or biting, or sucking, or crunching, they paused near a group of the Big Guys who were hanging around in front of the store. They stood close enough to the Big Guys to hear everything that was being said, but far enough away (they hoped) not to disturb them.

Included among these Big Guys was a lad who was not so much a stranger (for he was one of those nomadic types who thought it nothing to wander three or four blocks from his own block) as what you might call a "border figure"; he hung around enough so that he was no stranger, but still he did not belong, because he did not live on the block. There was always an element of suspicion attached to one who did not live on the block. He was called "The Gate," or when he was addressed directly, "Gate." This nickname apparently referred to the figure he once had, wide and formidable. There were some signs of that old figure, out of which he had grown, and yet he kept the nickname (like a tall "Pee Wee" or a gray-haired "Red"). A later school of sociologists may decide that the nickname "Gate" refers to the blocking maneuver, founded on superstition, or suspicion, in a dice game.

Now the conversation of the Big Guys was not of a particularly profound sort. It related to given individuals, mixed praise with the most severe criticism, the foulest maledictions, and was punctuated by expectorations geared for aim or distance. But to Davey and his friends, age conferred, if not dignity, a certain awe, because of that extra measure of experience, the activities just beyond them, so they listened, hoping to get closer to the unknown, the forbidden, and to be initiated painlessly into the mystery of the stage ahead.

But this cynical adoration on the part of the youngsters (for it was not exactly improvement they were looking for) did not predispose *all* of the Big Guys in their favor. Some were pleased, some paid them no mind, but The Gate, who looked around and saw these blemishes on the landscape, said: "Whatta you kids hangin' roun' for?"

At this question the four of them, in a kind of reflex movement, seemed to come closer together, but nobody made a move, for it was clear that the taunter was not serious in his intentions.

The scattered interchange of praise and invective went on; two of the older fellows lit up cigarettes, but The Gate was not one of those two.

"Beat it, you shrimps," he said.

This statement was not yet the one requiring flight (though it was a move in that direction from the previous question) because it was a command, but without a threat attached.

None of the Big Guys showed much interest in The Gate's annoyance, they looked at it as a kind of eccentricity, but with a sure knowledge that there *was* a motive, inexplicable to be sure, but the kind of motive that could induce any one of them, under similar pressures, to behave quite the same way. One of them said, tolerantly, "Aw, leave the kids alone, Gate."

But this friendly admonition only angered him the more. It was as though he was being opposed not only by the silent four, but by these contemporaries of his in whose company he was still somewhat of an outsider, where he still had to prove himself.

"Get goin'," said The Gate, "befaw I roon yiz."

Here was the command, and the threat, but no overt move. The Gate's rhetorical string was played out—his next move was pursuit. Again one of the Big Guys put a cautionary word to him, asking: "What's the diff if they stay here?" implying the acceptance and even enjoyment of the kids' somewhat idle homage.

"Because they're a buncha wise kids, that's what," said The Gate, and it was just then that Davey tossed up his ball, catching it in his backward-cupped hand.

Here, finally, was a reason, an act of insubordination to justify The Gate's wrath. He had been publicly humiliated.

"Aw right now," he said, and then he made his move. His intentions were obviously to disperse this group, swiftly, by this move in their direction, and then to return to the charmed circle, quietly triumphant.

To his surprise (and deepening chagrin), one of the four detached himself from the group, and advanced toward him, on his toes, in the approved boxing stance. The taunter was being taunted. In the few seconds between Davey's first move and his near approach, The Gate realized in what an absurd predicament he now found himself, forced to do battle with a kid three years younger and maybe thirty pounds lighter. To take on four of the kids was one thing; to find himself isolated with the one was monstrous. A victory could be only hollow and meaningless, a defeat catastrophic. He had no way of coming out at all. He looked longingly at Chick, Allie, and Richie, hoping they would move in to do battle, but they had stopped in their headlong flight, and were watching in fascination as their comrade-in-arms advanced on the enemy.

"Go way, ya runt," said The Gate to Davey, "go back tu da cradle."

In reply, Davey threw a left jab, which grazed The Gate's cheek.

Some of the Big Guys snickered. It was quite easy for them to turn against this suspect border figure.

The Gate had to protect himself, for to be hit by the kid

was in itself an embarrassment, perhaps not so bad as slough-ing him, but certainly shameful enough. The Gate's position was deteriorating fast, he could find help neither from his friends nor from his enemies.

Davey, meanwhile, was desperately trying to remember everything he had read about his hero's style. "Keep jabbin' him," he said to himself, "jab him crazy, look for the opening, and if you don't find it move back. Then jab away again."

He followed his own instructions to the letter. The Gate had to adopt a fighting stance in order to avoid the ignominy of being hit. Davey was fighting against an immovable target, for if The Gate were to start moving forward that would con-stitute an offensive, and The Gate realized that after he was out of this absurd predicament he would have to be able to say: "The kid went crazy, I just kept blocking his punches."

But that turned out not to be the case, for every now and then one of Davey's blows landed, and each jab was a mon-strous humiliation for the older boy.

Davey was in a kind of euphoria, imitating the image of himself, and every now and then realizing that it was all real, that he had fled the imaginary world where victory was dearly but surely won and was struggling here in the street, where the issue was always in doubt. Once more he jabbed at The Gate, struck him lightly under the eye, and danced off, but not before The Gate, helpless and infuriated, struck out blindly and hit Davey high up on the cheek.

The Gate advanced threateningly.

"Why doncha grow up?" he asked, but Davey's answer was a long left jab. One of the Big Guys snickered.

This ambiguous bout was brought to an end by a passer-by, one of those gents whose sense of justice is outraged by the sight of an obviously unequal struggle (as contrasted to one of those gents whose sense of exactly what is outraged by the sight of an obviously equal struggle).

"Here, break it up, you two."

The Gate turned toward this gentleman with a look of the deepest gratitude. "You are a veritable Nestor," he seemed to be saying, "a depository of the most profound truths buried in the heart of mankind."

Davey was perhaps less pleased with the turn of events, and would have been even more less-pleased had his cheek-bone not begun to swell and cause some discomfort.

"That'll loin ya," said The Gate, as Davey walked off with his friends, but this remark was meant for what record?

Davey was considerably cheered, he understood as well as the next one that the Big Guy had pulled his punches, but he was pleased with his own exhibition. Looking back, he saw himself in the classic weave, felt the acclaim of his invisible mentor.

"That was nice goin'," said Richie admiringly, and Davey felt also the approbation of the others. Then they walked each other home, and finally Davey and Chick stood together in the early darkness. They spoke seriously of matters of import, of the latest trade in the American League, of the next club meeting, of the distance of the furthest star.

"So long," said Chick, "see ya."

"So long," said Davey, and he sprinted to the door of his apartment, then opened the door slowly, hoping to avoid at least a direct appearance before his parents.

He reached his room without being seen, and raised a warning finger to his lips at his brother Danny, as he opened and closed the door.

"Who socked you?" asked the younger brother.

"The Gate," said Davey, and he gave a blow-by-blow description.

Danny was proud, envious, and disbelieving.

"You don't have to believe me," said Davey, "just ask anyone tomorrow."

Then he got onto his bed and started on his homework.

He wasn't at it long when his sister Joan, who was between the two boys in age, entered noiselessly.

"Did you see my *Little Women?*" she asked.

Davey denied any knowledge of the whereabouts of this work; Danny denied any knowledge of the very meaning of the question.

"It's a book," she said, "and I'm sure you know where it is."

The last part of the sentence was directed to Davey, who had been facing the wall, but now turned round to meet the gaze of his accuser.

She gasped with interest.

"What happened to you?" she asked.

"Oh, it's nothing," he said, "but don't tell Mom and Pop about it."

"If it's nothing," she asked, "why can't I tell them?"

"Instead of being so smart," he said, "why don't you think of something that will help?"

"Beefsteak," said Danny, who was steeped in all sorts of esoteric lore, "that will reduce the swelling."

"That's the same as steak," said Davey to his sister. "See if there's any in the kitchen."

She went and returned with a piece of steak in her hand.

"Great," said Davey, and he applied the meat to his cheek.

There was an instant of silence; then he opened his mouth with every intention of shrieking bloody murder, remembered the danger of disclosure, and bit into the meat, his eyes shut in agony.

"What's the matter?" gasped Joan.

"It burns," he said, "real bad."

They both looked at Danny, whose look of puzzlement suddenly passed into the area of understanding.

"Naturally," he said, "Mom salted the meat already."

"You're a girl," said Davey to Joan, "you should know all about these things."

"Don't bother me," said Joan, as she beat a retreat in the face of her brother's repeated admonitions to say absolutely nothing.

"They'll see it in the morning," said Danny sagaciously.

But Davey was not taking such a long view. He asked Danny to bring in some milk and crackers, and they ate and drank together.

Then it was Danny's bedtime, and Davey, to avoid discovery and because he was tired, got into bed himself. Deep in his soul he exulted, having fought in the manner of his peerless champion, and for his vindication.

The Locking Gas-Cap

"They're at it again," said Rhoda, and then she waited for my question before continuing with her explanation, because she finds it more interesting that way.

"What now?" I asked, toning the question so that it fell in the middle ground between boredom and interest.

"The gas-cap," she said.

I must explain that Rhoda and I were engaged to be married and that we already owned a car in common. It so happened that a mutual friend was going to Europe for an indeterminate stay and was looking to sell his car. He had been the sole owner, and that (plus the attractiveness of the price) was a determining element in our decision to buy.

"The damage that one person can do to a car," I pointed out to Rhoda at the time, "is strictly determined, characterologically, I mean. He can ride the clutch, or ruin the second gear, but it's generally one thing or another."

So we bought the car. One of the first things I had done was to examine the pedals, to compare the treadwear on the accelerator, brake, and clutch. I saw that the brake pedal was pretty well worn down, and had the brakes adjusted immediately. And we had pretty good luck with the car, mechanically, I mean.

But we had a problem of thievery. There was a gang of kids in the neighborhood—satin jackets, totemistic tattoos and all—and they preyed on all the open accessories—aerials, mirrors, gas-caps, wiper blades.

Rhoda lived with her mother, and I lived in a room around the corner from them. On many of the occasions when she came unexpectedly into my room, the car was involved—either a parking question, or, as on this occasion, a theft.

Of course, at other times, she came up to discuss with me matters of a more intimate nature—our finances, our apartment-to-be, plans for the marriage itself.

But the car too had a certain intimacy—perhaps because we had no home of our own, the car took on some of the qualities of a home. It was a 1950 Chevrolet.

Rhoda's mother was ailing, and Rhoda, naturally, found it difficult to leave her. We had decided it would be best if we did not all live together after our marriage. Rhoda's mother was not severely ill. She complained generally and seemed to be recovering from an old nervous exhaustion. Sometimes it seemed as though the complaints were a way of keeping Rhoda close to her. It was something I could not say to Rhoda, since we were not married.

Rhoda's mother had a spinster sister, over on the West Side of town. But somehow she did not want to live with that sister (who was willing enough to share her apartment), and preferred to live with Rhoda, nor was that desire in any way diminished by the prospect of our forthcoming marriage. Our engagement was now drawing close to its sixth year, and we were beginning to celebrate that date the way married couples celebrate their anniversaries. As the years went by, we all continued to be very understanding about it, but now and then I wondered what it was that I was supposed to be understanding about.

When she came in and said that the gas-cap was gone, I was brooding over the past and worrying about the future. I was hoping against hope that she had come in with some significant news about the two of us, that perhaps she had come to some sudden decision which she wanted to share with me. Of course, as the years went by, more and more of the primary cathexes became attached to the secondary phenomena. We all understood that perfectly well, but the understanding did not prevent us from getting quite involved, even incensed, over the supercharged secondary phenomena.

Still, when she came in, excited as she was, I thought that possibly she might have something in the primary division on her mind. When she mentioned the stolen gas-cap, I realized that more and more excitement was being generated about matters that we could remember once not being excited about.

"Well," I said, "we'll have to get a new one."

"It's the fourth one that's been stolen," she said.

Ordinarily I would have been as much upset by the theft as she was, and I knew that as time passed I would become as much upset by the theft as she was, but at the moment I preserved a certain coolness, and could see that her feelings were simply an overflow. In my unaccustomed objectivity, I recognized the displacement. Long continued, this attitude of Rhoda's (and of mine) can wreck a perfectly stable unhappy situation.

I suggested a ride in the car. It was what we always did under the circumstances, and the one less upset generally recommended the course.

"What a wonderful idea," said Rhoda, and she seized me in a wild embrace, meaning, as she invariably meant under the circumstances, that this was the perfect solution to all our problems. Also, I think she was genuinely fond of me, though I must say she seemed unusually aroused by the theft of these accessories from our car. I flung my arms around her and kissed her in an abandon that fell quite short of believing that this ride would solve all of our problems. I wondered whether her habitual displacement or my new-found objectivity was the superior attitude. I hoped that she would not ask her mother along, though if she did I would have understood, for her mother and her aunt had just had a furious fight over a detail too petty to mention at the moment. Naturally, that reduced the imminent possibility of their sharing an apartment. Sometimes I thought (without ever expressing myself) that Rhoda's mother had ulterior motives in these quarrels, which generally started up when the question of their living together arose.

We got into the car and swung over to the East River Drive and then downtown on that thoroughfare. It was the route we always followed under these circumstances; the busy little river seemed to have a calming effect on us, the busyness at a distance calming the turmoil close at home.

I turned on the radio, rolled past the football games to the opera broadcast. It was a late Saturday afternoon in October and I asked: "How is your mother today?"

This was as though to say: since it is on account of me that your mother is not along on this charming drive, the least I can do is talk about her and so bring her presence into the car. Rhoda understood this reaction perfectly.

"She's feeling badly on account of the awful row she had with Loretta."

In this way she was saying that it was not really on my account that her mother was not along on the ride and that I ought not to feel guilty about it.

It was part of the obliqueness of our relationship that we set up for each other these continual problems of translation.

"I wonder," she said, "why they are always picking on our car."

"They're not really picking on our car at all, everybody on the block is complaining."

"I bet," she said, "that more gas-caps have been stolen from our car than from any other car in the neighborhood."

"That's possible," I said, and I could not help thinking that she spoke about these thefts with shame, almost as though she had been stripped in public.

Suddenly I had a brilliant idea.

"Let's get a locking gas-cap," I said, "they come with two keys and the kids will never be able to get that lock off."

She did not respond, probably because the iron logic of my proposal left no loopholes and acted as an absolute damper on discussion. She did not even raise the obvious objection of the inconvenience of having to unlock the cap every time the car needed gas, realizing how insignificant this factor was compared to the outrage of the accomplished theft.

"Another thing," I said, "we avoid the dangers of foreign substances being poured into the gas tank. Do you know that a pound of sugar poured into the tank will absolutely ruin the motor?"

For some reason I felt constrained to set forth every conceivable advantage of the locking gas-cap. I had more than the layman's knowledge of this accessory, because for a few years I had worked as a salesman for an automotive supply house.

"Another thing," said Rhoda, adding aloud to what she had been saying to herself, "tomorrow is the anniversary of Father's death."

She meant that this was an added factor to explain her mother's upset condition. Rhoda's father had died when she was a child of six, and she spoke of him with the adulation you would expect from a normal child of six. She had never grown up enough in his presence to be disappointed by him, and she clung, over the abyss of the falling years, to her childhood image. I understood this very well and naturally hesitated to intrude into this worshipful sphere, the touching marriage of a long-gone child and a long-dead father.

He had been an engineer, and Rhoda spoke glowingly of bridges thrown over rivers in various European cities. He appeared as a powerful, kindly, successful, and handsome man. You could see him, in rough construction clothes, hands on hips, on the banks of the Danube, surveying his handiwork in the sunset of a buried day.

He had not left very much money, for Rhoda's mother had to work right along as a seamstress and had given up her work only after Rhoda began to earn enough for the two of them.

Rhoda's attitude toward her father did not make things easier for me. I felt that I was forever being judged against an ideal which no merely living man could hope to reach.

I swung off the Drive and went up a side street.

"There's a garageman on this block," I explained, "who carries a full line of auto accessories—I'm sure he'll have the locking gas-cap."

I parked in front of the garage, and we went into the office. That is a particularly nice quality of Rhoda's that she will accompany me wherever it is I am called. She has none of that squeamishness which many women have in the face of "man's work" or "man's world." She acts out of a sense of companionship as well as out of an objective interest in the business and institutional life of the city.

"Hello," I said to a youth in the office, "is Hymie around?"

"He's upstairs in the other office," said the tousle-haired, somewhat untidy lad of about nineteen. His collar was open, he was poorly complexioned, not so much by nature as by neglect, and had a rather direct, almost insolent manner.

"I know him, I used to do business with him," I said, and the youth looked at me without much interest. It *did* sound like a pitch for some kind of discount or favor. You could tell, however, that he was interested in Rhoda, by the way he did not look at her. Then there would be a sudden glance, furtive and bold.

"Well anyway," I said, "we need a locking gas-cap for our car. It's a Chevvy, I think it takes the 'A' type."

My knowledge failed to impress the youth, who began to make a search of some disorderly shelves for the cap. He fished out a box and saw they were radiator caps.

"I guess they're upstairs," he said. "Hymie keeps a lot of stuff up in that office."

He went out, and we sat around in the office. On the desk was a calendar showing a substantial woman naked from the belly up. Under the picture was the imprint of an auto body outfit. There were some price lists and yesterday's paper. The radio was on, up to number 23 of the 40 "Hits of the Week."

Let's go up too," I said to Rhoda. "I'd like to see Hymie again."

The youth had already disappeared up the dark incline that led to the first level of the garage. We made our way up, and then for the second time that day, either because of the cave effect (she being full of romantic conceits) or because she appreciated my efforts to protect the inviolability of the car, or maybe to show that she was indifferent to the blandishments of the young garage attendant, Rhoda seized me and we exchanged a kiss.

When we reached the level at the head of the ramp, the youth was standing against a wall close to a door. Against this wall was a cabinet where they apparently kept most of the smaller-type accessories—spark plugs, bulbs, the gas-caps—those which could be more easily pocketed by the numerous strangers (for the garage did quite a transient business) who went in and out of the downstairs office.

"Here's your gas-cap," said the youth, as he handed me an object wrapped in some brown tissue paper.

"Where's the box for it?" I asked.

"No box," he said, "that's how they come."

It wasn't much of a cap compared to the line I had handled, and I assumed it was cheaper.

"That's $2.49," he said, though I had sold a much better cap to the trade for eighty-five cents, and it listed at $1.49.

"They've *really* gone up," I said.

"I don't know," said the attendant, "that's the price."

"Where's Hymie?" I asked, and that was not so much to make the saving (for I was sure Hymie would give a better price) as to impress Rhoda and to drive another wedge (for every now and then I tried to drive a wedge) into the congealed idolatry which characterized her attitude toward her father.

The youth waved loosely in the direction of the door. I knocked and walked in, Rhoda beside me. To my surprise, Hymie was reclining on a couch. He nodded to me without expression, though I had not seen him for many years. "How are you?" he asked. I introduced Rhoda, and he rose from the couch only to half recline again. He did not ask us to sit. Thin, wiry, studious in appearance, Hymie's brightness had lost contact with all reality except the commercial one. I was by now amazed at his attitude, because we had been quite friendly, and in those days I had always assumed (though this had never been put to the test) that our relationship transcended our business dealings.

"Your man gave me this locking gas-cap," I said. "He wants $2.49 for it."

"Danny knows the price," he said. "He's been with me almost a year."

"You used to buy them from me for eighty-five cents," I said, half-jokingly, for I was certainly not going to make an issue of it, but I did expect he would warm up a bit and deal with me on a friendly basis.

He shrugged (I saw where Danny had picked up *his*

shrug), saying, "Everything has gone up in these five years."

He was uninterested and unbending. I hid my disappointment as well as I could and put down $2.50.

"Keep the change," I said, "good-luck penny," and I turned to go.

"How've you been?" he asked, and we paused for an instant.

"Oh, all right," I said, and that was about as far as he went in any expression of friendliness. I certainly did not encourage any further interchange.

"I don't like him much," said Rhoda, as we walked down the ramp toward the street. "His soul has shriveled up."

That was as good a criticism as I could make, but I knew she made it because she understood that I was hurt at not having impressed her with the power of my connections and so failed to weaken the idolatry which she knew to be my opinion of her relation with her father.

I remained silent, and then when we reached the street I took out the cap and tried both keys. They fit. I screwed on the cap, and then, ceremoniously, as though this were part of a double-ring marriage, or some primitive rite, I handed her one of the keys and asked her to attach it to her key ring. This ceremony was witnessed by Danny, whose ill-complexioned features I could see peering through the grimy garage-office window.

Then we got into the car and started to drive home. Though it was dusk, and though the lights began to twinkle across the river, awakening in even the meanest soul a memory of romance if not a hope of it, Rhoda acted in a rather petty manner. She *now* began to see all sorts of difficulties with the locking gas-cap. "Suppose I lose the key, or the lock jams, and I'll be stuck in some God-forsaken place without any gas."

Since we lived so close to one another, it was easy for us to share the car, and Rhoda had occasion to use the car on her own. We had to keep informing one another as to where the car was parked, and the car was a kind of bond and burden between us, requiring care and creating unity.

I well understood why she was suddenly running down the locking gas-cap, though it provided the safest answer possible to the thievery which had been plaguing us. She was bringing to my attention how I failed to measure up to the ideal of her father so securely entombed in her heart. The dusk —its memory and melancholia—sometimes had this effect on her. More immediately, we had planned to go out to a movie later in the evening, and I saw that Rhoda wanted to take her mother along, because of the quarrel and the death-day anniversary. She was running me down, creating a distance between us which I could narrow only by agreeing to the proposal which she had not yet made.

She made that proposal soon enough. "Don't you think I ought to take Mother along with us to the movie tonight?"

"Of course," I answered. "She's very upset about the quarrel she had with your aunt, and the anniversary of your father's death."

Then, relieved of the anxiety, she began to appreciate the charm of the dusk lying over the East River.

We were able to find a parking space quite close to Rhoda's house, which meant that she and her mother wouldn't have far to walk the next day (we *walked* to the neighborhood movie) when they took their usual Sunday afternoon drive, perhaps even to Rhoda's aunt, because the quarrels between the sisters blew up, and then they were together again. I told Rhoda I would pick her up later in the evening, a little before nine, because we had checked the starting times of the features, and Rhoda and her mother like to get in at the beginning of the complete show. I sometimes felt the same way. Occasionally, I felt as though I'd like to get in during the middle of the picture.

The Other Office

1.

Walking down the corridor (from the elevator) to my office, I passed a familiar figure going the other way. Had we been going in the same direction, been able to glance at one another, size one another up, and then maybe one of us ask— for he had looked at me with that startled recognition stymied by a mnemonic dead-spot—"say, don't I know you from somewhere?" I would have immediately found out that this was the same Randall who, some fifteen years back, had the tiny office right across the way from mine. Another building, another time.

But since we were going in opposite directions and since the quick glance picked up a familiar contour and then came to a halt against that dead-spot, the way it is when the recognition is not immediate, I did not come to that recognition for another two weeks, when we both stood waiting for the elevator to take us down. The recognition was not immediate, but it was simultaneous.

"Randall!" I cried, as we pounded each other in the jovial and sadistic manner sometimes adopted by old friends who miss one another, appreciate their separation, and are unexpectedly reunited, "Randall, you dog, where have you been hiding yourself?"

He replied in kind, though the fact is that neither one of us was in hiding, both our names being listed in the telephone directory.

"I've thought of calling you," said Randall, "but you know, one thing and another."

The one thing and the other is the inclination canceled out by the disinclination, but we were genuinely glad to see one another, if by fate rather than volition.

"Is Miss Daniels still with you?" I asked, after the thumping had subsided and we both recognized that of all possible meetings, this was not the most impossible, particularly since we were both alive, lived in the same city, and had offices in the same building, in fact on the same floor.

Miss Daniels was his secretary when, in trying out on her a nose ring which he thought might have commercial possibilities, if not universal appeal, he had kissed her, and she had criticized this kiss, saying that his sexuality had fled into his commodities.

"Oh no," he said, "I'm married now" and I fully understood the dialectic of this non sequitur.

We asked each other about our work and I discovered that we had remained in our respective lines. What his line was I could never quite understand; he was in the business of dreaming up commodities with a conceivable universal appeal.

When I went to his office a few days later (around a long corner) I noted on his window, in small, dignified gold lettering, the inscription:

RANDALL DEVELOPMENT COMPANY

and found him alone, stretched out on a sofa, listening to some awful semiclassical music on the radio and reading (for I glanced at the book which he tossed aside) a copy of Sapphic fragments.

As I now learned from our conversation, his work was, if anything, more abstract and unlikely than it had been, for in the old days, as I understood, he was involved in the fabricating of the products he conceived, but now he apparently sold his ideas and then worked on a commission or royalty basis with the manufacturers.

He was, as usual, vague about his projects (either out of professional secrecy or for character reasons), but I heard from someone in the building (it was the elevator man) that Randall had dreamed up the Hula-hoop, but my informant said that the way you ascribe some specific attribute to an abstraction, in order to bring it into the realm of the meaningful.

I recalled that when I had known Randall previously someone had said that he was the creator of the Yo-yo.

Whether he was indeed the creator of these remarkable toys I do not know, but certainly that was the way his mind ran—toward the creation of the absolutely simple, what answers a universal emotional need, the kind of thing that, once on the market, causes people to say:

"Absolutely obvious. How come I didn't think of it?" without realizing how hard the perfection is to come by and how hard it is to wed the perfection to the obvious, the universal.

"Look at movable type," he said to me, flicking off the radio. "What a rare and brilliant mind conceived that. Without that mind we might be living to this day with the archaic woodcuts, in the world of goblins and incunabula."

I considered for a moment the possibility of a world without movable type.

"Such pure intuitions are in the air all around us," he said, "we have only to pull them down to earth and use."

I looked around me, for what palpable configurations? Noticing a number of baseball box-scores cut out of the newspapers (on the desk, as my glance slowly moved downward), I asked Randall when he had become a baseball fan, for it was not an activity in which he used to show much interest, and I have never known of anyone who became a baseball fan late in life.

"Oh, that's my bread and butter," he said. "I work up the statistics for one of the wire services, there is a woman, a friend, who comes in a couple of days a week and gets them into shape, types them up."

2.

A few days later, I dropped into Randall's office again and met "the woman" he had mentioned. I found her working, rather serenely (she gave the effect of playing an organ) at the typewriter, on the *Earned Run* averages. Randall introduced us, her name was Mrs. Miliukoff (that was how it sounded, I've never seen it written). She nodded and went on with her work, giving no sign of being disturbed by the conversation behind her. She was a rather stately woman, in perhaps her late forties, fastidious in dress, elegant in manner, with the keenness that comes from long absorption in something you are interested in. When she rose and left the office a few minutes later, I asked Randall about her. He gave me one of those swift descriptions, which includes all the pertinent information and yet leaves out most everything important.

She was the widow of an architect, a man quite successful in his profession, though he had apparently thought at one time of following Thomas Hardy and giving up architecture for a writing career. He was now dead for five years, victim of an airplane crash. There were two boys, twins, in their junior year at the University of Pennsylvania. Mrs. Miliukoff was born and grew up in a small Connecticut town, her father having owned and managed a small, but unusually successful, factory. Married quite young, she had devoted herself to her husband and children; she and Mr. Miliukoff had moved in a society formed mostly by his professional associates. Randall and his wife were old friends of the Miliukoff's, having met them years back on a Mediterranean cruise. She was now working not so much for the money (for both her husband and her father had taken good care of her that way) but because . . .

Here Randall faltered, he was not quite sure why she was working but guessed that she wanted to fill up part of her day, part of the week, being alone in the house, the boys coming in only for holidays and frequent weekends.

"That's not the most interesting work in the world," I ventured, "typing up the *Earned Run* statistics. Is *she* a baseball fan?"

"No," laughed Randall, "there isn't a baseball fan in the place. She's a bit odd, enjoys the work, finds it soothing. So do I, in fact."

"You make it sound like therapy," I said.

"Oh no," replied Randall, "don't you find certain kinds of mechanical work relaxing?"

I learned that she came in pretty much when she felt like it (though there was a given amount of work that had to be done every week) and prepared for the press the figures that Randall worked up from a calculating machine, which, he told me, he had designed for precisely this purpose.

"It's a pretty expensive machine," he said, "but worth every penny of it. In fact, I've had a few others made up, and sold them to other statisticians in the trade."

He idly touched a few keys; there was an electronic whine.

"What do you know?" he asked, "Williams is hitting .357."

3.

During the next three weeks, I was quite taken up with my own work, and never did get a chance to get over to the Randall Development Company. When I say I didn't have a chance I mean I was somewhat disturbed and didn't think I ought to go there again, or so soon. During this period Randall had dropped by at my office so there was no question of social reciprocity involved. It is that you sometimes stay away from places to which you are drawn, out of confusion, lack of self-knowledge. Then you find that you are very busy, but the busyness is a cover for the confusion.

I am a distributor of encyclopedias, dictionaries, reference books, employing six salesmen who sell mostly on a door-to-door basis (as far west as Wisconsin) but also through selected retail outlets. My task is to coordinate their efforts, do the buying (which involves some travel), and handle certain promotional work (prizes, cut-price super-market come-ons, etc.), besides manage a small office staff, deal with the banks, etc. It is not the most adventurous way of making a living, but I get a certain pleasure (if not basic) out of buying cheap and selling dear, and as long as that pleasure lasts the business day can never be unbearable. Having been in the same line for a number of years, there are always people coming to me with all sorts of deals and buys—right now I am negotiating for quite a large quantity of foreign dictionaries, army surplus which has been kicking around for a number of years in various depots around the world. I am feeling out the market, checking with the big dealers in the city, for this involves a sizeable investment, and I like to sell off a certain amount before going into a deal of this size. In this way I more or less cover my expense and get an indication of the market mood.

But it's always one thing or another, and particularly if you want to make yourself busy in order to cover a prevailing confusion. As a bachelor, I am, so to speak, occupationally drawn to women, but after a while, so rigid is the frame of bachelor life, so circumscribed and demanding its habits, one is invariably drawn to a certain kind of woman, of a certain age, and a given disposition. It is easy enough to be specific, but the fact is that Mrs. Miliukoff did not fit into this neat bachelor scheme, and being drawn to her I was wary of upsetting what had come to be a very formalized, and in a way, easy life. But that life is what I really wanted to destroy.

So, feeling the way I did, I stayed away from Randall's office, put off repaying his visit. One afternoon, however, as I walked past the Development Company, Randall, who had caught up to me from behind, called out. He had a bag in his hand.

"Come and join us," he said. "We're having coffee."

I could have pleaded busyness (I was in fact on my way down the corridor toward the office of a man in the export field) but it was a hard invitation to turn down, so I accepted it. We entered, coffee was brewing on a small range, a container of milk appeared from the water-cooler freezer, and Mrs. Miliukoff served the coffee and the assorted Danish pastries, which Randall had in the paper bag. Gracious living was everywhere, we sat around a coffee table which, legs folded, had been lodged off in a corner.

4.

Facing Mrs. Miliukoff, I realized all the more why I had stayed away from this office, for I was very affected by her presence. She looked to be the age of my mother at the time that I was twelve or thirteen. It was then, for reasons I never clearly understood (though I now assume it must have been related to some crisis in the family life), that my mother turned toward me with a love, affection, and, yes, need, of an extraordinary intensity. I think she realized that this feeling was too powerful for my own good, too powerful for her own good, but she seemed unable to control herself. I was impressed, flattered, as well as confused by this torrent of affection. Never since has a woman loved me the way my mother loved me for that unforgettable year; she wanted me near her all the time, made up pretexts (as I, even though dumbly, understood then) to accompany me on errands which I could easily have accomplished by myself, and on my coming home from school or some place where I had been alone (that is, without her) she swept me up into her arms as though I were miraculously returned from some extraordinarily dangerous mission, if not from the dead.

During all this time my father looked on from a distance with an air of angry tolerance which I have never been able to understand. (Of course, these inabilities to understand may be forgettings, or refusals to remember.)

Never, I say, have I felt so wanted, so needed, never have I been made to feel so absolutely essential to the well-being, almost to the continued existence, of another person. She went with me to unlikely places, up to the Yankee Stadium, for example, to look at those games about which she could not have been more ignorant, from both a technical and historical view. There she sat at my side, gazing at this complex choreography, occasionally asking questions, less out of desire for knowledge than to make it appear that she was interested, and so, she thought, adding to my pleasure.

In going out with girls, I have always felt a little uncomfortable in being with those of my own age or younger and have shied away from those older, though it was to these older girls that I was most strongly drawn.

Mrs. Miliukoff's curious involvement in the baseball world (for the sight of the *Batting Averages* on the desk had revived that old scene where my mother sat with me in the grandstand) was an added factor in this confused attraction.

"Are you interested in baseball?" I asked her, and looked at Randall to show I had not forgotten that I had asked him about this matter, but in this look I was unable to show him why I *was* asking this question.

"Oh no," she replied, "I get a kind of pleasure in typing up the names of these people about whom I know absolutely nothing. As for the game itself, I have just about learned the meaning of a *Batting Average*. It is all very relaxing for me, something like Equinol four times a day. But I really find the names themselves—their shapes and sounds—most interesting. Did you know that one of James Joyce's great pleasures was to have friends read him the telephone directory?"

"Next to doing work that absorbs one fully," she went on, "it is best to find some mechanical work which keeps your mind and imagination free."

"And I am lucky," she said, smiling toward Randall, "that I have found the perfect job."

"That's why I have to double check all her figures," said Randall. "Sometimes the imagination moves in on the mechanics, and all sorts of curious switches appear, batters who can't hit the size of their heads are leading the league, and what not."

(During this interchange I thought how curious it was that she continued to reaffirm what I had already heard from Randall.)

I envied Randall at this moment, he seemed so at ease, almost indolent, the very apotheosis of low-pressure living, gave the effect of no tensions all the way down the line. I know very little about his life, but I am sure that anyone who can act this way during his working hours must have sources of pleasure buried deep in his twenty-four-hour life.

Now, Randall is not of the pure scientists—he will never come up with a law of motion or some original space-time theory—but there is a kind of purity in his practical scientific search, he is always seeking some practical instrument, machine, or what to transform the lives of all of us. I had heard that he was now thinking in terms of the mechanism that would replace the TV as the great mass-medium communication. The TV interested him as a social phenomenon not a bit, he never looked at it, and couldn't care less. But there was something that had to come into people's homes, following the phonograph, the radio, the TV. I couldn't imagine what that thing would be; when, in a conversational break, I asked what this successor to the TV might be, he laughed.

"Who knows," he asked, "maybe the whole mechanism will be internalized, our imagination become the Big Picture Tube."

I knew, from idle remarks he had made (and from the elevator man) that Randall was also interested in a portable cardiograph, for use by cardiac and noncardiac cases alike, easy enough for the layman to read (the instructions to be that explicit), so that the reader would know enough to go off to the doctor if necessary; in a springlike contrivance that would do away with our laborious method of parking between two cars by enabling the car to slide sideways into the empty space; in a special dye (coming in various colors) which would change, overnight, the shade of a suit or dress, doing away with the problem of the right *shade* for a given affair; in a new hot drink to supersede coffee and tea as well as taking the play away from cocoa, hot chocolate, and postum; in a book designed to be read in a bathtub (or under a shower); in a solution powerful enough (though not injurious to the skin) to destroy all garbage (hard and soft) and allow it to go down the kitchen drain, thus putting an end, once and for all, to garbage collection and incineration; and no doubt in alchemy, perpetual motion, and eternal life.

There was never any sense of urgency in his behavior. I contrasted it with my own working activity—the spot decisions that had to be made, the drafts that had to be met, the never ending time limits, the continual need to consummate one deal and then start another (there's no standing still, you either go ahead or retreat), the never ending burden of expense which demands constant buying, constant selling, and constant profit.

And contrasted his ease, his sybaritic manner, with my confusion before Mrs. Miliukoff, my attraction and withdrawal (for I wanted to leave), my absurdly simple and perplexing problem with this unusually attractive woman (I wanted to stay).

Drawn toward and desirous of leaving, one remains. Caught between remaining and departing, one lingers, particularly since the atmosphere was so congenial (I nearly said relaxing), so unbusiness-like. And sitting there, over the second cup of coffee, I thought how wonderful it would be if I could become a part of this organization. It was really more like a family, with the serene Mrs. Miliukoff (who might learn to love me, and need me) and the far-off Randall. How nice to recapture, even for a moment, an old situation of bliss. The coffee was warm. I could make myself useful here in some way, my knowledge of baseball would come in handy, but there was no rush about that, this was the lowest of all the low-pressure enterprises I had ever seen or heard about. Leisurely lunches, these charming coffee interludes, nights without worry, the master of one's time, if not of one's fate . . .

Someone knocked, nervously, on the plate-glass window of the Randall Development Company.

"Come in," said Randall, and it was my secretary who opened the door.

"Oh, I'm glad you're here," she said (what she meant was: "I'm glad I found you"), looking with ill-concealed amazement at our little coffee party, "there's a long-distance call from Rio de Janeiro. It's about some of those Spanish-English dictionaries. Somebody said you might be here."

(Who could have said that? I had never mentioned Randall to anyone in the office.)

I rose swiftly, began to make my apologies, but my secretary, who is of a rather sympathetic (the current word is *empathetic*) nature and falls in easily, pleasurably, with the surroundings in which she happens to find herself, said, "No rush, take your time, it's a person-to-person call, and I have the operator's number."

She wanted nothing more than to be invited to join us

in (or for) a cup of coffee. She gazed at Randall with some interest, if not curiosity.

"You get that party on the phone," I said crisply, "I'll be right in."

She left, I thanked my host and hostess, and felt a little foolish that I couldn't invite them to my office and reciprocate their hospitality. The best I could have managed was coffee containers in an office where there was no coffee table and where the phone was continually ringing. I looked with awe at Randall's silent phone.

"See you," I said, and walked slowly out of the office, then streaked down the corridor, for I knew that my secretary, returned to her desk, had already put through the long-distance call, and was nervously awaiting my return.

Ball of Fire

Eleven years ago—I remember the date because of an occurrence which is not pertinent to this account—an old friend, that is, someone who used to be an old friend ("he used to be a very good ex-friend of mine") mentioned the name *Oblomov*. I had heard the name before, its mention now (eleven years ago) struck a chord familiar but unclear. I knew, for example, that the name related to a book, but I was not sure whether Oblomov was the title of the book or the name of the author. I knew it to be the name of a person rather than a place, and so if it *were* the name of the book would refer (presumably) to the main character in that book. Because of the Paperback Revolution (which I will come to in a moment), my readers undoubtedly know that *Oblomov* is the title of a book, even that he is the main character in that book. It is not unusual, by the way, for the title of a book (even where the author is known) to be more familiar to the public than the name of that author. Is not *Don Quixote* better known than Cervantes? And would it be *too* surprising if, say 500 years from now, *Hamlet* were better known than Shakespeare? Explanations take one far afield, but this phenomenon—of the created object becoming more memorable than the creator—has some bearing on the value that mankind puts on the process of creation. So many worship the world over the God who made it, forgetting His name. But explanations take one far afield.

A little more than a century and a half after the French Revolution came the Paperback Revolution. Books that you could buy for a quarter, put in your pocket, read on train or bench and then throw away if you felt like it, now began to sell for $2.45, and mostly too big to fit a pocket. That was the Paperback Revolution. True, all sorts of books began to be published (Out-of-Prints, Hard-to-Gets, etc.), and among these books was *Oblomov*. There were dozens of the books in a store in which I was browsing, for the economics of the situation demanded that these books be printed in five, even six figures. At any rate I bought a copy. (There is no better price in buying more than one copy.) Though my ex-old friend had praised the book rapturously, he had not offered to loan it to me, and I did not ask to borrow it, because I am the kind of person who finds it difficult to return books and does not like to be asked for them, which the admirer of *Oblomov* never hesitated to do. I remember asking for the book along 4th Avenue (the one they have not yet succeeded in calling Park Avenue South; at least, they have not succeeded in having people call it Park Avenue South), but the booksellers had never heard of it, or it was out of stock, out of print, and so time wore on and I more or less forgot about the book, which joined that group of books that one plans to read. Many books are praised, and, generally speaking, books praised by those who know what they are talking about should be read, and the recommendations of friends are generally more interesting than the recommendations of reviewers and critics. One thing leads to another, circumstances and situations change, there came the Paperback Revolution, and I bought *Oblomov*, at an airport newstand, where the choice of books is beyond understanding, almost beyond confusion.

I was on my way to St. Louis on a business trip. I started

to read the book on the plane, and after a few chapters I fell asleep. That was the perfect physiological, even esthetic, reaction to this work, and I am sure the author, I forget his name at the moment, would have been pleased at my behavior. I do not mean that he was a propagandist for somnolence, but he surely saw it as a kind of Lesser Evil.

To those of you who are acquainted with this book, the idea of reading it in a jet plane, traveling at the speed of 500 miles an hour, is preposterous enough. I do not want to spoil the work for those who have not yet read it ("don't tell me how it ends"), but I can't be giving much away by pointing out that Oblomov is the essence of inertia, procrastination (the scene wherein he puts off everyday tasks is most amusing), the very apotheosis of ennui—that French neurological ailment, of a kind of golden boredom. Not altogether to my surprise, I discovered, in the introduction, before I fell asleep, that "Oblomovism" has a generic meaning in the Soviet Union, that the famed theoretician Bukharin (I am not quite sure whether he has achieved posthumorous, that is, posthumous retaliation, I mean rehabilitation, or not) used the word in criticizing the bureaucracy.

True, sleep was an ideal bit of criticism, but I was exhausted, too, for I'd been on a very rough schedule for weeks. I am a keen contender in our famed rat race, but understand the importance of the cat nap, which is one of the marks of the successful man of affairs. Because of the time elapsed and the intensity involved, this sleep of mine turned out to be much longer than the typical cat nap. Indeed, I was plainly asleep, and it was the instruction of the stewardess—a charming girl with a delicate Irish accent, from Kerry, maybe, or the Aran Islands themselves—"safety belts on, we're about to land," that woke me from my stupor, which is to sleep what sleep is to a cat nap. We were circling over the landing field, and it was quite a beautiful sight. This was a night flight; I had completed a busy day, and my appointment in St. Louis was for nine in the morning. It would have been more sensible to leave earlier in the day, but the press of business forbade. I could have taken the train, too, slept the night in pullman or roomette, but the fact is that I travel *only* by plane, become very restless in the slower vehicles of communication. The sight of the city not quite asleep was impressive, to say nothing of the circling lights, those searchlight rays on the field itself. My plan was to get right to the hotel and go to bed, and that I did. However, I was not able to fall asleep (because of the long nap, or short sleep on the plane), so I picked up *Oblomov* again. But it was not a good choice, because the author writes too engagingly of somnolence, one becomes entranced (my sleep on the plane was due, basically, to exhaustion), the way a master describer of the state of boredom puts the reader in a state of excited awareness.

Oblomov does not like to move, he has plans that he shelves, he gets into ridiculous arguments with his man-servant about this detail or that, he thinks of his house and serfs in the province, of work that must be done, of letters that must be written (the way they had to be written yesterday and the day before). He smiles and falls back in a benign coma of indifferentism—one of the better kinds of coma. This is a task that can wait—if not today, tomorrow will do just as well. Here is a task that *must* be taken care of immediately, he lifts up his pen, is baffled by the demands of grammar, sentence structure, puts down his pen, the message loses its urgency, it too can be put off till tomorrow (but no later!). He is happily somnolent again, has made a clear decision to procrastinate, a powerful exertion of will, something to be proud of. How nice that matters can wait, and, then, if they are left waiting long enough, can be forgotten. Oblomov dozes, dreams cozily of a shelter, a Utopian childhood, but I realize—there in that St. Louis bed—that I have neglected some necessary work, work that I should have taken care of on the plane, that I had *planned* to take care of on the plane but instead I had started to read the book, and then the cat nap had turned into a nap, and the nap into the genuine article. . . . I leaned over and picked up my briefcase, which I always keep at the side of my bed, just in case I should wake up in the middle of the night with a business thought which I might have to check against the figures, for if one goes back to sleep it is difficult in the morning to remember just what it was you thought. You might forget a given number, or the commercial complex in which the number has a meaning, and these night-thoughts, so often forgotten, can be the most significant ones, so I have trained myself to wake, jot down the thought or number, and go right back to sleep. I don't require much sleep anyway. Thomas Edison's four hours are about my speed, too much sleep dazes me, put me at a disadvantage for the exigencies of the day. I took the papers out of my briefcase and began to work on them.

Then, before I knew it—I am among those who generally *know* when they are falling asleep—I fell asleep. I fell *off* into sleep with a suddenness which would have surprised me had I known that I was doing it. Then I went immediately into a dream that proved to me, even while dreaming, that I had read *Oblomov*, all of it, and very likely before it had been so highly recommended to me. There was Olga, in the dream, and Andrei Stolz (my somewhat altered ego), the not very bright, selfless Agafya, her villainous brother Ivan—all these, and others, appearing not at all according to the contours of the book but in my own form of distribution. And, this night, on the plane, I had only read to a point where some of these characters had not even appeared! So I had either read the book before or, in the dream, created characters similar, name and all, to those in the book. A quick look at the book, past my place mark, showed me that the names I had dreamed were indeed the names of the people in the book, that I had not, as we say, "dreamed them up."

I do not consider myself a mystical personality, I stayed

with the laws of probability. and the overwhelming evidence was that I had read the book before and forgotten that I had read it. Either it had had no effect on me, or, more likely, it had a powerful effect which I was interested in burying. But now the return had come in a dream. I moved (in the dream) among those maddeningly familiar figures in an atmosphere of anxiety. Oblomov was sadly reclining, removing himself from life's responsibilities, from its pettiness, coldness, and horrors. And there was Stolz, running through Europe like a madman, promoting one deal and another. I saw him in Prague, around a conference table (one of those covered with green baize, in fact, it was a pool table), driving home a point, for the deal was in the balance, the crushing point had to be made. It was just then that I awoke and looked at my traveling clock, with its phosphorescent face. The time was ten after two, and I was wide awake.

Then I did something quite unprecedented (for me). I got out of bed, dressed, and went downstairs to the hotel bar. I had stopped in this hotel before, and knew its bar. Had it been necessary to leave the hotel in order to get to a bar, I should probably not have dressed and left the room, because it was chilly out, but since there was a bar in the hotel I did not hesitate for a moment, and made my way down there. I felt that a change of scene might help me to think more clearly, and I did want to understand why Oblomov had been so completely erased from my mind; the fact is that I knew perfectly well, but wanted the comfort of whisky and a few strangers.

There were a few strangers down there, a precious few (as though a remnant, and therefore precious), and given the day (Monday), and the hour (already given), that was no surprise. There was a moody chap in the corner—they do tend to move to the corners—and a couple of men, either friends who had nothing much to say to one another (either because they never had, or out of exhaustion of subject), or men who had met for the first time that night and now had nothing much left to say to one another. At the one occupied table behind me a man and woman were discussing personal matters in rather loud voices—"You never did love me," "Don't tell *me* who to marry." It was warm, and comfortable, the way I had expected it to be.

The thing is—did I need this whisky to tell it to me?—that I am by nature indolent, to this day I must make an effort to get up in the morning, to get started. Once moving, I never stop, my reputation as a ball of fire is well deserved. But I move, as do so many of us who do not know the meaning of change of pace, out of anxiety, out of fear that if I don't start I'll never move, that if I don't move I'll never start, and if I don't keep moving I'll just stay put. As a kid I was as lazy as they came; I returned from school (on days that I wasn't able to beg off, feign illness, etc.) and liked nothing better than to lie down, with a book or magazine—something to incite my dreams—and spend the afternoon that way. My mother often tried to get me out of the house. I was, and remain, an only child, and she was pretty busy during the day, didn't mind having someone in the house, but at the same time she had my interest at heart, made efforts to get me out, where I could move around, mix in the life of the street, that perpetual movement from which I recoiled. Out on the street—for my mother sometimes struck a kind of insistent note which I was bound to obey—I usually wound up sitting on the stoop steps or on the curb (as a last resort, for there was no support for the back), watching the mad whirl. I never wanted to be chosen in, the kids after a while didn't want to choose me in, accepted my laziness, not without jibe and stricture, but now and then, out of desperation, where an extra man was essential, I was forced into the action, to the chagrin of the team to which I was assigned. I was not the stuff out of which the immortal heroes of the playing fields are made. My Eton would have led to *our* Waterloo. I was lazy in school, too, kept looking out the window toward the freedom, not of movement in far places but to dreams undisturbed, for here in class I was sometimes brought up sharply, by the insistent, even the insolent questionings of the teacher. . . .

My father worked hard, six days a week, often not home till late at night, and he took it pretty easy on Sundays. At first he used not to be upset by my Sunday indolence, figured maybe I needed rest, the way he certainly did. He wasn't looking for trouble, but then things began to get to him—remarks by the neighbors, made directly or overheard, a note from the school which he happened to see, though my mother tried to protect him from these difficulties. One day, he came home early from work and found me fast asleep. Another day, he watched in amazement from our apartment window as I sat dreamily on the stoop steps, watching a punchball game from which I had artfully extricated myself. I had to explain to my father that I had come out into the street late (homework to do), after the sides had been chosen. I was getting to be kind of fat, something hard to imagine if you look at me today.

Well, my father slowly came to understand what was going on, and finally he raised the roof. He accused my mother of protecting me, indulging me, said I would become a drone, a parasite, and they got into a furious fight, my mother taking the position, which she did not altogether believe, that I had my own special way of doing things, that not all kids were alike, more about "specialness." "No kid of mine is going to turn into a bum," he shouted, "I'll see to that." Since I was his only child, he must have been referring to me. And he certainly did see to it. He had to get up before I did, but he made sure that I was up and dressed before he left the house. When he came home, he demanded to see my homework, cuffed me sharply if he was not pleased, was not averse to putting the belt to me. He wanted to know how I had spent the day and applied the corrective measures if he didn't like what he heard or didn't believe what I told him. That went on for six months, maybe a year, and it certainly got me moving. I haven't stopped since. And all on my own, too, for I have up to now avoided marriage.

So it was not difficult to understand my forgetting Oblomov. It was a fear of returning to that old indolence, those golden hours of forgetfulness, all that avoidance of growth and responsibility, which the author of *Oblomov* has so unforgettably described. That is one way in which develop hot shots, demon salesmen, promoters, wheelers and dealers, operators forever on the way, that is one of the elements in the creation of the rat race, the orgy of restlessness with which we are all too familiar.

I guess Oblomov is a kind of secret hero of mine; one must admire the courage, so to speak, of his laziness, to say nothing of the lovable qualities with which his creator endowed him—his sweetness, his innocence, his absolutely unconniving nature, his loyalty, his infinite trust.

Not difficult, I thought, to understand why it was that I had read a book, forgotten that I had read it, and then realized (through the mechanism of a dream) that I had indeed read that book. But, for the life of me, I could not remember when. I no longer had a copy of that book (could I have loaned it to the friend who had so unreservedly recommended it to me?), couldn't remember the shape, the texture, the color or binding of it. Was it a library book? Maybe. But what difference did it make? Yet, I was puzzled. One doesn't like to imagine that whole areas of experience have disappeared like islands into a sea. Why, I thought, that is a kind of death to unremember what it is that has happened; it makes experience unreal, almost meaningless, means that what I am doing now may well be forgotten, that this moment at the bar, trying to remember, may itself disappear. And why shouldn't it be forgotten? Do you call this experience? Here, a stranger among strangers? The couple at the table behind me were making a phony effort at reconciliation. It was probably because the man (maybe husband) wanted a little action in bed that he was coming to agree to matters in which he didn't have much interest, meaning: we're together, we're friends. What if they were making a phony effort at reconciliation? I mean, what difference did it make whether these strangers got along or didn't get along? Somebody else's experience. We oughtn't to live off the experiences of others. The moral note.

It was pretty late, and I had to get up pretty early. The fact is that it is not easy for me to get up in the morning. I have trained myself to let the alarm wake me, but at the moment of waking there is a powerful urge to return to sleep. Now this is not uncommon, and we most of us give in to another few minutes sleep. These tend to be the most delicious moments. But my habit is to throw the covers off immediately and jump out of bed, as though there were a demon beside me. There is such a demon, the imp of indolence, urging me to return to dream, to the softness of bed and sheet, to the warmth and darkness. Prenatal you say, and I would not deny it. But I am a true son of the West, my father saw to it. I am deaf to the siren murmur of prenatality, to the charm of Oblomovism, but at the same time I take no chances and go right for the cold shower (nothing like a cold shower to destroy the morning remnants of prenatality), rub myself vigorously, look out the window to see what the weather has in store for me, so that I may choose from my carefully chosen wardrobe. Of course, the weather is only one element in this choice—it is more a matter of who it is I am going to see, the impression I feel I ought to make, etc. Then downstairs for a quick but nourishing breakfast (for I have come to believe what the sellers of breakfast foods want me to believe, that breakfast is a key meal, sets me up for the day). Many a day I have completed my business in the first hours of the morning, taking advantage perhaps of the somnolence of the man across the table, the sleep is still in his eyes, I lay out the papers, I talk fast, convincingly, his mind is off somewheres, he is shaking out the night memories, the night horrors, and I am fresh as a daisy—the shower has paid off, also the brisk rubdown, the intelligent breakfast.

But here—in this bar—it is close to three in the morning, and I am not sleepy. I must be up at eight in the morning. How nice it would be if I could sleep through the day. And then I hear Stolz say: "Where are you? What have you become? You must come to your senses! Is this the life you prepared yourself for—to sleep like a mole in a burrow?"

But why is Stolz talking to me this way? Why is he saying that "in another four years there will be a railroad station there?" [on Oblomov's estate which Stolz has been managing] and that "your peasants will be working on the line, your grain will be carried by rail to the landing stage. And after that school, education. . . ."

My peasants—what an idea. I, who log seventy or eighty thousand miles a year of air travel! Well, of course, Stolz is not talking to me, he is talking to Oblomov, thinking about Oblomov. It is time for me to get to bed, for I have a rough day ahead. How come that ex-old friend, that old ex-friend, hadn't offered me a copy of *Oblomov* (assuming, of course, that he hadn't borrowed the book from me in the first place)? Not too nice of him, was it? Water under the bridge, ships that pass in the night.

In reading a book where an "I" is telling a story, I have often wondered how it is that the writer expects his readers to believe that a person who is not a writer by profession should be able to write in such a persuasive, even brilliant manner. The narrator may be a worker, a farmer, a merchant, a lawyer, and, yet (as in Dostoevsky), one is quite carried away by the style. The writer, of course, is acting, and we the readers must accept the double role—we know that there is a writer behind the farmer, and we more or less accept the convention, wondering, meanwhile (for we forget that there is a writer behind the narrator), how a merchant, or a lawyer, could write in such a persuasive, even brilliant manner. Sometimes the writer, recognizing that his narrator is not a professional author, tries to write clumsily, the way a farmer, or engineer, trying to be a writer, might write. But that effort at *complete* identity rarely works; it is somehow better when the writer treats the narrator as though he were a writer, recognizing that he is not a writer, doubling up, so to speak, on the fiction.

Sometimes the "I" is the writer himself, writing in an autobiographical way, an as-if autobiographical way, an imaginative autobiographical way, etc.

Sometimes, too, the "I" is indeed the writer himself, but he is not a professional writer, in the sense that he does not work steadily at writing (though all those who work steadily are not necessarily professionals). He can be one who "wants" to write, or a blocked writer, or a failed writer, or even what I believe the Italians have called a "ceased" writer, one who has tried and given up, who does not plan to return.

I bring these matters up because I am not a professional writer, though indeed, like so many in my line of work, I fall among the as-ifs, the blocked, failed and ceased. I am in the book business; it is possible that a keen reader might have guessed the "line" I was in by the knowledge I showed of the book business. Yes, I am in that line (it is abundantly clear by my manner of expression that I am not a professional writer), am a salesman of books, and, as I've pointed out, a very successful one. I knock down twenty-five, thirty G's a year, even more in an exceptionally good year. I suppose that I was drawn to the book business because I've always wanted to write, have worked up a few things on and off, but in a very sporadic way and never with any sense of the work having any real worth. Unfortunately, I deal in classic texts a good deal, sell to the colleges and universities, so I am always comparing my work to the best (that may be an error, perhaps it is proper to compare your work to the best *you* can do). At any rate, I've faded away from writing, done nothing at all for ten years, but this Oblomov business somehow stirred up my writing interests, and I've been moved to set down these happenings.

I left the bar just a few minutes before it closed (don't like to be in places when they close), and going through the lobby on my way to the elevators I saw a great automatic book-vending machine, lit up like a juke box. This machine was filled, it goes without saying, with paperbacks, selling mostly for $2.45. The machine makes all manner of change (may even, for all I know, accept checks, money orders, letters of credit), and the book comes zooming down at you. It is not quite like picking up a dusty book off a shelf in a used-book store. *That* book you can examine at your leisure and return. *This* book you must choose and buy before touching. No browsing here. And no way of returning it. How is it possible to return a book to a machine? The title *Literature and Revolution*, the author Leon Trotsky, caught my eye, caught both of them in fact. One of our serious competitors—I mean a competitor who published serious books—had issued this volume, which was not calculated, sales-wise, to make furrows on the brows of the publishers of Ian Fleming. I felt that I ought to read this book and went to the hotel cashier, conveniently located near the machine, and got the necessary change (for the change mechanism on the machine looked tricky, and I prefer to do business with people). The book came down at a terrific speed, all fresh, new, absolutely sanitary. It seemed to me that the vending-machine manufacturers had missed a bet. Why not a strain of music corresponding to the work purchased?

I then went upstairs to my room (having first to waken the drowsy elevator man, slumped over his stool in the corner of the cab, next to the controls. In this hotel, the selling of books was automated before the elevator). I went into bed and glanced at the book I had just bought.

I was nine years old at the time of Trotsky's death, so he is for me a figure out of history. Any person about whom you have not read in the daily papers, where his current activities are described, is a figure out of history. Russian politics have never particularly intrigued me, but I was, of course, aware of the significant, even tragic role of this man. Some of my older friends have a passionate attachment for him, though they seem to have slowly given up any political allegiance, and even seem to have lost interest in his political position, or meaning. But I had heard a great deal about his literary style and verve, and I felt that he would create a dialectical opposition to the Oblomovism in whose quiet backwaters I was somewhat fearful of being immersed. A little too much of that immersion would make me a dead duck (by drowning) in my country, in my time.

I looked through the book idly, and there, sure enough, was the statement: "One has to put an end to the romanticism of Oblomov and Tolstoi's Karataiev."

I was not familiar with the name Karataiev, obviously not an outstanding fictional figure because the name of his author had to be mentioned. But the name Oblomov stood alone—no need there for the author's name.

Then, a little earlier in this book this passage drew my attention, because it was what I wanted to read:

> *Futurism is against mysticism, against the passive deification of nature, against the aristocratic and every other kind of laziness, against dreaminess, and against lachrymosity—and stands for technique, for scientific organization, for the machine, for planfulness, for will power, for courage, for speed, for precision, and for the new man, who is armed with all these things*

True, true, just what I wanted to read, just what it was necessary for me to read, to avoid the perils of Oblomovism, this feudal swamp into which one can sink, and vainly struggle, and slowly die. This was modernity, even "futurism," which I vaguely recognized as a literary movement of the past. Of course, there is no need for an American to struggle to write this way, for we have no tradition of Oblomovism. There is a laziness approaching sloth, even sloth itself, but this is an individual phenomenon, not a social, nor even a group characteristic. In our business world the qualities of will power, speed, precision are taken for granted (only the word "courage" strikes an odd note). These qualities have been, so to speak, internalized, and coming out in favor of such qualities would be, in the U.S.A., a tautological absurdity—if all tautologies are not absurd—telling people what they have been brought up not to believe but to live. Dreaminess and lachrymosity are not serious problems in our land; it is indeed the excesses of speed and precision that draw the criticism of some of our social observers.

But the Russians had Oblomovism to contend with, and after (even while) putting down the book, turning off the bed light, I thought of this problem as an individual, if not a social, hazard. There were hints of it in my own psyche, a tendency toward the vegetative.

The attraction of Oblomov is, however, more than that of stupefaction and death, for he was, to repeat, a kind of hero —he was trusting, he recoiled from all conniving, the working of the angles, the sly washing of one another's hands, the subterfuges, the psychological elisions which go along with the speed and the scientific organization.

Yes, I thought, staring up at the hotel ceiling, hearing through the window (so I imagined) the flow of the mighty Mississippi, ours is a society of the morning, most of our work is done before noon, we rise swiftly from our beds at the sound of an alarm clock (think of it it, having to be roused by an *alarm*), while Oblomov, fearful of this tricky morning speed, rose late and fell back, worried about those intricate responsibilities not yet internalized, then shaking off the worry in a species of somnolence, as though what is put off does not exist.

He was a good fellow, ready to do anything for a friend, but seriously deficient in a sense of responsibility to the immediate. He almost achieved the responsibility of love, but not quite, and that drove him back to the fantasies and comforts of childhood, if not of prenatality. He found a wife who was also a mother—more a mother than a wife—an angelic creature, and she, in her own innocence, cradled him against the storms of reality. And so he died:

> *However vigilantly the loving eye of his wife watched over every moment of his life, the perpetual peace and quiet, with one day sluggishly moving onto the next, gradually brought the mechanism of his life to a halt. Ilya Ilych apparently died without pain, without suffering, like a clock that stops because someone has forgotten to wind it. No one witnessed his last moments or heard his dying breath.*

My eyes closed, the long day took its toll, I wooed sleep, found and conquered sleep, then fell into dream. I was in a pine glade, shady and warm, as comfortable as could be, half-asleep, looking up into a patch of blue sky. I had no place to go, nothing in prospect (I had in fact buried my appointment book deep in an unmarked place in the forest), I was quite unanxious about the passing of time. A little way through the woods was a lake, whose gray glint I could glimpse. Then I walked to that lake, which was frozen, and I skated on it, first gliding at my ease, then with mounting anxiety as the ice began to crack under me. "What an absurd mechanical dream," I thought to myself in my dream, very critical of my dream, as though I were a movie critic unhappy at what was being shown. Meanwhile, the ice continued to crack very insistently, and I woke to the insistent demand of my alarm clock. I jumped out of bed and tore into the shower, rubbed myself vigorously, then swiftly dressed, for I wanted a good breakfast before my early appointment. I put the two books on the bureau, the one by Trotsky, the other *Oblomov* (by Ivan Goncharov, translated by Ann Dunnigan, with a foreword by Harry T. Moore. A Signet Classic paperback published by the New American Library, 1963. 95¢).